ALSO BY CHRISTOPHER LAINE:

Seven Coins Drowning Series
Uncle Willingston
The Black Chili
The Trove

Tales of the Garden Path
In the Realm of the Midnight Gardener

christopherlaine.net

D1537219

SCREENS

SCREENS

CHRISTOPHER LAINE

garden path

Published by Garden Path

 GIRL FRIDAY
PRODUCTIONS

Edited and designed by Girl Friday Productions
www.girlfridayproductions.com

Cover design: Christopher Laine

ISBN (paperback): 978-1-7356992-0-2
ISBN (ebook): 978-1-7356992-1-9

For **James,**
who taught me to undo
their imposed sanity.

For **Frank Belknap Long,**
who made THEM real to me.

[LISTEN]

*I have absolutely no pleasure in the stimulants
in which I sometimes so madly indulge.
It has not been in the pursuit of pleasure that I
have periled life and reputation and reason.
It has been the desperate attempt to
escape from torturing memories,
from a sense of insupportable loneliness and a
dread of some strange impending doom.*
—Edgar Allan Poe

(The following printed pages were found in an unmarked folder at an apartment in Mumbai during a counter-terrorism raid, Jan 14, 2019. Fifteen suspected terrorists were killed in the raid. No charges or evidence were ever made public as to the accusations against the supposed terrorist cell.)

DISCLAIMER: By reading this letter, you are placing yourself in extreme peril. We urge you to fully consider the risks you are taking by even receiving this letter delivered to the address provided. Please ensure you have taken all possible precautions so that your reading will remain a secret from everyone. Take any and all measures to ensure you are not being tracked or observed, including but not limited to the means outlined below.

A NOTE ON PRECAUTIONARY MEASURES

* If you have followed the instructions found on the card, then this letter has been automatically printed and mailed to the anonymous post box you were instructed to set up. If you have not yet done so, immediately deactivate the anonymous post box to minimise potential risk to yourself.

* Before reading any further,
please TURN OFF ALL SCREENS. This
includes, but is not limited to:
televisions, tablets, laptops, PCs,
mobile phones, digital clocks, any
electronic device with a digital
display of any kind. If you can read
a digital display upon a device, no
matter how small or rudimentary, you
must turn this off before proceed-
ing. THEY are watching you. THEY can
see what you see, and it is believed
THEY are able to read working memory, though not longer than several
days.

* After completion of this letter,
destroy all traces of it immediately.
We recommend incineration, manual
destruction of ashes, and distributed disposal of the remains over an
extended area. Wait at least seven(7)
days after reading before turning
on any of the aforementioned devices
again.

* We recommend never again turning on any of the aforementioned
devices.

WHAT IS THE MANUSCRIPT?

It is believed that sometime in 2016,
posts began to circulate in dark web
forums, as well as on less-
frequented subreddits and message

boards. These posts made reference to a forbidden manuscript. This
manuscript was originally found in
a public place, left there by an
unknown source.

The Manuscript was said to then
have been redistributed physically
from person to person over the
course of that year. The actual ori-
gins of the Manuscript are unclear,
though it is believed to have been
written by an individual residing
in San Francisco, CA, USA in the
years prior. Similar on-line posts
also made mention of physical copies of the Manuscript having been
made since. Each of these copies was
painstakingly re-typed on a typewriter or even hand-written before
being distributed on to the Network.
The Network is thought to be an
anonymous system of mail routes and
courier drops set up for just this
purpose. All attempts to digitise
and electronically transfer copies of
this Manuscript were thought to be
immediately tracked and eliminated
at the source.

By the summer of the same year,
all posts on the internet, as well
as all comments or queries to the
Manuscript had been wiped from digital existence. Anyone known to have
any association with these posts,

the Manuscript, or even claiming to
have communicated with one of its
readers have disappeared or been
killed under strange and suspicious
circumstances.

After this, all mention of
the Manuscript, as well as those
involved with the Network, have been
considered a joke, or at best, the
perfect example of fake news. The
Manuscript and the Network became
urban legend, and like all things on
the internet, the lifespan of interest in the Network or the Manuscript
soon all but disappeared. Any seri-
ous discussion or investigation
into the Manuscript or the Network
is likely derided as trolling or is
systematically removed, and those
involved are soon discovered to have
disappeared or been killed.

These original and any subsequent posts are indeed correct and
thus had to be silenced by those
who could not allow themselves to
be exposed. There are, at present, a
number of copies of the Manuscript
in print. Originally in English, it
has since been copied and translated into any number of other lan-
guages, especially braille. There are
also believed to be tape-recorded
audio versions in circulation,
though these are far more rare. The

Network, of which we are a part, is
an anonymous group of individuals
who have either read the Manuscript
or one of its copies and are now
involved in the dissemination of
information about or related to it.
We use our anonymous and highly distributed system of non-digital communications to move information.
Much of what one receives on the
Network's mail system is verifiable,
but do not trust sources implicitly.
We disseminate information, we do
not verify it for you. Conclude for
yourself.

WHERE IS THE MANUSCRIPT?

This letter is not the Manuscript.
This letter's only purpose is to
reassure you that copies of the
Manuscript do indeed exist, the
Network is real, and that something
is happening of which everyone must
be made aware.

WHAT IS IN THE MANUSCRIPT?

It has been the judgement of the
Network that the Manuscript's contents are for you alone. We cannot
divulge any precise details of its
contents, nor can we tell you much
beyond what we have outlined above.

It is for your own safety, that of
the Network, and the continued survival and distribution of the last
remaining copies of the Manuscript
that no details be revealed about
its contents in this letter.

WHERE CAN I GET A COPY OF THE
MANUSCRIPT?

It is impossible for us to provide
any details on how to procure a
copy of the Manuscript. Copies move
across the Network at random, as to
diminish the potential of its discovery and destruction. We can only
say that at the time of this letter's
printing, copies of the Manuscript
do still indeed exist. We have no
information on their circulation or
whereabouts, or even about anyone
else on the Network. All communications, like this letter and the
transferal of the Manuscript, are
distributed through anonymous mail
drops or via secret courier.

  If you intend to procure one
of the remaining copies of the
Manuscript, please know that this is
an especially hazardous endeavour.
Any number of would-be seekers have
gone missing or have been murdered
in the last two years. There is no
reason to believe this might not be

the case for you, even with the most
stringent of caution. Do not accept
any offer to personally receive it,
from anyone known or unknown to you.
Do not discuss with anyone directly
your interest in the Manuscript,
irrespective of how close you know
them personally. If you manage to
get and read one, do not discuss
its contents with anyone. Above all
else, do NOT mention the Manuscript
on any digital platform whatsoever.
There is no amount of anonymity
which can ensure your safety were
you to do such a thing.

Be aware that if you do manage to
find one, the copy might be in one of
the aforementioned formats or lan-
guages. Prepare accordingly. Copies
being few, you will have to take
what is given. You will never find
access to a second.

There are also indications on
the Network that many of the copies might be poorly-translated, or
even have omitted key information.
The Network can neither confirm nor
deny this, as the anonymous and disparate nature of our interactions
makes such statements impossible to
verify.

Above all, do not keep the
Manuscript for yourself. It was the
author's express wish, as well as

the unanimous wish of those of us
who have read it that it moves on
for others to read. The sooner you
are rid of it, the safer you will
be, and the greater likelihood of
the Manuscript surviving to reach
another. It is imperative that as
many of us who survive continue
to spread its contents to those of
humanity who will listen. We are
unsure how much time is left for any
of us. The Manuscript does not make
such details clear.

FOR WOULD-BE SCRIVENERS

While there are those brave individuals still out there who will
attempt to keep manufacturing new
copies, the number in circulation
are inextricably always in decline.
Those who would stop us are vigi-
lant and intractable. We are always
playing a losing game in regards
to THEIR control and surveillance.
The Network takes all precautions to
protect the remaining copies, but we
are watched constantly. Copies which
have been seized are immediately
destroyed. Any forensic evidence on
such confiscated copies is used to
track anyone who has been associated
with it. If you fear for your life,
do not let yourself become one of

those discovered. Leave no trace of
yourself or any relation to it once
you have completed reading it.

If you intend to copy the
Manuscript, that is your preroga-
tive, but know it is a dangerous
one. Every person who has ever kept
a copy for more than the briefest of
time has eventually been discovered.
Those who wish to keep its secrets
unknown are forever tracking it and
us in newer and more ingenious ways.
There is no reason to believe THEY
are not already closing in.

Note that all digital reproduc-
tion of the Manuscript is impossible without detection. Any attempts
to do so are vehemently dissuaded.
Everyone who has attempted to digitise the Manuscript has disappeared
or been killed. If you manage to
procure a copy of the Manuscript, do
not attempt to reproduce it digitally
in any form. You will NOT succeed,
irrespective of what hopes you might
have.

FINAL WORDS

What we can tell you is that the
Manuscript is explicit in its warning. All life upon the Earth is in
the greatest peril. Greater than
climate change, greater than nuclear

war; greater than any calamity our world has ever faced. What is coming is the end of all things, the coming of something out of nightmare.

May future generations have mercy as they remember us, we the unwitting conspirators in the ruination of our species and our world. If the Manuscript is to be believed, what has been done cannot be undone. Mankind's time is up; it is only a matter of time before everyone realises it. We cannot stop what has been foretold. We can only warn one another and hope we might save something of our people and our world.

Good luck to you, to everyone and everything we hold dear.

If only luck could save us.

—The Network

THE NOBODY

You've found this, Chumley. Good for you. Now take my advice and put it back down.

This manuscript isn't meant for you. You don't have the stomach. Go back to your safe little life of TV and mobile phones, of Facebook and Twitter and YouTube pouring down your gullet by the gallon. Back to the web, to your game console, your favourite binge-worthy channels. That's a cozy little spot for the likes of you. You don't want any part of this.

What I'm about to tell you, this gets messy, and the last thing someone in this post-modern iron age wants is messy. Messy messes with your worldview. Messy messes with the neatness in your head. Messy doesn't get episodes played; it doesn't get you levelled up. Messy isn't responding to that comment on a comment on the bottom of some meme. Messy doesn't fit into a tweet. Leave messy alone. Put this down, before it's too late. Neatness counts, after all.

It's better this way. Put the manuscript down, walk away. You'll stay happy and stupid, a well-fed moron who doesn't want to know. The only way you're going to get to stay safe is if you just don't know. Don't dawdle. Go on. Walk away. Go back. Get back on the grid. There's a good little Chumley.

Trust me. You don't want to know. The batshit accountant told me that, that I didn't want to know, and you know he was right. I didn't want to know. I wish I'd listened to him when I had the chance. But no, I had to know for myself, to find out, and that didn't work out so swell for me. So, learn from my mistake. Take it on the lam.

And yet you're still reading. Because you can't stop, can you? No. You worked so hard to get your greasy little mitts on this in the first place. You heard about this manuscript, this one something you can't find on the internet. A pack of tattered pages in a manila envelope, being passed from one hand to the next. You've heard whispers of it, awful rumours, of things you shouldn't want to know. And so, you got your hands on it, and you read on, even though I told you it's not meant for you.

But after all, you're sure you know what you're getting into, right? You're positive you can handle it. Pardon me, but how the fuck would you know what you can handle? We're just here at the beginning. Everybody is sure they can handle everything at the beginning. The beginning is chump change. It's the end that really matters. That's where the rubber meets the road. That's when you'll know, when you'll really know what I know, and you'll be desperate to be gone, and to leave this manuscript behind, never to mention it again. Back you go, little Chumley. Back you go.

So, who the fuck am I, you ask. Who am I to tell you anything? Why I'm fucking nobody, that's who I am. My name is James, but what does that matter? It's just a name after all, and I'm a fucking nobody with a nobody's name. I'm not famous or rich or a celebrity. I don't have a blog, or a social presence, or an IPO. I have no Bitcoins, no venture capital. I'm not boot-strapped, or angel-invested. I don't have any followers, or stars, or likes. I don't have a channel of any sort, not a podcast, not an Instagram feed, none of that bullshit. Nothing about me counts for shit in your dismal digital world. I'm a nobody who's long dead, an anonymous statistic on an obituary you'll never find. I'm John Doe, a white chalk line on a murder scene floor. I doubt you could even find a trace left of who and what I was, no matter how many times you asked Google or Siri or Echo to find me. I am untraceable, a departed soul across an anonymous VPN. I do not register on your monitor, your search screen, or your smartphone. **404: narrator not found**.

And guess what? I've got a secret. James knows something you don't know.

I found it out, and now I'm dead. Keep reading, Chumley, and it's a good bet that you'll end up the same way too.

I bet you can't wait to get to the end now, can you? Yeah, I'm sure your dumb ass can handle it. Sure, you can.

You'll be fine.

James believes in you.

(Found plastered on walls and telephone poles at various locations around the globe)

WHAT IS KNOWN OF THE NETWORK
INFORMATION LAST UPDATED: 05.01.2019
* * * * * * * * * * * * * * * * * * * *

Sometime in latter 2017, rumours began to spread of something referred to as 'the Network'.

The Network was claimed not to be a computer system of any kind. It was not part of the dark web, a hacking organisation, or any kind of digital system. According to what details can be found, the Network has nothing to do with any form of modern technology. It is, in fact, a non-digitized channel of communication.

The Network is said to be an anonymous exchange of physical information, in the form of photographs, tape and vinyl recordings, drawings, but most of all, writings. Much of the writing comes in the form of letters, personal narratives, diary entries, as well as requests for information and general warnings

to other members of the Network.
Information is purported to travel
via traditional postal routes, and
via an anonymous volunteer courier
system supported and safeguarded by
the Network's members.

No member of the Network is
thought to be in direct personal
contact with any other. No names,
addresses, any personal information
is ever exchanged between members,
or included in any communications.
Drop locations for parcels and letters are rotated weekly. Volunteers
assigned to courier any communications to their next point in the
Network are changed after each distribution. Anonymity and security
are considered sacrosanct, critical
to the safety of all members and to
the Network itself.

Any breaches in the Network's anonymity or security in a given locale
has led to the complete dissolution
of any local activity indefinitely.

The Network is, in the public eye, little more than a rumour,
unsubstantiated and unconfirmed by
any source. There is no information
whatsoever about the Network to be
found on-line or in official publications of any kind. All public and
private digital systems are said
to be empty of any details about

the Network, its contents, and even
speculation on the subject. Even the
Dark Web is clean of any such data.
Any information, questions, posts
or media related to the Network are
believed to be removed immediately.
Anyone posting such information,
even to local LANs, or even disconnected PCs, are said to either
vanish or die under mysterious and
suspicious circumstances. News agen-
cies refuse to cover, or even sub-
stantiate claims of the Network's
existence. Journalists who persist end up fired or are silenced in
grisly ways.

What little information we have
on the Network is passed from person to person, or from the few members of the Network who are willing
to divulge small bits of information outside the Network itself. Such
divulgences are scant and isolated
to a single piece of information. It
is believed that the Network oper-
ates entirely outside the flow of
modern communications, that its members have disassociated themselves
from all digital media and technology, and that while its existence
is disavowed by all governments, is
most likely to be considered illegal
and banned at the highest levels of
power.

While details of the Network remain shrouded in mystery, one thing is clear. The Network was formed and continues to operate around a single primary contraband, the source of its membership and existence. The Network is a conduit through which travels copies of what is known only as the Manuscript.

THE LONG ROAD TO THE ABYSS

I don't remember when I first came in contact with the name of Halpin Chalmers. I'm pretty sure that name had been in and out of my life since college, maybe even my teens. I'm sure I'd read the name more than once in my life, though I couldn't tell you exactly where. I'm positive in all my fringe reading, the name of Halpin Chalmers must have crossed my path. But it was that old mutual friend who brought Halpin Chalmers to the forefront of my life. Goddamn him for that.

I was always a big reader when I was a kid. My mom was a librarian, so I remember books before I can remember anything else. I was reading books by the time I was four. By the time I was six, I was reading things years ahead of my age. My mom was only too happy to ply me with books. It was the least she could do for her alienated, anti-social son, given her and my dad had moved to that sewage tank we called our hometown. It was a toilet dressed up like Hometown USA, a Northern Californian burg full to the brim with every stereotypical racist, sexist, macho dickweed one could imagine.

Jocks, rednecks, white trash mullet heads, dirty cops, gang-bangers. Around every hick town suburban corner, down every side street or vacant lot, there was someone looking to take a beat on me. Strangeness and solitude mark you in a dump like that. It was a fucked-up place for a weird kid like me. I took beatings and abuse almost daily, and when I didn't, it was only because I knew how to hide, how to run, how to know when vicious things were on the hunt. None of it made any sense to me. I was a bookish little freak, and none of what happened in my hometown or the next couple of toilet towns around it added up to what was in my books. Even when the math did add up, it wasn't an equation that I wanted any part of. I was a lonely kid. I was lonely and strange and buried in my own little world, so I had no friends beyond my books and a penchant for a dark imagination. Those two things kept me sane living in that hick town, held a buffer between me and the incessant abuse I dealt with from the hillbillies and white trash. It was books that kept me going, and yet it was my loneliness and my bookishness that made me a target.

Childhood stumbled awkwardly into teen angst, and I was no less bullied, no less alienated or anti-social. But with enough time, even a bizarre, four-eyed freak like me manages to make friends, the gods know how. The friends I made were obviously freaks too, harassed weirdos and punk rockers living on the edge of the poverty line and the social norms. We banded together, scraped by on the sidelines. We smoked behind the basketball courts; we snuck slurps from a pint bottle of shit whiskey. We smoked weed, snorted crank, listened to Dead Kennedy's albums in black-lit rooms. I traded my glasses for contacts, my short-shorn hair for a black and blue dye job on a straggly mop. Me and my friends gave each other shitty needle tattoos and crummy piercings. We hated our lives together, and scraped keys across redneck trucks. Robitussin, ether rags, bikers buying us beer. Nickel bags, dime bags, books and the

Butthole Surfers. When I wasn't high to the rafters, I spent all my time playing chess and reading any weird shit I could get my hands on. Punk rock and Robert Anton Wilson; joints and brews and Lovecraft. I liked the dark stuff, in music, literature, and in my skull, strangeness that pushed the envelope. All that punk rock and drugs and sullen superiority made me hated by all my teachers. My intelligence and acerbic tongue made it clear that yeah, I was a smart-ass little punk, but I was smarter than most all of them. They hated me for that.

Time teeny-bopped past, and soon enough, I pushed on from high school and bailed on my shit hole hometown. Through some miracle of my high IQ and constant reading, I managed to eke my way into college. I moved to Sonoma. I'd do two years at community, then roll to some bigger school in a place that didn't have me sick to my guts.

It was there that I met her. She was like me, dark-hearted and smart, railing against a system she didn't quite under-stand. She was studying psychology; I was keen on philosophy. We became a couple in short order and moved in together as people do. We partied and went to school, worked our shit jobs to keep us afloat, and even in that rural backwater, we began to have something you might call happiness. It was fleeting, and we were dumb and self-obsessed, like everybody in their late teens, but we were together, and we were living life on our terms. It was as ideal as any relationship can ever be.

Years ticked by, and I rolled out of Sonoma for San Francisco, to get my bachelor's degree. My girlfriend was a year behind me, so she had to stick around Sonoma, but I went on ahead. I spent a year living in the dormitories, waiting for her to come down, and when she did, we got a place on Haight Street and Divisadero, a one-bedroom overlooking the inter-section, sitting atop a liquor store.

I sank into the dark intellectual life of San Francisco. It was the latter part of the 80s, and there was nothing one couldn't

do in that haunted place. The 60s and 70s were long gone, so
any hippies or swingers were rapidly bloating into middle age.
San Francisco had fallen out of favour and was largely ignored
by the world. It was the fucking best. This was an in-between
time, a brief moment when San Francisco was able to hide from
the rest of America. Rent was cheap. Things were cheap. San
Francisco was underpopulated. There was no real major industry, and it subsisted on tourist trade, and the internal dabble of
locals. It was a place lost in Avalonian mist. The city smelled
like old cigarettes, sea air, engine grease, jasmine tea, antique
shops, and library books. It was quiet for a city, introspective
and strange. I fit right in. It was a freak's wonderland, and I
bathed in its aberrant juices. I went to gigs, I smoked weed and
snorted speed. I scoured bookstores, libraries. I saw black and
white movies and listened as professors entangled my mind in
Hegelian babble. I drank shit whiskey in gulps between swigs
of orange soda. I read, and wrote, and lived the life of a city
which, back then, seemed like time had given it a wide berth.
I rode Muni trains to nowhere and wandered up and down
every place I could find. I saw gods and spirits appear and disappear from street corners and graffiti-stained alleys, and no
one thought anything of it, no more than they considered the
stragglers in faded all-night diners or the sad call of a ship's
horn from the churning mouth of the Bay.

So, for three years, she and I lived together while we
worked part-time, and went to school. We were 22, the future
was out in front of us, and what more could a douchebag like
me have wanted? We ate cheap takeout and bought crappy
clothes from thrift stores. We spent our days being free,
and our nights together in our cramped apartment. We fell
asleep to the crackle of sparks and the grumble of traffic. We
emerged in the day to a city that was our playground. That
time flitted by.

In due course, I graduated and then so did she. By this point, we'd been strung out on higher education, and the both of us wanted to be out on our own. We took Joe jobs, anything to fill the gap. We wanted to save some money, and with it, make our next move. We worked, and we met for dinner, and we went home night after night. Another two years went by, and we should have been happier than ever. But no.

In between all this domestic bliss, I was secretly drifting.

With school behind me and a degree in philosophy under my belt, I'd taken a job as a bike messenger. If you're too young or too stupid to know, there was a time when important packages and documents got from one company to another across town, and these were called bike messengers. We hauled ass on shitty bikes to get packages from one end of town to the other, as fast as possible. Dodging traffic, jumping curbs, racing between the buildings as we dashed to get in another delivery, make another buck. It was the perfect gig for a guy who wanted to forget about education and wanted to get soaked up in the grime of the city. I rode mornings and afternoons, with breaks for laughs, beers, and drugs to keep me hauling. It was a lifestyle more than a vocation, but the deliveries paid enough that I could have stashed some spare cash if I worked hard and kept expenses down. I worked hard enough, but expenses, they kept rising.

My habits kept up from high school and college: speed, weed, beers, and a dalliance with psychedelics. I was working 12 hr days, so the speed kept me moving, and the weed kept my head in the game. The psychedelics were for marking weekends, and the beers were for a job well done. I had a grip on it, had a system. I had a cog in my head that kept nodding along and telling me I was in control, I wasn't sliding. Maybe it was right. I managed to surf that edge since my teens, and if my dosage had risen somewhat, so had my productivity. I was carrying that weight, doing the job that needed doing, and I was managing to do so with an IQ in the genius band, an intensity and understanding of what is actually going on that evaded most of my peers. I needed to keep my mind occupied, and with books set aside, I needed the chimerical zing of recreational drugs to stave off boredom and madness.

Then that little cog in my head got wrong real fast. I found heroin.

I won't bore you with the details. If you're a square, you won't get it, and it's not my fucking job to educate you. If you're in the know, the story won't be any surprise. Some, gone to some more, gone to more than is smart, gone down, down, down . . . Down I went. Not all at once, but yeah, I fell. I went from snorting to needles in the span of six months. For a year and change after, the H just took over. My paychecks were soon a baboon's breakfast, with almost all of it going in my veins. I wasn't a messenger anymore. I was a full-on junkie who rode packages and lived a perpetual lie, just to keep the Habit happy, and the Sick at bay.

My girlfriend pretended like she didn't notice but come on. I might as well have had a fucking sign around my neck. I barely slept. I had no sex drive. Our bank account was gone. I looked like shit, smelled even worse. I was hocking our stuff, sneaking around nightly. I was lying to her constantly, and I didn't have the wherewithal or strength of character to even be good at it. I gaslighted her into all of it being her own paranoid crap, that she was the one with the problem. She loved me, and she trusted me, but she wasn't a fucking idiot. She worked out what was happening, even if it was too late by the time she got there.

And when it all finally cracked, when she caught me in our bedroom with the tie still on my arm, and the needle in my hand, I lay there in a glazed stupor while she cried and packed and left.

It was 1990, and I was a junkie, and I was all alone. It would be a good long while before I changed that station. I just lay in my own existential filth, listening to the end of the same song playing over and over and over.

(Message in a bottle, washed up on a beach in Raglan, New Zealand)

THE NETWORK AND MODERN SOCIETY
INFORMATION LAST UPDATED: 09.12.2019
* *

The Network is not modern society, or perhaps better put, it runs parallel to it, inside of it, but is not connected to its digital mainline.

While members of the Network appear to act and function within modern society, their primary differentiation revolves around the Manuscript and any information which corroborates and validates what we believe to be true.

Much thanks is owed to Network members, especially those who work tirelessly to ensure that the Network and its members are kept safe from discovery, that all communications and correspondence remain anonymous, and that copies of the Manuscript continue to remain in circulation. Without their tireless efforts, there is a strong possibility that the Network and its members would

have long since been discovered and
eradicated.

Contributors on the Network
appear to be of all walks of life.
Some content has been specifically
written for the Network (such as
this document), while other content
appears to have been found and circulated for its direct relation to
the Manuscript in some way.

Content circulated appears to
come from all corners of the world,
with some of it from sources which
had no knowledge of the Manuscript.
This could be either because it was
published before the Manuscript had
come into existence, or the content's
author was never made aware of the
dire situation unfolding since the
Manuscript's first appearance.

Whatever the case, and whatever the source of the content,
all is copied and kept in circulation through anonymous couriers and
private mail routes. The system by
which anonymity is maintained is
complex, rotated regularly, and the
work distributed collectively so as
to minimise the impact of the loss
of any specific members.

Any member will likely be called
upon at any given time to take up
some service for the Network, in
whatever capacity they are needed.

Do not shirk or shy from this unless
you are unable to assist or in danger of discovery. The Network can
only continue as long as our anonymity is maintained and as long as
members are willing to sacrifice for
the survival of our species in whatever form possible.

What one will receive from the
Network comes in many forms. Copies
of the Manuscript are not the only
items distributed along the Network.
Any documents, photographs, recordings or other non-digital communications which are ancillary to or
corroborate what the Manuscript's
author tells us move between the
Network's members.

The Network has only one purpose: To safeguard some resistance
to THEM, to ensure that even some
insignificant portion of our world is
somehow saved from ruin.

THAT OLD MUTUAL FRIEND OF OURS

So, what the fuck does any of this have to do with Halpin Chalmers? I'm getting to that.

Cut to the latter 90s, and I was a full-on drunk. Almost a decade had passed since my girlfriend left me. I was back to doing the bike messenger thing, burning tread by day and bar-flying by night. It was into my thirties, with me looking back on my twenties from the bottom of a vodka bottle, the mouth of a bong, and the sting of a syringe.

For the heroin, the reason my girlfriend left me and the reason my life turned to paste, it was in my past, if only just. After she split, I spent five years in a tenderloin shithole with a needle in my arm. I'd sold everything I owned and lived on the fringe like some kind of ghoul. In the end, I bailed on San Francisco, and spent fourteen months back in my hometown, hiding in my mom's basement, waiting for the withdrawals and the need to pass.

And pass it did, but that heroin urge, it never really lets go. Once a junkie, always a junkie, no matter how long you stay clean. I knew once I walked out of that basement, I'd cave. It'd just be a matter of time clean and sober before I'd be back on the fix. Eventually, I'd either OD and end my game, or end up as a street junkie, begging and stealing for a fix. Call me a prideful prick, but as much as the junk had its claws into me, the idea of turning up like that was too much to bear.

So, I made a choice. Rather than go back to the H, I'd let booze fill the gap. Both my parents were life-long drunks, and they lived a decent enough stretch. I figured if I paced myself, I had a good thirty or forty years to slowly kill myself on booze and smokes, rather than racing out of the game with H.

The bad shit was in the past. I liked to tell myself that I was on the mend, which was clearly a joke. I'd replaced heroin for generic vodka, but I was thirty-two and needed any little hope I could find. At the very least, now I was imagining a fresh start. It was enough hope to get me out of my mom's house, out of my hometown and back to San Francisco. I was riding again, a quasi-productive member of this laugh we call a society. As long as I kept the hooch to a minimum during business hours, I was fine. It wasn't an ideal recovery scenario, but any ex-junkie will tell you, there is no such thing as an ideal recovery. Better than nothing, right?

I'd been back in San Francisco maybe seven months, riding for a buddy who'd started his own messenger company in Hayes Valley. I was making decent cash and blowing most of it on my liquid "recovery" juice, two to three pints a day. The job, the booze and staying busy kept my mind off the junk. I wasn't asking for anything else.

Anyway, I was out one Friday night, and what do you know, but I ran into that old mutual friend of ours. You know the guy. Everybody knows him. That boon companion from college days and after, the skinny thinker with the terminal kind heart and penchant for self-destruction second only to your own. He was the old mutual friend, the guy who knew my girlfriend and me through thick and thin. He's the guy everybody knows and likes but can never quite get a bead on. That misfit that doesn't even fit in with misfits. A little too good-natured, a little too sensitive and well-meaning. He's not a bad guy; quite the opposite actually. It's his fundamental goodness which keeps you off-kilter, makes it hard to work out how someone can be so earnest and trusting in this sinkhole of a society. And the oddest thing about that mutual old friend of ours, you just can't help loving the guy. I'm not a sap, but yeah, he'd been my best friend, even if I couldn't figure out exactly why.

It had to have been close on eight years since I last laid eyes on him. Me and him went in different directions not long after my girlfriend split. I sank into the needle, and he was busy falling in love.

So, there it was, the decline of the 20th century, and there I was, drinking at the Covered Wagon after a long day riding, when he walks in. Just like that, that old mutual friend walks in, a pal from better times. If I'd imagined a hundred people that might have crossed that sill, he'd have been the last one I'd have picked, but there he was. I have to say, it was a welcome surprise; a long-lost reunion I'd never expected.

I saw him before he saw me, and ran across the place, nearly tackling him. I was so excited to see his goofy face, I picked him up and swung him around, cheering. He laughed and hugged me and told me it was great to see me. We got a spot at the bar. He bought me a drink, and we got to talking. After a couple rounds, he asked if I wanted to head over to his house. Truth is, I think he felt bad for me. It wasn't a minute past eleven, and I was already slurring and rambling in my excitement to see him again. He was probably just trying to get me clear of the sloppiness of the bar and my wasted messenger friends to someplace where we could talk like people. He'd always been an intellectual. Our discussions and debates in and after college had meant as much to me as they did to him.

He was always quieter than me, though. He favoured talk and thought over loud parties and stomping until dawn.

Last couple of weeks, I'd been in a rough patch with the willpower. Heroin was blowing on the wind around the City. It was everywhere, going cheap. I had four offers that week alone. The only thing keeping me from slipping back was the vodka, and I was hitting the sauce hard. I needed my head so boozed up that I couldn't bother chasing smack . . . or thinking about loneliness.

During and after my needle days, I'd lost connection with pretty much everyone I'd known, either through their disgust or the junkie's isolation. It'd been a long while since I'd seen anyone from college, let alone an old friend. Time (and class-A addiction) has a way of separating people. Seeing this guy, this old buddy, someone from a better time in my life, it felt like a lifeline. Despite my loaded state, I went along.

We rolled to his place, and I passed out on his couch almost immediately. What a reunion, right? I don't even remember getting there, but woke up on the couch just around four am. He was sitting there in a lounge chair, reading. It took me a minute to work out where I was or even who he was. When it hit me, I was excited to see him all over again. He was happy to see me as well but asked me to keep it down. He must have told me at the bar, but he had to re-explain that he was a dad now, and his wife (I'd met her back in the day when they were first dating) and baby girl were asleep down the hall.

It was a strange feeling, seeing our old mutual friend in that context. Here was a guy who I remember from our twenties. It had been drug-fuelled debates, hallucinogenic bops through Golden Gate Park, drunken nights chain-smoking and talking politics. And here we were, a decade from when we first met, and everything was different. Here was a guy with a wife and a kid. Mostly the same, but older, fatter, responsibility on his shoulders. But it was him. Even in all my bike messenger bravado, and his doughy husband and father routine, I was genuinely glad to see the guy.

He got me something to eat and a glass of water. It was quiet in the living room, with something playing on the stereo. I asked him what he was listening to, but I already knew. "Erik Satie's Gnossiennes," he replied, handing me the album cover. Leave it to him to have been listening to that, and on vinyl. Even back in the day, with all the rock and grunge and punk, he had a fetish for old music, and for vinyl albums.

The record must have been old and not in the best shape. I could hear it crackling like a fire, and the cover looked like it had been in a few too many tumbles on the garage sale circuit. I listened to the music, listened to that sad, awful piano dirge of **Gnossienne No. 3**. It hung in the back of my skull like a bloodied bedsheet. I lied and said I'd never heard of Satie or this music. I wondered if he knew I was lying. I'm sure I'd told him at some point in our friendship that my mom was a librarian and a piano teacher, and that Satie was one of her favourites. I knew those pieces only too well. But that was a long time and a lot of drugs ago. He'd most likely forgotten that I was probably the one who introduced him to Satie. I looked him in the eyes. If he remembered, it didn't show. He looked back at me with a calm, happy smile.

I glanced at the book he was reading. "Funny that we met tonight," he said. "This would be right up your alley." He handed it to me. "Guy's name is Halpin Chalmers. He was a small-time journalist and horror writer back in the twenties. Turns out he had a long-time interest in one of your favourite subjects: mind expansion and the occult."

I wanted to know what the book was about. "It's a collection of his writings, mixed with a sort of biography of him. The guy was a nut, but a major big brain. Bit of a tormented genius type." He smiled again, giving me his signature wink. "Sound familiar?"

I laughed, saying my genius days were behind me, that all that intellectual crap didn't pay the bills, blah, blah, blah. A hungover attempt at working-class heroism.

He shrugged it off. "Dunno, man. I think you'd be into it if you gave it a read." He thought for a second, then handed me the book. "Take it."

I tried to refuse, but he insisted. "You might still think all the Jungian stuff is bullshit, but for me, this is synchronicity. Me seeing you, me reading this book, you coming here. This book is far more you than me. I've been thinking of you the whole time I've been reading it. You'll connect with this Chalmers guy." He laughed. "He'd have been with us in our heyday."

The baby monitor on the wall started in with a little whimper. "Shit, man. I need to feed her." He looked tired then, careworn. I could see that fatherhood had taken a toll on his sleep, but he smiled. "I better get her."

I was never much on the sentimental shit, but I felt tears in my eyes watching our old mutual friend go down that hall, now a father caring for his baby. I felt wistful then, seeing him changed so much, seeing the distance which time had put between us. The years, they do have a way of getting away from us, don't they?

But he'd soon be coming back, and I recognised a moment for me to skiddoo. I threw on my jacket and boots and was ready to jet when he came back in with his baby girl. He saw I was going and didn't say anything to stop me. He did force the book on me, though. "Take it, man. Come back when you finish it. Tell me what you think of it."

I took the book if just to finish up and get out of there. I was feeling unnerved, out of place, seeing him like that. I lied and said I'd read the book, that we'd see each other again real soon. We both knew it was a lie, but he gave me a hug, told me it was amazing to see me again, and when I looked at him, I could see his eyes were filled up with tears. "It's great to see you, man," he said, choking a little. "I—it's been too long." I nodded and muttered something stupid in reply, patted him once on the shoulder, and I was gone.

The sun was just starting to glow somewhere over the East Bay. Birds were starting to chirp. San Francisco was waking up. I stuffed the book in my bag, jumped on my bike and rolled.

(the following is a condensation of two announcements which appeared in the Partridgeville Gazette, Partridgeville, New York, July 5, 1928)

EARTHQUAKE SHAKES FINANCIAL DISTRICT

At 2 o'clock this morning an earth tremor of unusual severity broke several plate–glass windows in Central Square and completely disorganised the electric and street railway systems. The tremor was felt in the outlying districts, and the steeple of the First Baptist Church on Angell Hill (designed by Christopher Wren in 1717) was entirely demolished. Firemen are now attempting to put out a blaze which threatens to destroy the Partridgeville Glue Works. An investigation is promised by the mayor and an immediate attempt will be made to fix responsibility for this disastrous occurrence.

OCCULT WRITER MURDERED BY UNKNOWN GUEST
HORRIBLE CRIME IN CENTRAL SQUARE
MYSTERY SURROUNDS DEATH OF HALPIN CHALMERS

At 9 a.m. today the body of Halpin Chalmers, author and journalist, was found in an empty room above the jewelry store of Smithwick and Isaacs, 24 Central Square. The coroner's investigation revealed that the room had been rented *furnished* to Mr. Chalmers on May 1, and that he had himself disposed of the furniture a fortnight ago. Chalmers was the author of several recondite books on occult themes, and a member of the Bibliographic Guild. He formerly resided in Brooklyn, New York.

At 7 a.m. Mr. L.E. Hancock, who occupies the apartment opposite Chalmers' room in the Smithwick and Isaacs establishment, smelt a peculiar odor when he opened his door to take in his cat and the morning edition of the *Partridgeville Gazette*. The odor he describes as extremely acrid and nauseous, and he affirms that it was so strong in the vicinity of Chalmers' room that he was obliged to hold his nose when he approached that section of the hall.

He was about to return to his own apartment when it occurred to him that Chalmers might have accidentally forgotten to turn off the gas in his kitchenette. Becoming considerably alarmed at the thought, he decided to investigate, and when repeated tappings on Chalmers' door brought no response he notified the superintendent. The latter opened the door by means of a pass key, and the two men quickly made their way into Chalmers room. The room was utterly destitute of furniture, and Hancock asserts that when he first glanced at the floor his heart went cold

within him, and that the superintendent.
without saying a word, walked to the open
window and stared at the building opposite
for fully five minutes.

Chalmers lay stretched upon his back in
the center of the room. He was starkly nude,
and his chest and arms were covered with
a peculiar bluish pus or ichor. His head lay
grotesquely upon his chest. It had been completely severed from his body, and the features of his body and head were twisted and
torn and horribly mangled. Nowhere was
there a trace of blood.

The room presented a most astonishing
appearance. The intersections of the walls,
ceiling and floor had been thickly smeared
with plaster of Paris, but at intervals fragments had cracked and fallen off, and someone had grouped these upon the floor about
the murdered man so as to form a perfect
triangle.

Beside the body were several sheets of
charred yellow paper. These bore fantastic
geometric designs and symbols and several
hastily scrawled sentences. The sentences
were almost illegible and so absurd in content that they furnished no possible clue to
the perpetrator of the crime. "I am waiting
and watching," Chalmers wrote. "I sit by the
window and watch walls and ceiling. I do not
believe they can reach me. but I must beware
lest THEY break through."

On another sheet of paper, the most
badly charred of the seven or eight fragments

found by Detective Sergeant Douglas (of the Partridgeville Reserve), was scrawled the following:

"Good God, the plaster is falling! A terrific shock has loosened the plaster and it is falling. I never could have anticipated this. The stranger has done this to me! It is growing dark in the room. I must phone Frank. But can he get here in time? I will try. I will recite the Einstein formula. I will—God. they are breaking through! They are breaking through! Smoke is pouring from the corners of the wall. Their *tongues*—ahhhhh—"

In the opinion of Detective Sergeant Douglas, Chalmers was poisoned by some obscure chemical. He has sent specimens of the strange blue slime found on Chalmers' body to the Partridgeville Chemical Laboratories; and he expects the report will shed new light on one of the most mysterious crimes of recent years. That Chalmers entertained a guest on the evening preceding the earthquake is certain, for his neighbor distinctly heard cries in the night, just around the time of the earthquake. Suspicion points strongly to this unknown visitor and the police are diligently endeavoring to discover his identity.

THE FADED GLORY

I rode for the Mission with that book in my bag, but my mind was still on our old mutual friend. He'd changed so much in the years since I last saw him. He wasn't the guy I knew any more.

I mean, yeah, he was the same guy. Same goofy smile, same big heart, same loyal dog-like friend my girlfriend and I used to make fun of when he wasn't around. He was the same guy with the same baffling but endearing innocence for someone who was so self-destructive. Yet now he'd lost some of that edge. The addict in him was gone. He wasn't the same jittery-handed bundle of self-destruction. That fire seemed to have gone out, and in its place, he had the wife and kids, the extra fat, the quiet life.

It happens. People change. That fire in the belly of youth just goes out for some folks. They lose their taste for the darkness. Having a family and doing the responsibility and respectability thing, it does that to plenty of hardcores. They just wither a bit, go soft and safe. That's what I'd seen. A guy who'd found his comfortable decline.

It made me sad to see him like that, all middle-class dad at the age of thirty. Me and other messengers made fun of dudes like that. It was like a bad joke. How many nights had I guffawed at the thought of me ever ending up like that? It was absolutely ludicrous.

It all boils down to what you can buy and what you can't. This clown-car we call a society has this pitch it runs. It pitches this idea of addiction, and of people getting sober, and the whole thing is a laughable myth. It's been fed to us since the days of the after-school special. In books or movies or TV shows, it always plays out as per the script. Some asshole who gets into booze or drugs eventually finds their life ruined by addiction. It starts out all fun and games at first, but the party has to end. Somewhere around the middle, the morality play cuts in. The sunken eyes, the smeared makeup, the losing of home and job and respect. Soon the poor junkie is selling grandma's jewellery or sucking dick in an alley for a fix. Drug dealers, money owed, threats of broken limbs or shallow graves.

And eventually comes the rock bottom moment, where our protagonist comes to their epiphany about their addiction. Lying in a pool of their own sick, bawling their eyes out, they see now how all their addiction focuses back on some painful childhood moment. Mommy burned her with cigarettes. Daddy didn't offer the requisite love and support. Uncle Wilbur snuck into his childhood bedroom at night. Money and stress led them to despair. The tears, the admissions, it all boiling down to a realisation that they had to change.

Then there's the montage sequence of tough recovery, of rehab and group therapy, of things very slowly coming back together. The music slowly starts to turn major chord. Time goes by, and they start to see some hope. Voila! After a few months in some white-bread clinic, our hero/heroine emerges, a better person for it, healed and ready to move into that bright and wonderful future which only sobriety can provide.

This is the lie about addiction we've been sold. Variations on a theme, sure, but at their roots, they're all the same bullshit. It's a script written by people who don't know the first thing about being an addict, written for suckers and buy-ins to the Just Say No mentality.

Take it from a lifer. There's nothing predictable about being an addict, about abusing any or all substances. Just because people drink or do drugs, doesn't mean they had a fucked-up past. Look at me. My parents didn't beat me. They didn't molest me or treat me like shit. I had a reasonably normal life growing up. I didn't do drugs because my life was fucked up. I did drugs to fuck up my life, my normal, lower-middle-class life.

And just because you've got addictions, it doesn't mean you'll end up hitting rock bottom. Not everybody ends up in an alley with track marks up and down their arms (I did, but that's not the point). Not everyone ends up ruined or turning tricks. 99% of addicts are functioning addicts, doing what's expected of them. Paying their bills, going to work, sorting their shit. Look around. Everybody is an addict, addicted to something.

If it exists, someone is addicted to it. Booze or drugs or cigarettes. Gambling or sex or TV or computer games or chocolate. Attention or validation or just your own fucked up thoughts about life. That's human beings. We like addiction. People like habits, particularly habits which make you feel good. Why not? That's normal. Humans like the good and dislike the bad. And I dare anyone to tell me otherwise. We get off on our need to get better than what the world gives us for free.

Look at you, Chumley. What are you addicted to? Maybe look at that mobile phone in your hand, that screen you're gawking into. How much of your life is wrapped up in that digital bong hit? How many binged episodes a week does it take before you start calling it an addiction? A shit ton, apparently. How many likes and shares did your posts get this week, I wonder. You better go check.

And yet the addiction morality play, that after-school special, it sticks to most everyone in some banal way or another. The whole society has been repeating this fairy tale for so long, it's hard for some not to regurgitate it when the chips are down. I've watched way too many fuckwits with flagging guts, or dim imaginations let a little spiralling out of control send them running for the safety net.

They find Jesus or Islam or power yoga or some such crap. They go all tears and contrition and shame, and that'd be it. Gone Daddy gone, road-running for the sure shores of moral redemption. Out of the scene, off the radar for at least a year. Sooner or later though, they'd turn up, looking like Ned Flanders or Louis Farrakhan, or dressed in yoga pants. They'd be buying organic green tea at Whole Foods with their newly-found gluten-free, vegan nag-bitch in tow. They'd have that forced, sappy smile, and the relieved look of someone who had escaped vertigo with their conformity and fear intact. They'd tell me they'd never felt better. What a relief to be clean and sober. They'd say it was good to see me, but I could see their forced smiles wavering as they looked at me. I was a thing to them, a pariah. I was a sickening reminder of that edge they'd pulled back from, and they were not going to get too close to me. Addiction, after all, is catching. They had a new heaven, and my hell had no place in it.

And that's what always made me laugh. I'd have rather died of an overdose than become an existential joke like that. I always saw myself going out in a blaze, heart popped or liver damage or an overdose. Anything with a little bit of an edge.

But I wasn't laughing about our old mutual friend. He'd always been a good guy, even if he was a little on the tender side, and to see him retracting the good works we'd done back in the day, it broke my heart. I wished him well in his comfortable, safe life. It wasn't for me.

I prefer the outer edge. That's where the lifers are, the real addicts who aren't giving in or giving up, hell or high water. Where do you land, Chumley? My money is on self-denying lifer, head all stuffed in digital dope. Go ahead. Prove me wrong.

(handwritten pages found in the ruins of an apartment building fire in Beskudnikovo, Moscow. Author believed to have died in the fire. Translated from the Russian)

To you, the reader,

My name is Renata B————, and I am a senior official at a prestigious corporation in the Russian Federation. Or should I say, I was a senior official.

Now, I am no one. I am without name, without hope, without anyone who can help me.

I have read the Manuscript. It has ruined my life. I warn you, do not read its pages unless you too would be ruined.

I did not know what the Manuscript was when I began to read it. It was accidental that it came into my possession. I had no interest in radical or dangerous things. I was successful and happy. My career was excellent. I was married to a good man. He was an engineer at my company, and we were wed six years ago. We had a four-year-old son, who was strong and bright. We had great hopes for our future.

That is gone now. My husband and child are gone, and I know not where. I do not know if they are alive or dead, but I have no hopes ever to see them again.

I am alone and running for my life. There is little chance for me. THEY are closer than I wish to admit.

The Manuscript came into my possession by accident. My husband and I were living and working in Moscow when I was contacted by my aunt. She was concerned for her son, my cousin, Matvei. Matvei was a troubled young man six years younger than myself. He had been involved in drugs, in crime. His only employment was with an old bookshop in Lyublino. We were close as children, but as time went on, Matvei drifted away from his family, and we lost contact.

My aunt had left Moscow a number of years ago and moved back to St. Petersburg for her retirement. She had only heard from Matvei from time to time since she'd left, but recently she had not heard from him at all. She was concerned and asked that we check in on him, to make sure everything was all right.

I was not interested in contacting Matvei or even going to see him, but my husband felt it was our familial duty to go. My aunt had been very kind to us when our son was a baby, taking him each day so we could work. I could not argue with my husband, for his motives were correct. That did not stop me from feeling something was terribly wrong. Matvei could be nothing but trouble for us.

We attempted to call what number my aunt had for him, but there was no answer. After several attempts, we drove to Matvei's apartment block to see if he was still living there. The superintendent told us that Matvei had not been seen or paid his rent in over two months. He had no idea what had become of my cousin, nor did he care. He was in the process of clearing out the apartment for a new tenant and asked if we would haul away Matvei's belongings, or they would be thrown out.

This is how the Manuscript came into my possession. We found it, a manuscript in a plain envelope, stuffed in a box of his things. How Matvei had gotten it, I cannot say. It was written in German (I learned German in university and used it frequently in my career in dealing with German companies) but was noted at the beginning to have been translated from English. My husband doesn't understand German but thought perhaps there was something useful in it which might help us locate my cousin. He suggested I read it to see what I might find out.

That was the beginning of the end for me and my family.

I never discovered what became of Matvei, but I can surmise. No good could come from reading that accursed book. I read its pages with growing anxiousness. I did not want to believe what I was reading, that any of it might be true, but as the days and weeks passed, as I read more, I saw signs all around me of what its author was saying. Damn him, and damn Matvei. What unspeakable horrors I was now learning, and in doing so, I withdrew from my life more and more.

I could no more face my work than I could face daily life. Each page drew me away from my sane, happy world. I could sense THEM, feel THEM, and feel eyes upon me as if everyone around me knew what I was reading. My husband asked me repeatedly to tell him what was in the Manuscript, but what at first was simply my innocent confusion of why Matvei would have had it, soon grew into elusiveness and fear. I could see it now. I could see it in the people on the street, in my colleagues and business associates. And yes, I began to see it in my husband and my child.

What I would give to undo what has been done. Help me, Father in Heaven. Take it away; let me be as I was once more. Let it be that I never read those pages, never heard of the Manuscript or its damned author. Let me return to my life, to the world which is innocent of all of this.

Let me not hear THEM coming for me. The breathing. That awful breathing, it is everywhere.

(letter burned beyond this point)

THE LIFE AND TIMES
OF HALPIN CHALMERS

I'm not gonna sugarcoat this. That book he gave me, it sat around untouched for a whole lot of years. It sat around on the milk crate I used as a nightstand next to my futon, gathering dust and cigarette ash. Given how far I'd drifted from my intellectual years, that book had no chance of getting read.

Thing was, I'd gone out of my way after college to drive myself into a cerebral dead-end. I'd turned my bike messenger lifestyle into a proletariat crusade. All that highbrow book stuff had gradually been denigrated to the ranks of either mental masturbation or pure bourgeois bullshit. The people I surrounded myself with since college were not exactly the book-read types. A lot of them had barely graduated high school. Any that had gone in for higher education, they overshadowed it when talking to other messengers with working man bravado and smug dismissal. I freely admit I ran this same game, and with the passage of years and the sinking into a paycheck-to-paycheck lifestyle, I'd all but convinced myself I believed it. That book sat untouched until I forgot it was there, just another bit of detritus in the pigsty that I called my life.

It was a one-night stand in the second year of the 21st century that brought that book back in the mix. I met some woman in a bar in the Mission, and god knows how, but I convinced her to sleep with me. Part of it was probably she was jacked to the gills on ecstasy or a small dose of acid. Whatever. Thing is, she came back to my place, we drank, we got naked, blah, blah, blah.

Once the deed was done, we were lying on my futon, and she picked the book up, the only book I had left in my life. "This is weird," she said, flipping pages. "You reading this?" She was too high to make sense of it. Her pupils were like black saucers, phasing in and out of focus as her blissed-out brain tried to comprehend the tiny typeface.

Now that the sex was over, I wanted her out. She was a stoned albatross, and my buzz was fading fast. She had next to no charm, and without my dick in the way, that charmlessness shone right through. I was giving her the stink eye (she didn't notice), when, in my woozy post-drunk, I started reading what I could while she flipped those pages. I was catching snippets, scanning the black and white prints and illustrations, reading blurbs of thought and insight, and I could feel something in what I was reading. I kept patience steady while I let her scan over the book with her drowsy, tripping eyes. Soon she faded out, and I picked up the book and started to read.

That was it. I was hooked. Every day, every minute I could steal between deliveries, every night at a quiet bar, or in my bedroom while my roommates romped and partied, I read that crazy thing.

The book was almost a thousand pages long, a seriously dense tome in tiny, single-spaced print, all of it information on and writings by Chalmers. The forward described him as an unsung hero of occult studies and fringe science, a man who wrote a lot in his time, and was respected only by those who could understand what he was trying to do. Many dismissed him as a shameless self-promoter, an imperious member of an elitist intelligentsia. Yet his writings did get published. Not in any mainstream publications, he was way too fringe for that. But Halpin Chalmers did get his work out to the world, and even during his lifetime, he garnered a wide following. Chalmers was well known as a regular fixture in Los Angeles during the heyday of occult revivalism back in the 20s. His essays on the police brutality against the labour movement were widely quoted and discussed in political circles. His occult writing was the inspiration for a generation of readers and writers. John Steinbeck met Chalmers back when Steinbeck was a starving writer in New York City, and Chalmers was a curator of some museum. Steinbeck called him "one of the most challenging, engaging men I have ever met, or ever will."

I dove in with gusto. In his journalism, Chalmers was a muckraker of the highest order who looked at the disenfranchised masses he defended in his writing as a pack of illiterate rabble. He wrote diatribes against corruption, what he called scientific dogmatism, and published extensively on topics ranging from the occult to mathematics to science to social and moral taboos. He was an intellectual elitist, but in the same breath was a quixotic champion for the uneducated masses. His writing was lengthy and, for a journalist, didactic. He extolled free-thinking and a kind of radical scientific approach which combined the sciences with the esoteric or supernatural. He'd reported or written monographs on everything out there. Science, war, politics, art, literature, crime, you name it. His journalism was varied and well-researched, but not just a little bit overreaching in its scope.

In his fiction and occult writing, that's where he was at his best. Chalmers wrote newspaper articles to pay the bills, but his occult writing was far and away superior. The book was interspersed with sections of something he'd written called "The Secret Watchers". It was off the hook. A lot of esoteric talk of creatures from alternate dimensions, things seeing through time, that kind of thing. It made for good fantasy. His work read like Allister Crowley, as if Chalmers wasn't making this stuff up, but actually believed it. From what the forward said, "The Secret Watchers" was banned until the late-60s, when it made a huge splash with the hippies and Satanists alike. I could see why. There was an intricacy and reality to his fiction, something which was hard to shake.

And yes, Chalmers was an avid proponent of mind-expanding substances to advance human consciousness. Admittedly, this is one of the things which really attracted me to him; I approached life in exactly the same way. He wrote articles on geometry and cosmology, and the use of psilocybin to enhance one's understanding of both. This was a guy who wasn't backing away from the edge. He was rushing at it screaming, and I was rushing right in there with him. I had to admit our old mutual friend had been on the money. I saw in Chalmers a kindred spirit, a hardcore free-thinker and critic of the system, a consumer of mind-altering chemicals to boot. If he'd been alive in my time, he'd have been into Bauhaus and methamphetamines.

There was a problem, though. Chalmer's writings only made up maybe half the book. The rest wasn't even written by Chalmers, but by his biographer and friend, Fred Carstairs. From what he wrote, Carstairs had a lot of respect for Chalmers, but at the same time seemed to be afraid of him, afraid of the places he went when he was under the influence, the things he did in the name of discovery. Carstairs was writing about the man he knew, but in many ways, he didn't seem to know much about Chalmers at all. They were friends and had exchanged letters over the years, but where Chalmers was a man on the periphery, Fred Carstairs was a man who only dabbled there out of studious fascination. Chalmers had travelled the world, lived life, whereby comparison, Carstairs had spent his whole life living in some Podunk town in upstate New York called Partridgeville. Our old mutual friend, he'd been my Carstairs. I'd always been the one swimming out into dark waters, while he stuck closer to shore. Whenever there's someone willing to push the envelope, there's gotta be someone nearby just not willing to go all the way.

In reading the biography, I felt like Carstairs kept a lot back in his writings, sticking to the facts and only dabbling into the personal when it was absolutely necessary. I was, by this point, nearing my second reading of the book, and I was sure there was more to Chalmers' life, but particularly to his death which the brief description and the bad print of Chalmers' obituary told. From the obituary, Chalmers' death was just another unsolved murder, but that was it. The case was never solved, and over the years since his death (particularly after the mid- to late-60s) a sort of legend had grown up around Chalmers, his writing and his death. The foreword said there was a small but dedicated following of Chalmers and his work. They held a yearly convention in Partridgeville (the town where Chalmers was murdered), with readings, panels, occult stuff, the works.

In total, I ended up reading the book four times. After the second reading, I started taking notes, highlighting passages, putting little comments in the margins. I was back in college again. I read it and re-read it, all the time hoping that maybe I'd missed something, that another read would shed some more light. But it didn't matter how many fucking times I read it. In the end, what I was after just wasn't in the book. Chalmers had been gruesomely murdered in some dingy apartment above a jewellery store, and somehow this book managed to gloss over every sordid detail. I needed to know what happened. I needed more.

So, I spent a good year of my spare time scouring book-stores. Nobody had much of anything. Books on or by eccentric occult writers from the 1920s wasn't what you'd call a popular genre. Even the darker, mustier bookstores had next to nothing. I did find a complete edition of The Secret Watchers, but it was only marginally longer than the excerpts in my book.

The libraries around town were even less helpful, though I did get a lead from a segment of a doctor's report on Chalmers' death in the microfiche section. I had to sit in this dingy little room in the library's basement to even view it. The clipping was from a bacteriologist named James Morton who'd been asked to analyse some blue goo the cops had found covering Chalmers' body. Here's what it said:

> 'The fluid sent to me for analysis is the most peculiar that I have ever examined. It resembles living protoplasm, but it lacks the peculiar substances known as enzymes. Enzymes catalyse the chemical reactions occurring in living cells, and when the cell dies, they cause it to disintegrate by hydrolysation. Without enzymes, protoplasm should possess enduring vitality, i.e. immortality. Enzymes are the negative components, so to speak, of unicellular organisms, which is the basis of all life. That living matter without enzymes biologists emphatically deny. And yet the substance that you have sent me is alive and it lacks these "indispensable" bodies. Good God, sir, do you realise what astounding new vistas this opens up?'

What the hell was that? How had Chalmers ended up covered in some weird slime? Carstairs never said anything about that in the biography. How the fuck do you gloss over weird slime at the scene of a murder?

I asked around for a long time, but it eventually became clear that the trail had gone dead. There was nothing more to read on the subject. I did research in all the places I knew. Hell, I even contacted universities and bookshops on the East Coast, but it was all leading back to a whole lotta nothing. I wrote to the Chalmers appreciation nuts, but no one ever responded.

I was still a drunk at this point, and the time I spent chasing the details of Chalmers' death slowly got swallowed up by my nightly dates with Mr. Vodka. The book, failing to give me anything more, even after my fourth read, sat once more next to my futon, gathering dust. Time marched on, and I stumbled along in its wake.

Then, about a year after the first read, I got a break even without looking for one.

(the following article appeared in the Los Angeles Times, June 21, 1929)

DISRUPTION AT HOLLYWOOD PREMIERE
Young woman hospitalized after apparent nervous breakdown

The premiere of the much anticipated "Hollywood Revue of 1929" was cut short last night when a young woman had to be removed from the theater during the second half of the movie.

Miss Sylvia Templeton, an office employee, was in attendance at the premiere at Grauman's Chinese Theater, when nearing the latter part of the second act, she began screaming uncontrollably.

Dr Arnold Fetzer, a physician who was also in attendance, attempted to assist with calming Miss Templeton but found her incoherent. "She wouldn't stop screaming," Dr Fetzer explained. "We had no choice but to restrain her." Several witnesses present corroborated the events which led to Miss Templeton's removal from the theater.

Miss Templeton was taken by ambulance to Los Angeles County Hospital. Her family could not be reached for comment, as it is believed they are with their daughter at this time.

Producer Harry Rapf was concerned for Miss Templeton above all else. "I only met her this evening. She seemed a lovely young woman. I hope she gets well soon. My prayers go out to her and her family."

All patrons present at last night's premiere have been invited to the MGM studios for a private screening tonight, so they might finish watching the film.

STARTING WITH A TYPEWRITER

I'm writing this on an old daisy wheel electric typewriter. I couldn't believe they actually still sold them, typewriters I mean. In the age of tablets and touchscreens, smartphones and laptops, who uses a fucking typewriter anymore?! Ha, I do apparently. But there you go. An electric typewriter. Pretty good one too.

When I first started writing this all down, I thought about ditching technology altogether. It was a panic move, one motivated by my need to put up as big a wall as possible between me and the nightmare. But to be fair, it wasn't just that. I've always been a Luddite. Most junkies and alcoholics are, but I was the king of the Luddites, worsening the older I got. Technology, all that fancy-schmancy crap, was a mainstream thing, for suckers and sell-outs. While I've mellowed with age, I'm still convinced younger me was on to something. Hell, why bother learning about yourself when you can just chase after the next shiny techno-toy? Why worry about our world, the human condition, about the environment, war, poverty, injustice? That stuff is a downer. Look over there! The newest bit of iShit has just gone on sale, and you can have yours too if you stand in a goddamn line for two days to get yours first.

When I began writing this, you can imagine that the idea of ditching anything electric had a romantic ring to it. You know the song and dance: Returning to the basics, writing by hand, nights by candlelight, all that Abe Lincoln writing with coal on a slate bullshit. Luddites lap it up. I know I did.

A taste of simplicity and that sentiment was short-lived. Fact is, I needed to write this quickly. There's a lot to get down, and it needed to be legible. Legibility alone ruled out me writing it by hand. Doctor prescriptions didn't have shit on my cuneiform. My handwriting was shit in my best days, and my best days are long behind me. I scratched by hand for three days, then spent another two trying to decipher what I'd written in the first place.

So, the ol' pen and ink were out, and a 1981 IBM Selectric II electric typewriter was in.

Electricity isn't the problem, Chumley. It's not electricity that draws THEM. If it was, THEY would have been on us back in the 1800s. No, it's the screens. That's what keeps THEM, lets THEM at us, those goddamn screens we love so much. The way we ogle them every chance we get with our piggy little eyes.

Addiction is a brain disorder characterized by compulsive engagement in rewarding stimuli despite adverse consequences.

Despite the involvement of a number of psychosocial factors, a biological process—one which is induced by repeated exposure to an addictive stimulus—is the core pathology that drives the development and maintenance of an addiction. The two properties that characterize all addictive stimuli are that they are reinforcing (i.e., they increase the likelihood that a person will seek repeated exposure to them) and intrinsically rewarding (i.e., they are perceived as being inherently positive, desirable, and pleasurable).

Addiction is a disorder of the brain's reward system which arises through transcriptional and epigenetic mechanisms and develops over time from chronically high levels of exposure to an addictive stimulus (e.g., eating food, the use of cocaine, engagement in sexual activity, participation in high-thrill cultural activities such as gambling, etc.).

There is scientific evidence that the addictive behaviours share key neurobiological features—they intensely involve brain pathways of reward and reinforcement, affecting motivation, which consists of the neurotransmitter dopamine. And, in keeping with other highly motivated states, they lead to the pruning of synapses in the prefrontal cortex, home of the brain's highest functions.

Complex conditions that affect reward, reinforcement, motivation, and memory systems of the brain, substance use and gambling disorders are characterized by impaired control over usage; social impairment, involving disruption of everyday activities and relationships; and may involve craving. Continued use is typically harmful to relationships and work or school obligations. Another distinguishing feature is that individuals may continue the activity despite physical or psychological harm incurred or exacerbated by use. And typically, tolerance to the substance increases, as the body adapts to its presence.

DeltaFosB (ΔFosB), a gene tran-
scription factor, is a critical com-
ponent and common factor in the
development of virtually all forms
of addictions.

Two decades of research into
ΔFosB's role in addiction have demonstrated that addiction arises, and
the associated compulsive behaviour
intensifies or attenuates, along with
the overexpression of ΔFosB in the
D1-type medium spiny neurons of the
nucleus accumbens.

Because addiction affects the
brain's executive functions, centred
in the prefrontal cortex, individuals who develop an addiction may
not be aware that their behaviour is
causing problems for themselves and
others. Over time, the pursuit of
the pleasurable effects of the substance or behaviour may dominate an
individual's activities.

Addiction exacts an "astoundingly
high financial and human toll" on
individuals and society as a
whole . . .

THE ANARCHIST
BOOKSHOP

I don't know how I'd missed it, especially because back in the day, I went into this place all the time. I was riding a package up to Upper Haight when totally by accident, I looked over and spotted it. Binding Pact, the anarchist bookshop. I slammed on the brakes so hard, I nearly got clipped by a cab. The driver gave me an earful of shitty middle-eastern English, but I was in no headspace to bother with a retort.

My hands were actually shaking as I locked up my bike. Seeing it, remembering the kind of crazy crap they had in there, I knew this was the place where I could get some answers. How or why I hadn't considered or even remembered this place, I can't say. All I knew was, after a year mixed up in trying to find out more about Halpin Chalmers, I'd found the one last chance I had to get something fresh. I hurried inside.

It was just how I remembered it. The place smelled like old newsprint and pretension. Something approximating music was lolling from overhead. Images of Emma Goldman, Leo Tolstoy and Che Guevara glared at me from the walls.

Anarchist and communist pamphlets and books, all of them badly printed or poorly bound, lined shelves. The front wall was an orgy of fliers and pamphlets, photocopied manifestos, you name it, on the "struggle" and every variation thereof. Nearby was a book section on feminism, LGBTQ, misogyny and sexism. Across from it, there was a section on government conspiracies, Noam Chomsky, the Illuminati, corporate greed. Row after row of bookshelves greeted me with every lefty concept under the sun. If it had a liberal agenda behind it, it was in there. The place was every conservative's nightmare, a Bakunin Barnes and Nobles. Everyone browsing looked pasty and pointedly vegan. Everything from anti-globalization meetings to radical poetry readings to save the freaking whales accosted me from all sides.

I hadn't been in that place in over a decade. I had to smile at how some shit never changes. Our old mutual friend and I spent a lot of time in here, more than once too blazed on 'shrooms to do much more than stare and giggle and get thrown out. No doubt, we bought our share of those lefty books, and we checked out the upcoming events on the over-crammed bulletin board. For the most part, though, we found those events so I could go along and mock everyone in sight, no matter what side of the protest you were on, and he'd go along and hit on revolutionary types (he had a kink for men or women with radical zeal) . We bought some of those books to read, but many more to keep us laughing while we waited for a dealer to turn up. It was a comfort to see the place, and that it hadn't changed. I considered grabbing a flier for the Social Justice rally at City Hall, just for old time's sake.

But I had bigger fish to fry. I had to see if this book hole had what I needed. "Where's the occult section?" I asked the pale-faced, black-lipsticked, pierced guy behind the counter. He gave me the up-and-down. I don't think he appreciated my looks, my clothes or my tone. He frowned and lazily waved in a direction, then looked away, bored.

I headed over and started searching for my prize. It was a pretty good-sized section: a whole shelf dedicated to the occult. But after tearing through the lot, my hopes faded. Occult, my ass. It was UFOs, the Tibetan Book of the Dead, Carlos Castaneda and Peace Magick for Wiccans. My excitement turned to squinting disgust. What the fuck? Unexplained Mysteries, copies of the Satanic Bible (expensive ones autographed by late Anton Lavey before he bought the diabolical farm), practises of modern Druids, a copy of the Tao of Pooh?! I couldn't believe it. I'd seen more occult shit at a Renaissance Fair. "Hey, haven't you got any other books?" I asked. "Older books? Good books?"

The counter emo still did not appreciate my looks, my clothes, nor my tone. But, being the patent professional of the emo book-selling variety, he sighed, then rang a bell in front of him.

Out of a back room came a fat guy with a ponytail and a greying beard. He looked like Gary Gygax, the inventor of Dungeons and Dragons, if Gary Gygax got all dolled up like a Caliph. He had on dark little glasses, Turkish slippers, a sarik, some cheesy ass robes and was sipping something from a teensy glass. The fat guy eyed the emo behind the counter, the emo flourished in my direction, and the fat guy came over and looked down at me crouched in my browsing.

I asked him if they had any real occult books. Caliph Gary looked down at me and said they had more copies of Peace Magick for Wiccans in the back. I explained that my five copies at home were just fine, thanks, but I was after something a little more authentic. Gary did a fantastic job of looking smug and aloof. I suppressed the natural urge to stand up and smack that little glass out of his hand and instead asked if they had any books on Halpin Chalmers.

Oh, that did it. Caliph Gary stiffened and told me 'no' a little too fast. The haughtiness was gone. His face was now squirming through a thousand emotions, all the while glancing around the place, at the counter emo, at the other customers. He looked stricken, beset on all sides. I was about to tell him not to get his panties in a twist, that I was just looking for a book on Halpin Chalmers, when he quickly handed me a card with a name and a phone number on it, then hurried back behind the door he'd just come out of, closing it fast. No one noticed the exchange, or for that matter, seemed to care. I left.

(graffiti on a wall in São Paulo, Brazil)

Nós somos os olhos e ouvidos! Nós somos o gado!

(Translation: We are the eyes and ears! We are the cattle!)

CALIPH GARY'S GIFT

So, I called. I wasn't exactly sure why I did. More than likely, ol' Caliph Gary gave me that card because he was looking for an anonymous hookup, but if there was a chance he had something, I needed to know. After a whole lot of rings, he answered.

Gary asked who I was, and I said nobody, the same nobody who he gave the card to at the bookstore. He asked who I'd talked to. Again, I said nobody. He asked me what I knew. I said lots of things, but if he meant about Halpin Chalmers, I told him about the book I'd read, and that I wanted more information on Chalmers, particularly about his death.

Gary changed tack. He asked me what I did for entertainment. I said I drank a lot and spent my nights calling bookstore weirdos who gave me their cards. He asked if I had a TV or a computer. I said not fucking likely. He asked where I was calling from. I told him a payphone; that my apartment didn't have a phone, or if it did, I didn't know where it was. He asked what I did for a living. I told him I was a bike messenger and then asked him if giving me the third degree was making him feel better or worse. Gary thought about this, then asked if I could come to the Mission to meet him. He gave me an address. I told him I was just a few blocks away.

Gary was a weirdo, no doubt, but from the looks of things, he was a rich, pampered weirdo. His apartment in the Mission looked dingy enough from the outside, but once past two metal gates and up a flight of stairs, I walked into a polished Victorian beauty. The place had either been in his family since the good ol' days and been kept up, or Gary had the dosh to fix the place up properly. Either way, it was like stepping in a time machine. It was polished wood floors, giant old rugs, shining brass lamps, the full catastrophe. It was the sort of place you'd expect to find a snooty butler in tails, or someone writing their memoirs by gas lamp.

Gary was dressed like Sherlock Holmes when he lounges around 221B Baker Street, except I doubt Doctor Watson ever turned up and found Holmes in a Greta Garbo turban or Turkish slippers. Gary was, and I had the good fortune of witnessing this.

"Sit down," he said. He handed me a drink. I asked what it was. He shrugged. "Does it matter?"

Fair enough. Plus, the Sherlock / Greta / Suleiman ensemble had me in need of some liquid fortification. I drank. It was brandy. Good brandy.

Gary ran over his phone questions again, almost word-for-word, then asked if I'd been followed. I asked if I had been followed, how would I know? He acknowledged the soundness of my logic, then paced about in front of me. The guy was on edge, trying to work out if he could trust me. It took a while, but in the end, he told me to follow him.

We went down the hall, into the kitchen, then to a door at the back. I was ready to clock Caliph Gary if he got fresh, but I only half thought it'd be necessary. Gary wasn't after any hookup. He was scared. As he worked a padlock on the door, I could see his hands were shaking, see the sweat on his fat neck. He got the lock off and opened the door. I peered in.

I'm a pretty messed-up guy, and I've seen some (read 'lots of') bizarre shit in my time, but the room on the other side of that door definitely took me aback. It was likely once a pantry, a small, dark space with a swinging bulb for light. My eyes adjusted to the dim, showing me a room with every corner intentionally rounded and smoothed with some kind of epoxy or something. It wasn't slapdash. This was a first-class job. Every angle was missing. Not a single edge was showing. The room was left with a disturbingly organic feel to it. It wasn't quite like being on the inside of an egg, but it wasn't far off, either. All the edges and corners were rounded out and perfectly smooth. Gary ushered me in and closed the door behind us.

"This is just a precaution," he said, grabbing a rounded jar and smearing stinky sealant in the door cracks with his finger. When he was done, the room was smoothed completely, stunk to high heaven of sealant, and my earlier idea to clock him was making more sense by the second. I stood nearby, seeing where this was going.

The room had one item in it, an old standing wardrobe which was equally rounded, top to bottom. Gary opened the cabinet and lying inside on a pile of cushions were five books, each mummified in bubble wrap. He unwrapped them one at a time and showed them to me.

The first one was a copy of the book I'd read. "You read this?" he asked, and I nodded. He nodded in return, re-wrapping the book and putting it back on the cushions. He unwrapped the next three, asking me if I'd read them, but they were all new to me, and I said so. He said they were less important, some more details about Halpin Chalmers, but nothing I couldn't work out from the first book. I reiterated that I wanted to know more, but he stopped me. "You said on the phone that you wanted to know more about how he died?" he asked as he re-wrapped the fourth book. I nodded. Gary unwrapped the last book. He sat staring at it for a long time, considering something, but hell if I knew what. I have to admit, at this point I was pretty keen to be out of there. The vacant look on his face, the muttering to himself, his whacky tabaccy get-up, the creepy rounded room thing, it was starting to play on my last nerve. I cleared my throat, asked what was up.

He snapped out of his haze and stared at me. Finally, he looked the book over one last time and handed it to me. It was a small, thin volume with dinky white and gold embossed text on the front and the spine. Gary forked over the book, then got up and yanked the door open, breaking the gooey seal. "You have to go now," he said, hurrying me out. "You can't be here anymore. Please don't ever come back."

For a doughy dandy, Gary was pretty strong. He had me down the hall to the front door like a nightclub bouncer. "You were never here," he said. "Do you have my card?" I fished it out of my bag. He snatched it from me and stuffed it into his robe pocket. "For my sake and yours, forget this house; forget about me. If anyone asks, you found that book. Don't let anyone see that you have it, and don't read it anywhere in public. Once you finish it, get rid of it. Destroy it, for all I care. Don't give it to friends. Don't give it to anyone you know or who could trace it back to you. Read it and move on. That's—" he stuttered, and I could see he was in a panic. "That's all the advice I have."

He shuffled me out the door and down the stairs, apologising repeatedly, pulling the gates closed behind him, and that was that. I was back on the street with the taste of brandy in my mouth, the stink of epoxy up my nose, a stupid look on my face and a book in my hand that felt as illicit as a briefcase full of cocaine and kiddy porn. I stood there, looking at the iron grates of his front gate, wondering what had just happened, and why it all felt so strangely familiar. Is it possible to feel too much deja vu? And was it me, or for an instant, had I seen the grin of a mouth from the shadows of those stairs? I jumped in panic, then leaned in for a closer look. Nothing and nobody.

I got on my bike and rode for home, pondering all the way. Gary was clearly the Grand Poobah of the Royal Order of Kooks, but that wasn't it. You live in San Francisco as long and as rough as I have, meeting crackpots is par for the course. Sure, Gary was an eccentric, even a little off his nut, but whatever I'd just witnessed crossed into a whole new territory of unhinged. Gary was spooked something fierce by the whole business, and scuzzy as I looked, I don't think it was me doing the spooking. That complete fiasco with the rounded room and the bubble-wrapped books was hard to ignore. It wasn't me; it was the book he'd given me, the topic of Halpin Chalmers, that had Gary turned inside out with fear.

I got home with my new prize, but Gary's dread had me wondering what I was getting myself into.

*(a file found in an abandoned public health clinic, Coney Is-
land, New York, 2003)*

For over 30 years, I have been a
practicing physician. I began my
career in late 1972, at Queens
Hospital, where I worked for six
years, then spent just over twenty
years in private practice, and for
the last four years have worked
here at the Wilford Free Clinic
in semi-retirement. In that time,
I have seen patients born, signed
death certificates for others, and
have taken care of the sick and
injured in every imaginable situation. I consider myself a person of
science, someone who believes that
facts are the basis of all reason,
and reason the base of all truth.
Contrary to those who would say otherwise, facts do not lie.

It was late in the 1980s that
I first began to observe a growing
phenomenon among my patients, and
indeed, across our civilization as a
whole. I have spoken with physicians
at conferences from nations all over
the world, slowly gathering data in
my own time to verify what I was

observing as a growing and troubling
health care crisis.

We are, in due course, becoming a
civilization of addicts. While many
of my peers were quick to dismiss my
concerns early on as scaremongering,
with time, most have come to concur
with my findings, if only in private.
Our nation, and yes, our world, is
slowly being consumed by a quickly
rising state of perpetual and wide-
spread addiction. I can see of no
other way to categorize our current
state.

While the danger of drug addiction is an ever-present threat to
public health and social well-being,
this is only one facet to the crisis within which we find ourselves.
Drug addiction is clearly on the
rise, with a staggering amount of
illicit drugs of every type flowing into industrialized nations
around the globe. The demand for
cocaine remains largely unabated,
a toxic industry generating nearly
$100 billion in revenues annually.
Methamphetamine addiction infects
millions around the world, with
adults and children clutched in its
grips. Add to this a shocking rise
of not only heroin use but of a sickening over-prescription of opioids
by so-called physicians who are in

the pockets of the pharmaceutical industry.

Alcohol consumption has risen to record levels in the decades since I began practicing medicine. Tobacco and nicotine use has decreased in some industrialized nations but has skyrocketed in other parts of the globe. Caffeine, particularly in coffee and tea, has been a staple among adults for centuries, but in the last 30 years has increased dramatically in children, mainly in part due to soft drinks, and their more recent vile sibling, energy drinks. Sugar consumption has increased by nearly 400 percent in the last 30 years. Obesity rates have risen from one in ten adults in 1970 to one in three.

What is driving this age of addiction is, by my best estimation, some change to our global experience, some unknown stressor which continues to assert itself upon the human race in ever-increasing force.

Dr. Sarah Myers
Queens, New York

THE DEATH OF
HALPIN CHALMERS

The book was slim, a grand total of fifty pages, bound in a crappy black cloth paper cover. It was printed back in the mid-70s by some cut-rate, backwater publishing house I'd never heard of.

It was the real story of the death of Halpin Chalmers.

The book was written by Fred Carstairs in his later years, explaining what had happened in the last few days of Chalmers' life. I'd wondered why Carstairs' biography of Chalmers had mentioned his death but had almost no details about how he'd died. This little gem, it seemed, was the follow-up, also written by Carstairs, but not meant for broad public consumption. It was clearly part of a single print run, one of a total of five hundred copies. This made it not only a first edition but a rarity at that. That group of Chalmers fanatics would most likely step over their own grandmothers to get their hands on it. And Caliph Gary had turned it over to me like the thing was covered in the plague, like he'd handed me something cursed.

The book was written as a memoir of sorts. Carstairs explained at the very start that he was recounting the details of Chalmers' death because he'd been silent for too long, that the truth needed to come out. He expected no money to come from book sales. Why would he? No one cared what had happened to a relative unknown like Chalmers almost fifty years before. Even fewer would believe what Carstairs was about to reveal, but he didn't care. People had to be warned.

According to Carstairs, Chalmers was an avid researcher in the realms of fringe science. Throughout his career, Chalmers had befriended or been in regular contact with any number of scientific outcasts: mathematicians chasing marginal theorems, scientists engaged in questionable work, physicians and psychologists who'd been banned from practice for unethical studies. Mix in with these types, Chalmers was obsessed with occult studies, and had attempted to convince others of the blindness of science to what he called "a more sublime reality". There was, according to Chalmers, far more going on in the universe than even the great thinkers believed, and that the occult was a means of re-education, a key to unlocking what modern man had long since forgotten.

In the years leading up to his death, Chalmers had gotten himself preoccupied with some fucked-up notions of space and time. He was tangled up in really esoteric shit, most of which Carstairs was quick to admit he didn't understand. It combined relativity, geometry, and a whole lot of concepts, symbols and formula from ancient texts, particularly from some banned book called the *Al Azif*, written in seventh-century Yemen. Carstairs found Chalmers all but giving up any semblance of a personal or professional life, spending all of his time locked away in his apartment, studying this stuff.

Chalmers had moved back to their hometown of Partridgeville and taken up digs in an apartment over a jewellery store. He was tired of New York City and wanted to throw himself into his studies without fear of interruption. Carstairs wrote that even with the both of them holed up in that little town, Chalmers and he hardly saw one another. Chalmers was a recluse, only reaching out to his friend when it suited him or he needed something.

One night, Carstairs was contacted by Chalmers, asking him to come to visit him at his flat. Carstairs went over. Chalmers then explained that he was planning on taking some ancient drug from China called *Liao*. Chalmers had been obsessed for years with the subject of time and was working on the theory that time was, in fact, an illusion. All time, the past and the present and the future, is happening at once, and it's only our limited consciousness that keeps us from seeing this.

According to Carstairs, Chalmers claimed Liao was the drug which Lao Tzu took when he was enlightened with the idea of the Tao, the flow of the universe from which all things pour and to which all things return. Our old mutual friend, he was a would-be scholar of all that Chinese mystical shit. He used to go on about it back in the day. According to our mutual old pal, Lao Tzu was one of the greatest minds of the ancient world. His vision of the Tao had shaken Chinese civilisation to its fundaments, not to mention his philosophy's impact on the world in centuries to come. And here was an occultist during the 1920s who was going to paddle out into those deep, dark waters.

Chalmers imagined that he could use this Liao drug the same as Lao Tzu. Not for any kind of spiritual enlightenment, but to discover the secrets and geometry of time that had eluded him and his studies for years.

Before Carstairs could stop him, Chalmers took the Liao and told Carstairs to take down all that he said and did and to shake him awake if danger was apparent. Chalmers had no idea what the drug would do but needed his experience to be recorded for posterity. His friend and biographer was not happy in the least, that it was a very dangerous game to be playing with some strange substance, but Chalmers refused to relent.

Carstairs said that Chalmers quickly sank into a wild-eyed stupor, and soon rambled about seeing all time as one, the past, the present and the future. He said he was aware of being in every moment all at once, that he was every person across every lifetime. He swore that he had bridged what he called *timespace*, a continuum of all existence which rested beyond mortal perception. Chalmers was seeing all time in a single moment, a great panoply of experience which could not be grasped, only experienced as he was experiencing it. He grew excited and wild-eyed. Carstairs was scared that Chalmers had gone too far, that the drug was overwhelming his brain, and tried to wake him from his visions. But Chalmers wouldn't relent, and went further back through this timespace, further back, back to the dawn. Back before humanity, before mammalian life, he hurtled back past the dinosaurs, back to the beginning of life on our measly planet, to the creation of the earth, to the creation of the solar system, the galaxy. He kept going back, back to the big bang, to before it, to the eternal oscillation of universe upon universe, all of it living and dying in an instant before Chalmer's wild eyes.

Chalmers said he was travelling along what he called the curves of timespace. According to Carstairs, Chalmers afterwards explained that all things in the endless expanse of all universes exist in the curves of timespace, but there is more to timespace than the curves. There were also the angles of timespace, and it was into the place where the curves and these angles met that Chalmers was going. He was babbling, saying things which Carstairs couldn't make sense of, strange ramblings and howling about infinity, about seeing THEM, that THEY had sensed him.

Carstairs reported that it was then that, while Chalmers was screaming and waving his arms, Carstairs himself smelled something horrible, a smell that hadn't been in the room before. Chalmers was all but a madman at that point, a drooling lunatic baring his teeth in terror. Carstairs couldn't explain where the smell had come from, only that it was overpowering and like nothing he'd ever smelled before.

Chalmers was ranting about having gone too far, and that he was witnessing some unspeakable deed committed at the beginning of Creation. Whatever this deed was, it had split all that was clean and living from all that was foul. The foul was trapped in the angles of timespace and thirsted for that which is clean and alive, that which was travelling along the curves. All life as we know it is thankfully restricted to the curves of timespace, and for quintillions of years, they had remained separate. But Chalmers had bridged the gap, stumbled across timespace into these gruesome angles.

And in his lunatic vision, on some distant, grey abyss beyond all human reckoning, on some splintered dimensional shore, he could feel them turn and sense him. These horrible, spectral things sensed in him what they had thirsted after across the eternity of timespace, and they gave chase. They made for him. Chalmers gave these things a name.

The Hounds of Tindalos.

He could not be sure what these things were, even if they had bodies, but he felt their awful breath upon him, felt their hunger as they chased him back across the countless aeons to the 20th century. All Chalmers knew was that these extra-dimensional things had found his scent and would pursue him no matter what.

Carstairs couldn't take any more. He'd shaken his friend out of his madness, terrified that Chalmers would hurt himself or would possibly lose his mind outright. Chalmers eventually came out of it but was badly shaken. Carstairs brought his crazy, brilliant friend a drink, then left half in terror of the madman who Chalmers had become.

Carstairs pondered in the book that whatever Chalmers had experienced, it had aged the man in an instant. Even after he'd drank some whiskey and calmed a bit from the experience, Chalmers was a shaking mess, sweating and in absolute terror. Carstairs said that in one night, he saw Chalmers go from a strapping, healthy man of middle age to a tremoring invalid, broken and aged and weak. He'd never seen anything affect anyone so terribly, and it was to haunt Carstairs to his dying day.

The next afternoon, Chalmers had called Carstairs and asked him to come back to his flat and to bring plaster. Carstairs did it but found Chalmers in his room in absolute fear for his life. All the furniture had been tossed out. Nothing remained in there but Chalmers and some of his papers. Chalmers claimed these things he'd seen in his Liao-induced vision were coming for him, but that they could only travel along angles of timespace, not the curves. The plaster was to be used to seal up every angle, every straight line in the room. They would curve the room so these things, these Hounds, would be unable to reach him. Perhaps then they would give up and go away, back to their ancient nether realm. Carstairs helped despite himself, but left Chalmers once they were done.

Late that night, after Carstairs left his insane friend in that rounded room and had gone home, there was an earthquake. Several buildings were levelled in the quake, and the entire electrical system was conked out. Pretty unusual for a quake to hit some east coast hick town, but no one took it as much more than a freak natural disaster.

The next day, Chalmers was found dead. A neighbour of Chalmers' was suspicious when he smelled something nasty coming from Chalmers' room. The cops were called. They found his body covered in the blue goo the autopsy described.

As for Chalmers, it was bad. His head was torn off and left on his chest; his body was mangled and withered. It was the worst unsolved crime in fifty years, particularly in a Podunk town like that. The cops, the doctors, the newspapers, they worked on the case on and off for five years, but from the start, they most likely wrote off the incident as the obvious conclusion to a muckraking drug addict's worthless life. No one bothered to dig deeper than the mundane, accepting his death as a murder or some freak accident of the quake, but not much more than that.

But Carstairs, he saw the body and saw what scribbled pages his dead friend left behind at his very end. Chalmers' last scrawled words said it was the plaster. The earthquake had caused the plaster to crack and fall off, revealing angles, and it was through this which these phantasmal things had come through to finish him off.

I finished the book. I was speechless. My heart was pounding, and my mouth was dry. It was four in the morning, and I was wide awake. I can't say what it was about what I'd read in that crappy little book written by Carstairs, but it rang true. I know, it sounds like a lot of crazy bullshit, but if you'd read it, if you read the desperation in his words, you'd have believed it too. I had to find out. Even as I put down the book and thought of how insane my idea was, I had to know.

Yeah, I know. Even if I clearly didn't buy the extra-dimensional (air quotes) "Hounds of Tindalos" crap, I had to know if the drug or whatever it was could open my mind like that. I knew something had happened to Chalmers, and I needed to know.

I had to get my hands on that Liao stuff.

(found in a recycling center in Wooster, Ohio)

A WARNING

I didn't believe. I didn't think any of it could be true. I got into this three years ago. I heard about it, but I was sure it was just another hoax. I intended to fake news this whole Network thing, debunk this Manuscript bullshit.

But the joke was on me. I dug, and I dug, and then found out it's not a scam or a hoax. It's all true, every word. The Manuscript is real. And what's more, everything in it is true. God, how can it be true? How can this be happening?

I've stayed hidden all this time, but I'm under no delusions. THEY will find me eventually. No one stays hidden forever. I've seen hundreds of us die too soon, watched THEM take people, turn them.

THEY creep at the edges of our reality, waiting just beyond the angles. THEY feed on us, use us as their eyes and their ears. And when THEY have taken everything they can from us, THEY turn us into those things, those corpses that won't die.

I've seen the departed, the grey dead. THEY hide in the dark, lurking in the forgotten corners of our cities and abandoned places. Their flesh is waxy and grey, hairless and sunken into itself. Their features are twisted, elongated. Sharp chins and noses, long sickening teeth behind blackened gums and lips. They move like ravening animals, loping on all fours sometimes, or slouched and rushing like horrid approximations of people.

My time is nearly up. I have hidden from THEM as long as I can. I know THEY will find me. No one hides from THEM forever. Listen, because it might save you even a short while.

Blend in, don't arouse suspicion. If THEY suspect you are disconnected, THEY will come for you. Whatever you do, don't look. Avert your eyes. If you see slouching shapes in the night, then it is already too late.

THE NEED

Oh, Chumley. My need to find that Liao, it must make some sense to you. Look in your desperate little heart and see if you can find it in you.

You know that need far better than you'd like to admit.

Digital mainline, electromagnetic fix. That mobile phone or game controller jittering in your hand, that weak hindbrain of yours desperate for another fix. You can feel it, can't you? That urge, that want. That need. Go on. Lift it up, have another look. Hit the restart button. Click to the next episode. Take another hit.

You and yours. A sea of blank faces locked on tablets and phones, gazing emptily at the TV. You're prisoners, slaves to the box, the phone, the screen. A human oblivion served up one pageview at a time. Your minds weakening; your sanity draining. You too stupid and convex to see that none of it is real, none of it is really happening . . . except in your heads. You're living in a distributed multi-interface dreamworld from which none of you seem to want to wake. Posts, and streams, and videos, and episodes and tweets and comments and memes and clicks and on and on it goes. All of it serves one purpose, to feed the fix. Keep you hooked. Keep you looking, docile, dim. Round and round, clickety-clickety, never looking up, obsessively swiping to the next page, clicking on the next channel.

So why are you bothering to read these tattered, yellowed pages, when there's internet crack still to smoke? Trolls and followers, celebrities and scandals, memes and gifs and posts and snaps. Turn back, little Chumley. Turn back the pages and be what weakness wants you to be.

Weakness, and THEM.

(the following is a classified document stolen from Los Alamos Laboratories. This is an excerpt from the personal journals of Prof. Willingston Willingston)

How does one understand time? This is an age-old question, but one which has, for all intents and purposes, been laid to rest by the masses.

Time, it is understood, is a line. This line proceeds from the past, through the present, and into the future.

Let us presuppose a moment that this is correct. It is, for the majority of human beings, the rational understanding. If we start from this vantage, and now introduce the idea of time travel, we are immediately struck with issues which rapidly become irreconcilable.

If a time traveller travels into the past from the future, why has not their influence on the past been known? If one travels to the past,

and thereupon murders one's grandparents before they conceived our
father or mother, then how could one
have been subsequently born, created
a time machine, and gone back to the
past to murder?

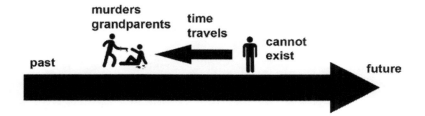

If time travel is someday
revealed to mankind, why have no
past eras shown signs of it? Have
time travellers simply perfected
their surreptitiousness to avoid all
discovery? Unlikely in even the most
generous of suspension of disbelief.

Could it be that time is self-
correcting, in that any attempted
changes to the 'timeline' by travellers would be nullified by interference from some divine underpinning
or requisite order of things? Again,
while a tempting premise upon which
to base one's thinking, it has no
merit or evidence in the natural order. The universe does not
self-correct to details, only to
overall patterns.

Were I to travel into the past,
and thereupon murder my own grandparents, what becomes of the timeline ahead of me?

Simply put, it splits.

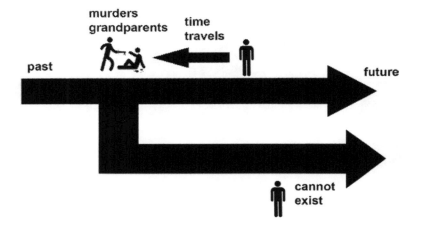

Each quantum event, each variation in time and space can be
thought of as a decision tree. Yes
or no, right or left, up or down.
Schrödinger's cat is alive or dead,
each a branch on the decision tree.
Our universe is comprised of an
infinite number of these variants
at any single moment. For any path
from which the future thus becomes
the present and what was present to
become the past, this infinite number
of variants must first be resolved.
On or off. One or zero. In or out.
Dead or alive. Imagine the immensity

of the variants simply to march
forward even an instant into the
future. The universe as we know it
is quantum state shifting, decisions
being made, the falling of a leaf or
it remaining another moment on the
branch.

*And both variants in any of those
quantum events is true.*

On the surface, this is the pin-
nacle of folly, nonsense. How can
both A and B be correct? One must be
true, and one must not. Schrödinger's
cat is either dead or it is not.

But what if each of these variants at the quantum level, each
variation in action / reaction, this
or that, was a splitting of the
timeline, a creation of two distinct
reflections of a previously joined
universe, with each representing
some variant in the quantum fluctua-
tion, each new universe spawned from
some subatomic variant in the endless sea of all such variants.

Imagine the universe splintering
again and again, each quantum-level
decision tree branching to more and
more branches. Imagine the universe
not as a single thing, but as field
of infinitely diverging sibling universes, all of them similar but for
one quantum variant, and continuing
to vary again and again from there.

The cosmic constant is not a number, but fission, an ever-branching radiation of realities which flood away from one another, creating even more variance, even more diversity.

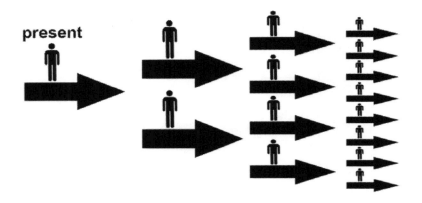

Futures (all true)

present

We refer to this ever-expanding diversification, this endless splitting of universes by quantum decision as *the Potentiality*. It is impossible to calculate how many universes there must be, as we are unable to even calculate all the quantum-level events which comprise a single microsecond of our universe, let alone all of their permutations.

How would your present appear then? What future are you headed into? Your universe is one of a nigh-infinite number of offspring of some previous universe's quantum

variances, and so shall your universe be the source of such infinite
offspring. Are you marching into the
future, or simply creating reflections of all the quantum decision
trees which must be resolved?

And if the nature of the universe is one such that it is forever
splitting itself into more and more
universes, each spawning an infinite
number more, what is the nature of
the self? What is the fundamental
nature of existence if we remove the
contaminant of human ego, the folly
of the whole and indivisible self?

If I owe my universe's existence
to the by-product of a quantum variance which preceded this moment,
what relation does my 'self' have
to the unimaginable other instances
of myself created at the same time?
I will have come into existence at
the same moment quintillions of
others of me have appeared, all of
us quantum variants of a fractious
timespace. And from my universe,
with every passing moment, quintillions more of me will be spawned, *ad
infinitum.*

What becomes of the nature of
sanity, which is based fundamentally
on what it can grasp and reason, if
all that we are is an ever-branching
sequence of quantum clones, no more

related to our past self than any
other variant? How can we speak of a
self when we see that we are nothing more than a single division in
an eternally splintering multiverse?
Our timespace continuum is then comprised of infinitely reflecting mirrors. There is no more objective
truth, for all these universes are
both true and false, relative to the
observer.

In such a model of timespace, one
is now freed of such impediments
as 'time lines', since there is no
line. There is an infinite branching of lines, all of them expanding
from an infinite number of variations
which preceded it. One is capable
of traversing back across any timeline into the past, undoing the
cause of their existence, and there
is no paradox. There is no paradox,
for their actions in that past now
splinter timespace into even more
realities, new existences where the
time traveller was never born, none
of which relate back to the source
universe of our traveller.

And what becomes of the traveller? Decoupled as they are from
their originating timeline, they are
set loose in the radiation of time.
Ultimately, their fate is of no concern. They are no longer associated

with any timespace. They are set
adrift in infinitude, never to return
to their point of origin, for no
point of origin can ever again be
found.

The Potentiality is pure chaos.
There are so many variations in a
single instance of any universe that
they fall beyond calculation or measure. Each of these in turn lead to
the diversifying of the one into so
many minutely varied universes that
there is no sense in it which can
be tracked or even reasonably understood in all but the most rudimentary of ways.

Such small things, quanta, yet
their impact can now be seen to be
the fundamental nature of all timespace. The Potentiality is the result
of unending variance. The future and
the past are but ideas which cling
to primitive human cerebrums but
have no bearing upon the intrinsic
nature of reality. No force in the
multiverse can impact such random-
ness in any meaningful way, save to
increase the diversification, adding
more chaos to the spectrum.

With this said, in such a system,
there will still be patterns which
cannot be disassembled at the quantum level. Some variants are invi-
olate, in as that while all states

are made true, some states will, through infinite digression into the future from an infinitely digressing past, become unavoidable. In a chaotic system there is an undeniable sensitivity to initial conditions, and timespace is no different in this respect. There can be, even in such differentiation, a focal point from whence certain quantum diversification began. Such a focal point in timespace would be unavoidable. While variations would splinter away from this focal point, the nature of such a locus would be that it could not be undone by any amount of quantum diversification. Such a thing would be *sui generis,* a thing in the cosmic order which has no equal, and which sprang into cosmological existence from nothing but its own will to exist . . .

THE SEARCH FOR LIAO

I've done every drug they can think up, and I'd never even heard of this Liao shit. Not a massive surprise. Some ancient stuff from China wasn't exactly edging to be the next big street drug. I started with basic research, but it turned up squat. A reference or two in some old journals, and one mention in a book on Chinese mythology. Yeah, that was helpful. I might as well have been chasing unicorns, for all the chance I had of finding this crap.

I had to admit that there was a good chance the stuff didn't even exist, or if it did, that Chalmers got the name wrong. America in the 1920s wasn't exactly drenched in multiculturalism. What the fuck did anyone in America back then know about Chinese anything, let alone some obscure Chinese drug? If it wasn't Charlie Chan or fortune cookies, it didn't exist.

But I was living in San Francisco in the 21st century. Over twenty per cent of the population is Chinese or of Chinese ancestry. I figured if this Liao stuff did exist, I was in the right place to sniff it out.

I had plenty of Chinese co-workers in the messenger game, but most of them were like third or fourth generation.

Culturally, most of them were whiter than me. A couple of them asked for forks when we'd go for dim sum. I asked anyway.

"Dude," one guy explained. "I don't fucking know. What did you call it? Liao? That's like half of this town's last name. Besides, I only speak enough Cantonese to get good dumplings, bullshit my grandmother into giving me money, or talk smack with my cousins." This turned out to be the common theme. Chinese, schminese. These guys were just messenger dirtbags, same as me. They weren't gonna be any help. So, I asked if they knew anyone who might know. "Dunno, maybe my cousin's neighbour, but he doesn't talk to non-Chinese," This was a popular response.

Thing is, inroads into Chinese culture are hard as hell. If you're an outsider, your dumb ass stays an outsider. Our old mutual friend, he knew Chinese people all over town. He studied kung fu with some guy off Grant Street. He used to practically live in Chinatown. His teacher introduced him around, got him in. But I wasn't gonna drag him into this. He had enough shit on his plate, what with a kid and a wife and a Joe job. Plus, that ship had sailed. I wasn't going to get back into his life. Once was enough. I could do this on my own.

I kept at it. In my spare time, or on deliveries, I made discreet enquiries, but more often than not got dead-eyed stares or poorly-disguised frowns from anyone who might be able to help. At a Chinese herbalist, I got a condescending nod and an offer for qigong lessons to help with my energy flow. Another guy used it as a chance to sell me ginseng. One old lady on Stockton Street summed up my months of searching: "Go away. You bad luck."

Yeah, I was persona non grata where the Liao was concerned. Nobody had anything to tell me, beyond having no idea what I was talking about. Yet there were those odd moments, those couple of times over the months, I read the signs of shit being afoot. More than once when I asked about Liao, I saw brief flashes of shock, of the person knowing what I was talking about, and then they'd clam up real quick. I knew the tell. Liao was real, and they didn't want to be the one to let me in on it. Their stony silence only pushed me to look all the further.

It was nearly three months of no progress later that I finally got an unexpected break.

One afternoon, I was eating lunch, sitting on the steps on Market and Montgomery, when one of my buddies rolls up. "Dude, you still after that weird shit you asked me about? Liao or whatever." I told him I was. "I talked to my cousin's neighbour. He said he might be able to hook you up."

CASE STUDY: PATIENT JI-124568: DAVID TANNER
OVERVIEW

David Tanner is a 37-year-old Caucasian male who had been working professionally up until his admittance to this facility on November 15, 2015. Up to that time, David had no prior psychological conditions or records of treatment. He was admitted after being found in his apartment in a state of near catatonia.

David suffers from a persistent and highly complex delusion related to the subject of time. He is convinced that time is being consumed by some sort of machine, a time machine as he explains it. According to David, the machine was built and is being operated by a person he has never met, the uncle of an ex-employee at David's former place of employment, the uncle being named (bizarrely enough) one Dr Willingston Willingston.

Despite all attempts to convince him otherwise, David is sure

that this Willingston is travelling
through time on some secret mission. The time machine, apparently,
is powered by time, and so all time
near to the machine is being consumed as it continues to operate. He
believes the machine will eventually 'eat up' all time, and everyone
will be trapped in a final, unending
moment.

David is quiet, well-kept and
orderly, almost to a fault. He is
always on time, very careful with
his habits, and asks regularly for
tasks which he can perform to busy
himself. Beyond his delusion of
time-travelling antagonists and the
end of the world, David seems a very
pensive, studious man who appreci-
ates routine above all else. At this
time, my colleagues and I believe
David's delusion to be incurable.

DOCTOR:
    Good morning, David.

DT:
    Good morning, Dr Geiger.

DOCTOR:
    How are you feeling?

DT:

Alright, I suppose. A little tired.

DOCTOR:

Still with the insomnia?

DT:

Yes. Not much better, even with the medication you gave me.

DOCTOR:

Well, we'll have to see what we can do about that. If you don't mind, I'd like to pick up where we left off last Wednesday. Would that be all right?

DT:

I'm not sure what more I can tell you. We have been over the topic of Patrick and his Uncle Willingston quite a bit, wouldn't you agree?

DOCTOR:

   Yes, that's true, David. We have
been over it many times. And what
have we talked about?

DT:

   The fact that you say none of it
is real. There are no records of
anyone named Willingston Willingston
anywhere, and that my company—

DOCTOR:

   Your former company. You are no
longer an employee there.

DT:

   Of course. That my former company has no record of anyone named
Patrick Willingston ever having
worked there. But—

DOCTOR:

   But?

DT:

   I've told you, this uncle of his,
this Willingston Willingston; he's
travelling through time. He's changing things, moving things around. He

could easily have gone back in time, erased records, made himself and Patrick disappear from history.

DOCTOR:

And yet if everyone else has forgotten these men, what about you? Why do you still remember it all?

DT:

I've thought about this a lot. I wondered the same thing, but I think it must be because I am a part of it, I am caught up in the paradox.

DOCTOR:

You're speaking of a paradox in time travel.

DT:

Of course. I must be somehow caught up in this experiment Willingston is doing, or perhaps caught in its backdraft, its wake, if you see what I mean. I am not involved, per se, but because I was there at the beginning, I'm now a part of it. I can't be removed. I'm part of the equation.

DOCTOR:

Which brings us back to our last
session. You told me that you had
seen him. You'd seen (refers to
notes) this Willingston, seen his
experiment and what he was trying
to do. You said he was trying to
stop creatures from coming into our
world, creatures from the angles of
time. Have I got that right?

DT:

Yes, that's right. I see him sometimes, Willingston. As he moves
through timespace—

DOCTOR:

Where have you seen him, David?
Here? Here at the hospital?

DT:

Yes. But he doesn't look like a
man. He's a smile.

DOCTOR:

A smile?

DT:

That's right. He's an enormous
smile, a smile within a smile within
a smile. And I've seen what he shows
me.

DOCTOR:

What has Willingston shown you,
David?

DT:

I've seen these creatures, these
things that he is trying to stop.
They're not like us, Dr Geiger.
They come from a dimension made of
angles, unnatural angles. The crea-
tures, they are made of angles too.
Angles and hunger. Do you know what
I mean?

DOCTOR:

I'm afraid I don't.

DT:

Everything in our universe is
made of curves, slopes, rounded
shapes, but not their universe,
not them, no. They are all sharp
edges, refractions, splintered reality. They are as different from us

as any other thing could be. Even
alien life from our universe would
be made of the same basic stuff we
are, no matter how different. But not
these things. They are nothing like
us. I can hardly bear to remember
the sight of them; that's how awful
they are. Worst of all, it's their
breathing, the awful sound of their
breathing, and the blue of their
tongues and their lifeless, hollow
eyes.

DOCTOR:
   Have these creatures spoken to
you as well, David?

DT:
   No, thank god, no. No, if
they knew I could see them, that
Willingston had shown them to me, I
know they would come for me, come to
kill me, to do even worse to me.

DOCTOR:
   What do they want, David? What
do these angle creatures want? Why
is Willingston and his time machine
trying to stop them.

DT:

I don't know for sure. He hasn't told me that. But they are out there, and he is doing what he can. I know his machine is eating up our time, but you see, that doesn't matter. If it saves us all, if he can stop them, what does it matter if all the time is gone? Isn't that a small price to pay? If we can be saved?

THE COUSIN'S NEIGHBOR

My messenger buddy, Will, warned me not to get my hopes up, that he'd met his cousin's neighbour a couple times, and the guy was a sour-faced crank. Most likely, he was off his reclusive nut, and nothing was going to come from my meeting him, except maybe me coming to the same conclusion that this guy was batshit crazy.

According to Will, this guy had come to the US after China took Hong Kong back from the British, that he'd come over, bought a house in the Sunset, then holed himself up, only bothering to show his shaggy head when he absolutely had to. This guy apparently grew up in Kowloon, so he spoke English just fine, but he refused to speak a word of it now that he resided in the biggest English-speaking country in the world. He refused to interact with anyone outside of the Chinese community, and then only with other Cantonese. He said the mainland Chinese couldn't be trusted, that most of them were definitely "in on it". In on what, I wanted to know. Will said he didn't know, but was it ever a good sign when someone says a whole country of people are "in on it"? Good point.

So, Will and I rolled out to the edges of the city to meet this guy.

It was cold that day, that kind of San Francisco cold that seeps into your bones with the mist. The further west we rode, the closer we got to the Pacific, the colder and gloomier it got. By the time we hit 19th Avenue, we were shadow puppets in the late Saturday afternoon fog.

When we finally stopped riding, we were in the wind-swept, sand-strewn expanse that is the outer Sunset. If you've never been there before, there is a feeling to it which is hard to describe. Trust me when I say it has a ghostly, distant, unrequited feeling of loneliness where the sand meets the shore. I never go out there if I can help it. There's something grim and lost about the outer Sunset, a creeping feeling of unwelcoming eyes. When we showed up, it was quiet and thick with mist, and yeah, creepy as hell.

My buddy Will, he leaned his bike close to mine and spoke in a heated whisper. "Look, dude, I'll spell it out. I was just fucking with you the first time I said that shit about my cousin's neighbour. Jesus, man. I never figured my cousin's neighbour would actually know anything, particularly this dude. I'm not kidding here. This guy is definitely not playing with a full deck, I tell you what."

Will shuddered. "I met this cat at this party my cousin was throwing. She lives there." He pointed at one of the houses across the street from where we'd stopped. "He lives there," he pointed next door. The place was that rundown dump every neighbourhood collects over time. Browned and wind-weathered, it was a beach-worn 1950s bungalow, surrounded by dead weeds, exterior crusted with sea salt and flecking paint. It definitely had a vibe, let me put it that way.

Will carried on. "So, anyway. I'm at this lame-ass party of my cousin's a year or so back. My cousin throws this monthly party, some kind of social gathering where old Chinese ladies turn up and do the crap old Chinese ladies like doing. I grew up around this shit, man. No way I wanted anything to do with my cousin's party, and for a couple years, I did my best to dodge that shit. In the end, what can I say? They wore me down, dude. Every chance possible, my mom and my aunt would guilt the fuck out of me into going. Family is family, all that crap. My cousin really wanted to see me. Why didn't I like my cousin? Why was I being this way? They nagged at me until I finally cracked.

"So, I turn up, and it's exactly my worst nightmare come true. The place is packed to the brim with every old Cantonese lady in goddamn San Francisco, with some of Oakland thrown in for good measure. I mean like packed, man. It's cheap perfume, bad breath and too much fat old broad stuffed into too little Sunday dress, just as far as the eye can see. Mahjong tiles and gossiping Gerties, dim sum and old ladies bragging about their kids and grandkids. Everybody talking about how they saved three bucks on this, or five bucks on that. My cousin, my mom and my aunt are running all over the place, serving tea and clucking it up with the rest of the hens, and that leaves me in a corner of the kitchen, left to my own shit.

"I didn't want to be there, man. I mean, what the fuck, right? What, I'm gonna sit down and gab with old lady Fei about her grandson's piano recital? Smile and bow and bring tea and sesame balls to the army of the nearly dead? Nuts to that. So anyway, there I am, bored down to my tits camped out in my little spot in the kitchen, and there's not another dude in sight. That's how I met this guy. He's the neighbour. Guy shows up like halfway through the soiree, dressed in a suit and with a bottle of Maotai. That makes the old bitties perk up: free booze. Anyway, eventually dude ends up in the kitchen, and because we're the only roosters at this henhouse, we get to gabbing.

"Straight up, from the first, guy is dodgy as fuck. Suits a little run down, his hair's a little too shaggy, and he's got those fucked up psycho eyes, you know what I'm saying? I immediately pick up this "tinfoil hat" vibe. Whatever. Guy's livin' a little rough, gettin' a little nuts. Makes me no nevermind. Hell, he brought me a cup of hooch. Don't wanna be inhospitable, right? So, one thing leads to another. Blah, blah, blah. And he starts telling me his stories. He runs some bullshit on me about him being this big shot industrial cat back in Hong Kong. Whatever. Everybody says shit like that. Come on. Look at that dump over there. That dude ain't rich. Or if he is rich, he's like crazy rich, one of them Howard Hughes pukes who end up with their feet stuck in Kleenex boxes, all their money in a pillowcase. That kind of shit." Will laughed and nudged me.

I told him daylight was burning, so cut to the chase.

"Right, sorry. So anyway, it was about a year ago, and every month I gotta do my time at the musty tea party, and every time, the neighbour turns up with a bottle of Maotai, and we get to sippin' and gabbin'. Since it's mostly just me and him that aren't million-year-old ladies, we kinda got this thing going. He tells me the same stories again and again, spilling all this racist conspiracy shit, and I sit there and ask questions, since what the fuck else am I gonna do, right?

"Now, when he first started turning up to these parties, according to my aunt and mom and my cousin, they were all happy about it. He was quiet and clean, all that shit. Even when I first met him, they were still cool with him turning up, even though he looked a bit scunge. But every month on month after that, he'd show up, and he'd be a little bit weirder, his clothes a little mankier, his stink getting harder and harder to ignore. My mom and aunt wanted to somehow *uninvite him*. They tried asking me to do it. Fuck that. I'm not gettin' involved in all their shit. They wanted him gone, they could get rid of him.

Yeah, sure, I'll admit, the guy had a funk, but no worse than most messengers. All good by this brother right here.

"I will say this, dude. He was definitely gettin' weirder. Like talkin' to himself and staring around all Charles Manson and shit. But again, free booze. And it was fun seeing how much mumbo jumbo I could get him to say. Some of the shit he came up with had me trippin' bare balls. Dude."

Seriously. Daylight. Burning.

"Sorry. Anyway, a couple months back, there we were again, party time, and it hits me that you were asking around about that Liao shit, right? So, I figure why not. But then I ask him, and what the FUCK! Dude freaks! He grabs me by the jacket and drags me out into my cousin's back yard. He starts in with the twenty questions. Who the hell told me to ask him about that? Who was I working for? What did I want? So now I'm part of his whole conspiracy, you know? But I play it cool. I tell him it was a friend of mine who wanted to know, that I was just asking for a friend. He keeps on with the X-Files crap a while, but I keep telling him, no man. It's for a friend.

"That was too much for him. He bailed. Ran the fuck out. Next party, I turn up, and dude's a no show. Party after that, same thing. My aunt and my mom and my cousin are happy with that, but I needed closure, you feel me? So finally I go over there, and after like ten minutes of me hammering on the front door, he turns up on the other side of it, refusing to open it, telling me I'm one of them. I get his crazy ass calmed down some, and finally, I managed to get him to open the door and talk to me straight. Dude, that guy is fucked up now. Like next level shit nuts. Stunk like rice breath and cat hair. Nasty. Anyway, I tell him it really is for a friend of mine, and could he hook a brother up? Next thing, he wants to know all about you, who you are, how I know you, blah, blah, blah. And then he tells me he wants to meet you . . . in person. So, you're welcome, man. He's up there waiting for you, dude." Will settled back on the seat of his bike and looked ready to roll.

I wanted to know where the fuck he thought he was going.

"He wants to meet you, dude. You. He said point-blank that I was not welcome. This is a private dance, bitch. I got your foot in the door. Don't thank me, or anything. Just . . . Have fun." Will laughed caustically, slapped me on the back, and rolled.

And that was it. Will was gone. I sat there a while, looking at the grubby house where this guy lived. I'm not the superstitious sort, but that was the kind of house where bad shit happens.

It was not lost on me that I'd asked for all of this.

THE BATSHIT
ACCOUNTANT

I knocked on the dingy door.

It opened way too fast. The guy standing there looked like he hadn't slept in forever. He glared at me through grimy, dandruff-dusted hair, his eyes hard and unflinching. I looked back but kept the urge to stare him down in check. This guy had something I wanted; I wasn't about to provoke him into slamming the door in my face. Besides, he was teetering on the edge, ready to snap. I wasn't about to set that in motion. He was small compared to me, but size or no, Will was right. This guy had the look of a psychotic. I waited.

He looked me up and down, then looked past me, up and down the street. Finally, he grabbed me by the shoulder and pulled me inside, slamming the door and bolting it up tight.

If the outside of the house wasn't bad enough, the inside was downright grim. No lights, discarded trash everywhere. Not a stick of furniture in sight. The walls were bare of any decorations (unless filth is a decoration), anything to mark a normal life here. The dusty blinds were down on every window.

I backed over by the desiccated fireplace and stood looking at him.

For the man, he was dressed in a pair of frayed suit pants and a pit-stained button down. He was gristly lank, with a face and bared arms darkened by layers of filth. His nails were crusty and long. His teeth were stained a grungy yellow, flecked with bits of food. His eyes were dark but with too much white showing as he glared at everything, particularly me. He had this scraggly little beard with stray hairs pointing every which way. I could smell him from where I stood, and that was a couple yards' distance. Imagine if an accountant had gone batshit crazy, and you get a pretty close picture of where this guy was in the descent into madness department.

He yelled something at me in Cantonese. I stared, held up my hands, but he yelled it again anyway. I put my hands up higher.

"Your pockets," the batshit accountant yelled, in English this time. "Empty them!"

I turned them out. He pushed me back and rummaged. Crumpled pack of cigarettes, a couple bucks, my house keys and lint. He glared at me.

"Your bag!" the accountant demanded. I took it off and handed it over. The guy tore through it, searching frantically. He came out with my pager.

"What's this?" he screamed, throwing it at the dead fireplace. I jumped out of the way, as it shattered into bits, plastic flying everywhere. Great. Now I was out fifty bucks to get another one. I wanted the Liao, but there were limits. I started towards him.

He pulled a gun from the belt of his pants.

"Why do you have one of those?!" he wanted to know. "Why did you bring that here?" He kept the gun on me and dumped the contents of my bag on the floor, kicking through the contents with his foot. "Where's your phone?" He wanted to know

I told him I didn't have a phone. "Bullshit!" he yelled. "Everybody has a fucking phone here!" I told him not me. He dropped the bag, looked around like he was trying to figure out what to do next. "Let's go," he said, waving with the gun. "Move!"

I wasn't keen on going anywhere with this guy, but that gun made a strong case, so I went.

He led me downstairs to the garage, gun pressed to my spine.

I couldn't say then why I wasn't really scared. Okay, sure, I was scared, but not desperately, not like I thought this guy was gonna off me. There was something about him, about his desperation, about the way his hand shook while he was aiming the gun at me. This guy, like Caliph Gary, was scared.

He made me open the door and go in.

THE GARAGE

At the bottom of a flight of stairs, the garage was half in shadows, lit by five camping lanterns set out evenly around the place. The lanterns gave off harsh white balls of light, so the shadows around them seemed black, hiding things on the edges. There was that unsettling hiss and stink of burning kerosene.

The guy pushed me into the middle of the garage so that I was standing in the centre of the five camping lanterns. I got a sinking feeling in my gut and looked down at the concrete floor. The guy had drawn a pattern on the ground in paint, connecting the points where the five lanterns sat. Yeah. I was standing in the middle of a pentagram.

Not my best moment. I took a second to look down and make sure I wasn't standing on a patch of dried blood.

"They can't get in here," the batshit accountant announced, like that was supposed to make me feel better, or even mean anything to me.

I asked who couldn't get in here.

"You know who I mean!" he yelled. THEM!!!!" He pointed around the room. "No way in. This is the only safe place in this house, in this whole country!" He pointed around at his handiwork.

My eyes had adjusted enough for me to make out what he'd done. The walls, the corners, every straight edge in that place was smoothed and rounded. There wasn't an angle to be found. Plaster and sealant had turned that place into a series of flowing curves.

That sinking feeling. It can turn into a free fall if you're not careful.

"Tell me why you came." He said, then without waiting for me to respond. "Tell me!"

I admit it. I stumbled over my next words. That trigger hand was jittering something fierce, and even an idiot could see Mr. Batshit Accountant was close to snapping. I didn't want it to be because I cleared my throat the wrong way.

"Well?!" he shrieked.

I said that I was looking for Liao, and Will told me he knew how to find it, or at least about it. I didn't want trouble. I just wanted to find the stuff. That was it.

The accountant didn't like it. "You're full of shit," he said, nearly whimpering. "I'm not sure which of you is telling the truth. You might not be the same, it might be a different curve. You could be working for THEM!"

Ignoring the whole "which one of you" thing, I said I didn't know who they were, and I wasn't working for anyone. I was just a bike messenger. All I wanted was to get this Liao stuff. That was it.

The accountant gave me the stink eye. "Why? Why are you so interested in Liao? How do you even know about it? Most Chinese nowadays don't even know what it is. How come a *gweilo* like you knows about it?"

A what? I asked.

"A foreigner," the accountant explained. "A *gweilo*. A foreigner."

I pointed out that well, since he was the immigrant in my country, technically he was the foreigner.

"Shut the fuck up!" he yelled. I did what his gun told me. "No, you know something. You know." He turned and looked at the ground near my feet. "Not you," he yelled. "Him!" He pointed at me, still talking to the ground. He stood there and thought hard, waving that gun between me and that vacant patch of ground. Then the accountant gave me a hard, knowing look. "You read about him, didn't you?"

Him? I asked.

"Him, him!" the accountant clarified. "The goddamn occult writer. The one who was murdered."

Halpin Chalmers, I said.

The accountant nodded at me, then at the ground, and for the first time, a harsh grin crossed his face. "So, you do know. Yes, Halpin Chalmers. And what he saw, what he found out."

He looked me over and then lowered the gun and laughed. It was a ruthless, corroded sound. "But you don't know. I can see it on you. You don't have any idea what's going on, what you're getting yourself into, do you? You're just some idiot who that kid from next door knows, asking about this stuff." He laughed again, pulling a baggy from his pants pocket. "Yes, I have what you want." His eyes were locked with mine, and that grisly smile spread further up the sides of his filthy cheeks. "But you sure you want it? You sure you want to know?" He shook his head. "You should listen to me. You don't want to know."

I said I did.

He turned back to that patch of the floor. "He said he wants to know! Don't tell me what to do. He wants it. That means he already has it!" His eyes flashed back at me.

He started to raise the gun again but gave it up. He looked at the baggy in his other hand, then chucked it at my feet. "Take it. Take it and get the fuck out of here. Don't come back. You come back, you come near my property, I'll shoot you. I swear, I'll shoot you dead if I ever see you again."

He kept the gun levelled on me as I bent down and picked up the baggy.

He looked between me and patch of ground. His eyes were flinching. "I know!" he finally yelled at whatever he saw. "You," he said to me. "You have to find Wǔyè Yuándīng. Wǔyè Yuándīng."

I said I didn't know who or what that was.

"Just do it! That's what he told me to tell you. It's the only way you can stay safe long enough. Find Wǔyè Yuándīng."

The batshit accountant turned and told the floor to shut up, shut up, SHUT UP! "You want to lead them here?!" the accountant demanded. "I didn't have to help!" He was screaming at no one, and yet why for an instant did I see something where he was looking? Was it a trick of the dark and the fluorescent and the insanity of that moment, but did I just see the shape of something there on the floor? A jerking, snarling spasm of a human body. Naked and hunched on all fours. But no, it wasn't there. There was nothing there.

The batshit accountant turned his attentions back to me. "Out, asshole," he said, shooing me with the gun. "Time to go. Get the hell out of here. Me, I'm staying down here, where it's safe." I nodded, pocketed the baggy, and went for the stairs.

I was halfway up when he grunted for my attention. "It's bad," he said, his face crinkled in a madman's misery. "You don't know, but you will. It's bad. The end of everything."

Once up the stairs, I closed the door behind me, and that was that. It was unsettling how dead silent the place was. It was as if there was no one else here, that I was alone, a pilgrim in a dead god's temple. I could hear the sweep of the wind on Ocean Beach outside, the remote wheezing of traffic on Great Highway, not to mention the agitated rasp of my own breath. I quickly gathered my crap from the living room, opened the front door, took one last look at that crumbling dump, and was gone.

(the following article appeared in the Evening Courier, September 15, 1932, Camden, New Jersey)

MAN KILLED IN LABORATORY ACCIDENT
Worker killed at RCA Laboratories

A 24-year-old man was pronounced dead at the scene early yesterday morning when police were summoned to RCA Laboratories.

The victim, Eric Gunterman, was a resident of Camden, and a laboratory assistant to Doctor Vladimir Zworykin.

Mr. Gunterman died in an industrial accident while working on an experiment with Dr Zworkin, though the exact nature of the experiment is not known.

Princeton coroner Elwood Tarcie stated an autopsy would be performed, as the cause of death was not apparent. "We're not sure what killed Mr. Gunterman," Tarcie said. "We will release more information as it becomes available."

County Sheriff Harrison Myers, who was present at RCA Laboratories at the pronouncement of Mr. Gunterman's death, said he did not suspect foul play, but an inquest would be made. "The man died of something, and we need to get to the bottom of it, if just for his family's sake."

RCA president David Sarnoff was also present and said his prayers and condolences went out to Mr. Gunterman's family.

Mr. Gunterman is survived by his parents, Charles and Norma Gunterman, of Midland, Michigan.

A PONDERING PAUSE

I rode for home, brooding the entire way. I rode from the outer Sunset up to 19th Avenue, then took 19th down to Golden Gate Park. It was misty and cold, like so many dusks in this town. I was enveloped in fog, surrounded by the flow of 19th Avenue traffic, the only cyclist in that murmuring swarm of cars. The cold insectoid buzz of civilisation was all around me, but I was too absorbed to give it much thought.

This whole thing was playing out like a bad dream. All I'd wanted was to learn more about this Halpin Chalmers guy, to find this Liao stuff. Yet now I was looking down the barrel of a whole new gullet-wrenching world. Caliph Gary, the batshit accountant, those rounded rooms of theirs just like Carstairs said Chalmers had built. It all added up to a pretty fucked up scene, with me wondering what it was about Chalmers and Liao that had everyone so goddamn spooked. The Hounds of Tindalos? That had to be bullshit, just a psychotic break of a demented genius having a bad trip on some ancient herbals.

Funny. It had been my defacto explanation of what happened to Chalmers, but now the explanation left me cold. Something about Chalmers and his demented trip had these couple of kooks losing their shit, and now I had to wonder: what about me? Was that what I had to look forward to? Was that what this crap in the baggie had in store for me?

At that moment, I wasn't sure about anything. This whole thing was starting to feel like it'd gone off the rails, and thirty-something me wasn't as geared up for this psychic adventure as younger, dumber me had told me I would be. There was a creeping malaise to this that had me feeling paranoid and oppressed.

I spent the next couple weeks pondering.

That first night, after what had happened at the batshit accountant's place, there was no way I was going to take the Liao any time soon. I was too freaked out to consider any psychedelics, or whatever that shit did. I let Sunday roll by, and then I went back to work the next day. I did my job, drank my vodka, and one week turned to two, turned to three.

Whenever I was home, I kept taking the Liao out of my stash box and examining it. There were fifteen pellets, brown lumps the size of chocolate truffles. They looked like they were made out of clay and dried grass. They smelled awful. I'd look at them, smell them, even came close to licking one once, but no. I'd tuck the bag back in the stash box and move on.

Fact was, I knew what came next. Whatever happened, one way or the other, the moment I took the Liao, I was turning a corner, no going back. This was one of those moments which could not be taken back, and I think that's why I hesitated.

Chumley, unless you're as thick as I think you are, you must have had some moment like that. A prison sentence of a moment, where you just can't figure out what to do. I was trapped there, chewing and chewing at this decision every free chance I had. This was me crossing a threshold, and thing was, for all my bravado and even excitement, now I wasn't so sure. Maybe it was what I'd seen to get there. Caliph Gary and the batshit accountant were enough to put the heebie-jeebies in anybody, even a time-tested cynic like me. Maybe it was my advancing years. I had to admit, I'd had my fill of trying every-thing under the sun. I'd settled into a nice drunken funk, and I liked it. Going full tits on some unknown guano was enticing, doubtless, but it wasn't without its potential pitfalls. I wasn't scared so much as I was not so eager to go all Wile E. Coyote off the side of a cliff chasing another roadrunner. This all rumi-nated in my noodle, and yet a part of me was baffled by all this.

Yeah, all the excuses or reasons or whatever you want to call them were there, but none of this was virgin territory for me. I wanted this. The amount of fucking effort I'd put into get-ting this crap was proof positive of that. And sure, I was a little freaked out, but not so much that I was willing to back out and walk away. I still wanted this. And yet something kept my toes back from the edge. Something was eating at me, sweating me with a worry I couldn't name. That *was* new, and most of all, that's what had me unwilling to commit and follow through.

Three months went by. Then four. I ignored the baggy, and I ignored my inner nag raging after me to make a decision. But in the end, my hesitation was silenced by the need. The need to know, to go further, to push out to the edge. I lulled myself (as I so often did in my life) into thinking I was the smart guy, and whatever the Liao did, it would make me that much smarter than I was today.

Funny thing about smart guys. More often than not, they outsmart themselves.

(found at a protest in Budapest, Hungary, 14 Dec 2018. Translated from Hungarian)

**WHAT BECAME OF THE ORIGINAL
MANUSCRIPT?
INFORMATION LAST UPDATED: 10.11.2017**
* *

Questions have been raised by those of us on the Network as to what became of the original Manuscript.

Much like any book written and copied before the modern printing press, we can only speculate as to what may or may not have been changed, omitted, or mistranslated by those who have created copies of their own.

Modern printing in any form is impossible. All mass printing systems created in the last 20 years are digital in nature, and thus pose too significant a risk to its user. All earlier such devices are being systematically found and destroyed, along with those in possession of such machinery.

This leaves us with our only recourse, which is through copying the Manuscript by hand, a long and laborious task, and one fraught with the potential for human error.

This, of course, leads to a further complication of the potential for a dilution of the original content and intent. As successive copies are made, particularly copies of copies, we face the epistemological dilemma of generation loss, the loss of quality between subsequent copies of a thing.

Consider the children's game known in North America as Telephone. Ten people line up, with the first whispering a message in the ear of the one closest to them. This person then whispers the message as they understood it to the next, and so on, until the message reaches the last person. Invariably, the message has changed, often significantly, from the original. The more complex the original message, the greater the variance.

While several have claimed to have read or even still possess the original, it is impossible to verify these claims. It is unlikely anyone on the Network would seek to deceive on this subject openly. However, those making such statements may themselves believe they are correct.

Does the original still indeed exist? It is difficult to say, but rumours persist.

What we do know is that the original was typed on an electric typewriter, likely an IBM Selectric II or III. Handwritten copies are, therefore, copies of the original, and should be considered suspect to some amount of generation loss.

One rumour persists that the original can be identified by a slight smearing of the characters beginning every third new line, based on some flaw in the original typewriter's motor and daisy wheel.

In another, there are purported cup stains on pages 57, 123 and 166.

Another rumour is that there are residual traces of Liao or the blue ichor on the pages, though these are mostly dismissed as apocryphal.

The most lasting rumour of the whereabouts of the original Manuscript claims that the original Manuscript has been 'removed from play' by the individual known as Willingston. In some manner, Willingston has made the Manuscript inaccessible to both us and THEM. With little to no information available on this Willingston, or how he could have accomplished this feat, such a rumour is tantalizing but

otherwise is little more than the
wildest of speculation.

THE FIRST TASTE

It was a day shy of five months since my visit to *Maison de Batshit Accountant* and the procuring of the Liao. It was Friday late afternoon, and my last delivery of the day was done. I was biking from the top of the financial district back down to the Mission. And as I rode, I knew. I knew it like I always knew. I was going home, and this was going to be the day. I had smart guy written all over me. I was as ready as I was ever going to be. No vodka-swilling at a Tenderloin dump tonight for this bike messenger. No sir. It was all home sweet home and Liao sweet Liao.

I got home before any of my roommates. They were still at work, or more likely, out getting loaded someplace I should have been. The apartment was afternoon quiet. I went into my room and locked the door. I took a couple swigs off a pint bottle, then took five of the nasty-smelling truffles out the baggie and set them on a magazine. I just wanted to look at them for a second.

The urge to be as impulsive as Chalmers, it was tempting. Just upend the lot of them and let fate sort it out. I might have been a smart guy that day, but I wasn't that smart. I'd been down the rabbit hole before. I knew better than to take the plunge with a new drug without knowing how far I might fall. Chalmers went too far, and he lost his nut. I wasn't rushing in like a rookie. I was taking this scientifically, seeing what this shit could do.

I cut one of the Liao pellets in half with my pocketknife and downed it. I swallowed it whole, using more vodka to wash it down. Thank the gods for that vodka. The aftertaste of the Liao left on the back of my tongue and throat was nauseating. I'd thought it smelled bad!

I carefully re-stashed the rest of it in the baggie, hid it away in my stash box, and cosied down on my futon to wait.

It did not take long.

One minute, I was just me, a muddled, stupid, fucked-up homo sapien with the usual bullshit to weigh him down the same as it weighs down all of us. Next thing, I'd been shown a light switch.

It's like I'd been walking around in a dim room my entire life, and the Liao had turned on that switch for me. I went from the dark side of the road to the light one in a flash. There was suddenly no doubt in my mind. Everything was bright and clear. The world around me had blossomed as a flower I'd been waiting for my entire life, and I saw clarity as clarity has never been seen before. The world, my thinking, my understanding. I saw things clearly for the first time. Just as I could see the twinkle of my light bulb spattering white rays across my room, I could see space, time, the present, the past and the future, all of them in front of me. All of them making perfect sense. The Liao had come through and brushed away every cobweb from my skull. I was clarity's favourite child, and everything in and around me snapped into perfect alignment.

I'd spent my life scrambling, dosing myself on whatever new thing I could find. Why? Because the most pathetic need of anyone in this world, the most heinous of addictions in all of us is the need for meaning, for understanding. Smokes, booze, speed, hallucinogenics, heroin, none of it really made anything clear. It made shit fun, yeah. It made being confused more entertaining, but nothing got answered. None of them was it.

But this Liao, this was it. This was exactly what all addicts are after. Clarity, perfect lucidity and a sense of what is actually going on. I was peeking into myself, seeing the universe, leering up the petticoats of the cosmos. I wasn't high; I wasn't tripping. I was sharp and clear, and so was the world. What I'd tried finding every which way was now what stood before me, a state where nothing could be doubted or questioned. I could feel the cells in my body metabolising, see the wrinkles writhing on the grey surface of my blood-cloaked brain. It was a primordial sea, and I had tamed its tumultuous waves.

I never left that room for the six hours the Liao lasted, but what a six hours I spent. I saw my life, my place, as clearly as looking through the glass tank of an aquarium. Everything I considered made sense. I was able to work out problems which had plagued me for decades and untangle my own personal nonsense like spreading butter on hot bread. I had found my place in the universe, and it was that room. It was wherever I was. I was clear and sure of all things. The centre sprang from me, a well of understanding. I was able to discern the smallest detail, and I was able to work out the most complex concepts that loom a billion light-years away.

I busied my hands while this clarity rang an impeccable gong in my head. I tidied, I cleaned, all the while, my mind was unfettered order and equanimity. I saw every moment in the unblemished present. Past and future draped on each side, merging into the eternal flow of timespace in front of me. I could see my thoughts, my actions, the whorl of dust in the air, the bright flourish of street lights coming in my window, all of it in sync with the beating of my heart, the air rising and falling in my lungs. I saw in that room all of timespace, a perfect microcosm that embodied and encapsulated the world, the universe. I was the glowing, undeniable centre of everything, and I laughed. I laughed and cried and realised like I'd never done before. Nothing escaped me, not even myself. I breathed in the wisdom of the ages.

Soon, my room had gone from the scuzzy rathole I'd called a home for almost a decade into a paragon of orderliness. I'd cleaned it top to bottom. In six hours, I was picked up and dropped off on the other side of the insurmountable. And in the end, when I sat back on my spruced-up futon, all bright-eyed and bushy-tailed, mind and body and spirit in absolute alignment, I lay back, and immediately fell into a serene and dreamless sleep.

THE SECOND TASTE

I woke up Saturday, amazed and impressed. The purity of the previous afternoon and night was faded, but not gone entirely. I knew at last with this Liao stuff, I was on the right track.

It was 6am, the earliest I'd been up in many, many years. I didn't want any booze or weed or even a cigarette. I'd heard my roommates up late the night before, drinking and carousing. They'd be asleep for hours. I basked in the early morning silence. When I finally got up, I showered, got dressed and then snuck back into my room. I took the second half of the lump of Liao I'd had yesterday, and for good measure, I downed a whole lump more, gulping it down with water. I headed out to ride, not ready for this to end.

I was amazed at the tonic effect this Liao stuff had. Rather than feeling sluggish or sick or hungover in any way, I felt like I'd been cleaned out. This stuff made me feel like I'd done a six-hour ride on my bike and hadn't had a drink in months. What the hell was this stuff that it made me feel so good? How had Chalmers been driven to insanity by what he saw while he was on it? I felt amazing, whole, bright and in complete control. And he'd gone insane. What Chalmers had described was an uncontrollable hurtle through the expanse of consciousness, mayhem that ended in tragedy. I found the whole thing to be entirely in my control, a powerful but pleasant expansion of my mind, like twenty years of therapy and meditation rolled into a foul-tasting ball of herbs.

I shrugged it off. Who could say how close old Chalmers had been to the edge when he took it? He could have already been one step away from the nutball factory, and the big dose of Liao he took gave him one roller coaster ride too many for his teetering sanity.

That was Chalmers' problem, not mine. As for me, I grabbed my bike and was out the door.

It didn't matter where I rode. I let the Liao soak into my body, my sweat, the bike, the pump of my legs, the heat in my muscles, and the cool of the sweat on my face and back. It felt great, unfettered. I was free, and I had Liao to thank for it. Even more than the night before, I could see the radiant web, the perfect symmetry in a universe shown to the polished mirror of my mind. White-hot focus, seeing the world without the limiting blinders of normality.

I rode from the Mission down to the water, then hauled ass, all but laughing with joy, all the way up to China Basin. When I got to the ballpark, I followed a Muni train along the Embarcadero, then hooked back along Howard Street, zig-zagged my way to Montgomery. I pumped hard, my mind a flaming gem, and my body feeling righteous and fresh, all the way through the financial district, then up along to Columbus, into North Beach.

It was after 8am by then, and the North Beach cafes were just starting to open. I made for Cafe Trieste, locked up my bike, ordered an espresso, and camped it inside. I was in the vivid zone, from the Liao, the lack of crap in my system, the good night's sleep and the hour-and-a-half hard ride. I considered a cigarette but dismissed it. For whatever reason, I wanted to be with others, not sitting outside.

The photos on the walls, the work of the staff, the quiet, swishing flick of newspaper pages from customers, and the subdued sound of NPR playing in the background held me enthralled and grinning.

I'd never felt that good, that alive and connected. It was a stupid cafe with a sub-par coffee, and there I was with a giant smile on my face. That place was everything that mattered to me. I was on top of the universal peak, the focal point of anything and everything, surrounded by old hippies and beatniks, morning locals and the comforting mist of a San Francisco morning.

And then the three of them came in. I didn't think much of them, I mean, why would I? They were tourists, or close enough, nervous and talking too much and pointing around. They were well-off and tan, dressed in sporty clothes as no self-respecting San Franciscan would ever be caught dead in. They ordered drinks and counter food, sat three tables down from me, near the door, and once they had their drinks and food, the dad in the group took out a laptop. He plugged a camera into it with a cable, and they all sat there looking at the screen, chattering like happy little tourist mice.

I was aloof, a free and disinterested prodigy, so their arrival and actions were inconsequential. But eventually, my attention shifted their way nonchalantly, to their obtuse goings-on. The tippety-tapping on the keyboard, the glow of the laptop screen on their three faces.

My mouth gaped.

I couldn't help it. It was like a slap. A hard clunk to my imperturbable psyche. I leaned forward, looking at the faint blue glow shining from the laptop screen on to their faces.

I blinked, then actually rubbed my eyes. No, I wasn't imagining it. There was nothing wrong with my eyes. Everything was clear, crystal in fact. I could make out the tiniest details from where I sat. No blurred vision, no hallucinations. I wasn't tripping. Quite the opposite. I don't ever recall feeling so clear-headed in my life. And yet when I looked back at that laptop where those tourists sat staring over their coffees, it was still there. What I was seeing was still right there in front of me. It was real.

Whatever it was, whatever they were, I could see them as clear as I saw anything. Something was squirming up out of the laptop's screen, snaking up to lap at those tourists' eyes. What were they? Harsh fissures, discordant angles bobbing and pulsing from the computer screen. The light then splintered into strands, which roped together into ligaments made of some sickening energy. I could see these writhing shapes, like blind, hungry eels lashing up at those tourists' faces. I was made sick by the sound they made: a quiet but unmistakable wheezing was coming from the screen, as whatever was coming from it was breathing. As I watched, really focused in, I could see those writhing bands twisting and heaving as they rushed up and pressed into those people's eyes, feeding on them in some way.

It was horrific, and the more I stared, the more awful it became. It was like finding a parasite latched to someone's neck, a leech sucking itself bloated on the thigh of an animal.

I stood up and shambled towards the door but kept a wide birth from those people. What I must have looked like, a big burly bike messenger staring at them in complete terror as I edged out the cafe door. They looked up at me, and the twisting things retreated into the screen.

I ran out of the café, and without looking back, undid the lock on my bike and rode away as fast as I could.

AT THE BAR

I had to be back to Golden Gate Park. I didn't know why, but it called to me. It's a long way from North Beach to the park, but I was desperate to be there. I had to be away from what I'd seen. The cold morning fog clung to Van Ness, but I rode so hard that I soon worked up a hot sweat despite it. My legs and chest burned with exertion. My mind kept flashing back on what I'd seen.

It all felt so real. I was so clear and sure, but my brain was rejecting what I'd seen. How could it have been real?! I raced around it in my head again and again, but it was already fading. The ride on the bike, the connection I felt with the road, the air, the life and motion all around me, that perfect focus was coming back.

I laughed. What kind of a rookie was I? Now that I was out riding through the streets, away from the cafe, it was all so obvious. I'd hallucinated the entire episode with the laptop. Refraction from the screen, some trick of the light, it had fucked with my doped mind. I had mistaken what I'd imagined for reality. No matter how clear everything was, I'd just seen something that wasn't real, and it had thrown me hard.

Of course it was just a hallucination. What else? I kept chuckling with relief and feeling more than a bit stupid for how I'd acted. I'd been taking drugs most of my life, and here I see one weird thing, and I lose it? Moron. How could I have let myself get so carried away, so wrapped up in what was clearly a hallucination? Something about the mad flickering of that laptop must have triggered it. Teach me for screwing around with this fucked up Chinese drug. I needed to be more careful.

I got up around the Panhandle, and by then, I was feeling like a jackweed for my freak-out in North Beach. I could only imagine the terror I inspired in those fucking tourists. I scared them, that's for sure, but it could have gone down a lot worse. The cops could have been called. I could have started a panic, or the father-knows-best in the tourist family could have gone all hero and tried to take a swing at me. I swore at myself: Keep your shit in check, pal. There were still hours ahead of me. I needed this clarity. No fucking it up with freak-outs.

Still, it was strange, how everything else could be so sharp, and I'd still seen what I'd seen. The squirming coming up from the screen, the awful sense that I was seeing something which I oughtn't. It was a terrible, lonely feeling of loss and desolation. I'd never felt that way before.

But it was just a dream, a delusion. I put it out of my head. I decided the park would be a waste of time, after all. I needed the damp and musty of the park right now like I needed a hole in my head. So, I turned for upper Haight, for a bar I knew that'd be open at this hour. A beer would take the edge off.

It was early, so the streets were pretty quiet. I parked my bike and popped into the bar. It was dark, run-down, and quiet. Just a couple barflies and the bitter almond of an owner. He gave me the stink eye, but I ignored it. His surly vibe wasn't going to deter me. I ordered a beer. I was going to grab a table near the back, cool my heels, and regroup.

I was standing there, waiting for ol' grumpy to measure out my change. The barflies were watching the TV on the wall. I glanced up, not really fussed, and the beer fell out of my hand. The bottle hit the bar top, then went flying, beer spraying everywhere.

I backed away. There it was again, there they were, whatever I'd seen on that laptop screen. The TV writhed with phantom tendrils that crackled and roiled from the screen and clung to those barflies' staring faces. They were like leeches to exposed flesh. I could see chalky globs of pale energy being drawn from those drunks' eyes, flowing along those coils until they were lapped up by the squirming mass just at the surface of the TV. Worse still, sickening blue energy, a ghastly ichor, dripped back from the screen along that connection to the drunks' faces, where it soaked into their skin, absorbed by their unsuspecting flesh.

"What the fuck is wrong with you?!" the owner snarled, snatching up the bottle and mopping the counter. "You're makin' a goddamn mess! You want another, you pay for it!"

But I barely registered him. I was looking on in disgusted fascination at the nauseous pseudopods locked to those drunks' oblivious faces. I turned and looked directly at the TV, and a new writhing obelisk of that stuff snaked from the screen and came straight for my face. The angry owner was still yelling at me, but fuck him. I was too busy backing away in terror. It kept coming, undulating straight for my face, my eyes. I nearly screamed, stumbling back, then fell over, breaking my gaze on the TV. Grumpy had run around and pulled me up, hollering at me to get my dumb ass out of his fucking bar, but I wasn't paying attention. When I looked back at the TV, the thing had slowly wound itself back to the screen, unfulfilled. Only then, when I looked back, did it reappear and begin advancing once again. It could sense me, sense my staring eyes on the TV.

I don't remember rightly what happened next. I guess I shoved the owner and ran for the door. The owner's and barflies' screams chased me as I dashed out. All I know for sure is I grabbed my bike and rode like hell.

. . . In evolutionary biology, parasitism is a relationship between species, where one organism, the parasite, lives on or in another organism, the host, causing it harm, and is adapted structurally to this way of life.

Parasites reduce host fitness by general or specialised pathology, from parasitic castration to modification of host behaviour. Parasites increase their own fitness by exploiting hosts for resources necessary for their survival, in particular by feeding on them, often with lethal results to the host.

The *Ophiocordyceps unilateralis* fungus is a prime example. The fungus, found in tropical forests, infects a foraging ant through spores that attach and penetrate the exoskeleton and slowly take over the ant's behaviour.

As the infection advances, the infected ant is compelled to leave its nest for a more humid microclimate that's favourable to the fungus's growth. The ant is compelled to descend to a vantage point about 10 inches off the ground, sink its jaws into a leaf vein on the north side of a plant, and wait for death.

There is an incubation period where infected ants appear perfectly healthy and go about their business undetected by the rest of the colony.

The parasitic wasp *Hymenoepimecis argyraphaga* grows its larvae on spiders of the species *Leucauge argyra*. Shortly before killing its host, the larva injects it with a chemical that changes its weaving behaviour, causing it to weave a strong, cocoon-like structure. The larva then kills the spider and enters the cocoon to pupate.

Parasites that induce behavioural changes in their hosts often exploit the regulation of social behaviour in the brain. Social behaviour is regulated by neurotransmitters, such as dopamine and serotonin, in the emotional centres of the brain—primarily the amygdala and the hypothalamus . . .

THE UNRELENTING
HORROR

If I'd been scared in North Beach, I was petrified now. I shot up Haight Street, into Golden Gate Park, whimpering and barely containing a horrified shriek. What the fuck was I seeing? I stared around, half expecting to see more hallucinations, but everything was so clear, so normal and absolutely in focus. I couldn't reconcile what I was seeing now with what I was seeing on those screens. How could that . . . that whatever it was, whatever was snaking from those screens, be real?!

But I knew it was real. The certitude of the Liao, it was undeniable. That was the thing which had madness clawing at the edge of my brain. I knew what I was seeing was real. It wasn't some trick of the light, a bad trip. Those things coiled with a gruesome purpose, like predators feeding.

All of it raced through my head as I rode through the park. I was sweating and coughing like mad. I tossed down my bike and collapsed on a bench. I'll admit it. I was so scared, I was close to tears.

All around me was normality. Early risers on their way here and there were all around the park. Old people were doing tai chi. A couple were having a beat cop take their picture. It was as typical a day by the Academy of Sciences as anyone could imagine. I could make it all out with such absolute clarity. Everything was so perfect and beautiful and easy to understand. Everything except what I'd seen.

I sat there and smoked, looking at the ground, wishing this would just end. How I wished I could take back eating that Liao. I've regretted drug trips before, but not like this. With acid or 'shrooms or speed or booze, you know it will pass. Wait it out, and it'll pass. Some streetwise part of your brain always knows it will end, knows that it's just in your head. Those demons always fade.

This wasn't that. This stuff, it had cracked open something inside me which couldn't be uncracked. I was seeing what was really there, seeing reality as purely as it could be seen, and there was something awful writhing and feeding on the human race.

I'd pulled back that one curtain too many. I'd seen something I wasn't supposed to see. And you're good and goddamn right I wanted that curtain closed up again. I didn't want anything more to do with this. The smart guy who'd spent his life pushing up to the edge had finally found the edge that went too far. I was frantic to backpedal away from that chasm.

A wheezing came from behind me, and though I didn't want to, I had to turn and see.

There were two massive screens in the front of the entrance to the Academy of Sciences, suspended overhead, displaying a short video of what was inside. People were standing there, looking up, and I could see the sickly things reaching out from the displays to those interested, unaware eyes, leeching from them, spurting blue venom across their faces. Those screens squirmed with the things, their jagged, undefined bodies roping together in the revolting manner of frenzied eels. There was a look of shattered glass to them, of something ripping its way into our world. Every person who looked at those giant monitors was attacked, drained by one of those things clamped to their skull. I cringed as I saw the vomited blue slime drip down those writhing bands and on to the skin of those watching the video. As their skin absorbed it, I could see the darkening of the shadows around their eyes, the sinking of their cheeks. Something evil flowed back in that grim exchange, like malaria spread by parasites.

What could I do? Was I supposed to jump up, yell at them to look away? Should I grab a brick and try to smash the screens? What fucking good would that do? As terrified and desperate as I was, I knew what that would get me. They'd run from me. I'd be the lunatic who went off his nut. Someone would call the cops. I'd be cuffed, hauled downtown. And what would I tell them? That I could see what no one else could? That horrid things were feeding on people through screens?! They'd chuck me in the slammer, or more likely, in a nuthouse, and who the hell would blame them?

As I watched, one of those slithering, frenetic tongues lolled toward me from out of those displays. It wound across the open space, stretching, coiling, a voltaic pharynx that convulsed hungrily as it came. I only stared. Sickened to nausea as it advanced on me, I couldn't turn away. Some awful part in me had to know. It fed upon me in less than an instant.

It was something essential, I know that. I was drained of something . . . not quite memory, not quite life force. Something more essential than that.

In that one, brief moment, they drank from me, tore some essence from me. And not only me, but of the universe itself. Call it electromagnetism, call it quantum balance. What they had taken was a binding legalism between the forces of the cosmos. This is what they took, what they fed on.

A dumber soul would have thought of this in inherently selfish terms. What was taken from me. I'm sure had it been any other moment than that one, I would have thought of it the same. But in that instant, with the Liao fuelling my endocrine system, I knew better.

What they were stealing was not me, not my memories, or my spirit, or even my existence. What they were stealing was a chunk of my own transient pattern in the body universal. They were not simply dissecting me, they were taking away some small piece of the greater puzzle, consuming some tiny cog in the order upon which the universe rests. What was left in its place was enervating chaos.

These awful things devoured a fundamental part of me and of all life, all existence. It sent my psyche reeling. I was dizzied, saddened, and half-lost on a doomed wavefront. I stared into nothing, trying to puzzle together who I was, or for that matter what point there was to any of it. Why bother? Why exist? It was hopeless, a veneer across the skein of despair. Why was I so desperately thirsty just then, and in the end, when would my meaningless existence finally and so tragically complete? An unremitting sorrow came over me. I was the dementia patient desperately trying to recall how he got there, or even really who she was. I was at the end, looking at Doomsday, the final chapter of my miserably wasted life. My lies were laid bare, with no forgiveness waiting in the end. Only ignominy, childish blubbering and hypocritical calls for mercy. The clock had wound down, sounded its last alarm, and fell away with a dismal final tick.

And then that blue energy drained into me. My throat went bone dry, cracking and blown with hot dust and sand. My eyes burned; the edges of the world seared. I felt myself recoiling, snarling, lashing at everyone around me. Thieves, murderers, criminals, rapists, perverts. I was beset on all sides by their lies, their violence and skulking deviance. I hated them, wanted more than anything to wipe them out, to erase them from the equation. They were monsters, psychopaths, fascists, and they were all around me. Everything dimmed and went grey, streaked in fissures of blue. The world was a desiccating carapace, dying, collapsing, and the weak and the stupid ruled over everything. I was their enemy, full of hatred, desperate to slash and shoot them down. The world was a combat zone; rioting raged everywhere. War and destruction, and I revelled to see them, all of the enemies, thrown down, burned as I screamed laughter at their pain and anguish. Faces rushed up, talking heads, liars and collaborators. Scheming, plots, a worldwide cabal. An endless cacophony of blathering voices broadcast into my cerebellum. Everything evil and unclean bathed in blue light, my mind only holding together through hateful rage, my teeth clenched, and my lips peeled back.

I had absorbed it into me, whatever that toxin was. It was fading fast, but I could still sense it in me like a vile aftertaste I'd have given anything to vomit up.

I knew that the more this happened, the more they swallowed us up, the further we would fall. It would be a long while, a vampiric lifetime, but eventually, everyone would be drained. We would collapse in on that horrific space their feeding left in us, drowning in a pool of blue venom. With time, there would be nothing left but a vacant lot where we had once existed, *a dead emptiness.*

A dead emptiness and that blue energy, that carcinogen which was very likely twisting people's minds without their knowledge.

How long had these things been there? How long had we been their unwitting food source? I thought of the endless hours I'd spent staring at TV, of the billions around the world doing the same every day and every night. All of humanity staring at televisions, gawking at computers. All of us being drained and poisoned by these . . . things.

Who could say exactly what these predators were, but it wasn't all that hard to surmise. Some form of parasite, an awful type of anti-life. Were these the horrors of which Chalmers had spoken? The Hounds of Tindalos? I wanted to reject it out of hand. The ravings of a madman. But who was mad now? I was seeing them with my own eyes, something which no one else knew were there. Not a day before, and I hadn't known. I'd only stumbled into this by dim-witted accident and a dose of some fucked-up Chinese herbs. I knew that once the Liao was out of my system, they'd be hidden once more, an invisible threat that no one could see. No one would ever believe what I now knew.

The batshit accountant had known. So had Caliph Gary. They'd known what I hadn't, and they were cowering in fear. Was that my only option? Was I supposed to bow my head and make me a rounded room and hide?

No.

I wasn't going out like that. I felt anger curl back my lip. I stared back into that screen, stared right into the squirming mass of shards. Fuck you, I cursed. Fuck you, whatever the fuck you are. I know you're there. I know what you're doing. I'm going to figure out a way to expose you, to put an end to this. Maybe not today, or tomorrow, but I will do everything in my power to put an end to you gorging on us. Fuck you, I snarled at those mindless things on the far side of the screen.

Their rancid breath hissed back at me. Oh, how stupid I was. How arrogant. I could see it then. *They knew.* They knew I could see them, and they knew what I'd said. I could feel them through that tendril attached to my skull, hear it in the way their sickening breath wheezed at me. I could see into their vacant eyes and see the splintered intelligence which was at their core. They could see into my mind, and in that moment, all dosed-up on Liao, I could see into theirs.

That swarm of ravenous things beyond the edge of the screens, they decided this one time to reply.

No, they replied. Fuck you.

Intelligence. I hadn't counted on that. These things were not mindless feeders. These things were intelligent, an awful intelligence that, according to Chalmers, was ancient, extending back beyond the scope of mankind, the scope of our world, our galaxy, even our universe. All of the cosmos was nothing but a food source to them. We were the whirling school of idiot fish, and I was the one sardine who saw them, and pitifully tried to defy them. This they could not have. I could not be allowed to survive.

For the first time in my life, I really knew what fear was. This wasn't some hick or gangbanger or dirty cop. This wasn't a fight I could win, or even walk away from. These things weren't some movie villain and me the unlikely hero. I wasn't going to win or even survive. They knew who I was, and they could not abide a tattler such as me to interfere.

They turned as one, and I felt their awful breath fall upon me, felt their gaze bore into me. They meant to give chase.

I whipped my head and turned away from the screen, already grabbing for my bike.

I needed to be the fuck away. I leapt on, taking just one last look at those poor fools staring up at those projectors. My blood ran cold. One of the tourists who'd been staring up at them turned and locked eyes with mine. Her lip was twisted wolfishly as she regarded me, and even worse, I could see that her eyes were a lurid, glowing blue. From inside of her, those things were glaring back at me. They were inside of her, writhing and starved, and through her, they were leering.

That hadn't gone as I'd planned. Now, I'd have to do the only thing I could do.

I ran.

(published findings in the 2013 European Journal of Radiology)

BRAIN SCAN RESEARCH FINDINGS IN SCREEN ADDICTION

- **Grey matter atrophy** Multiple studies have shown atrophy (shrinkage or loss of tissue volume) in grey matter areas (where "processing" occurs). Areas affected included the frontal lobe, which governs executive functions, such as planning, prioritizing, organizing, and impulse control. Volume loss was also seen in the striatum, which is involved in reward pathways and the suppression of socially unacceptable impulses. A finding of particular concern was damage to an area known as the insula, which is involved in our capacity to develop empathy and compassion for others and our ability to integrate physical signals with emotion.

- **Compromised white matter integrity** Research has also demonstrated loss of integrity to the brain's white matter. "Spotty" white matter

translates into loss of communication within the brain, including connections to and from various
lobes of the same hemisphere, links
between the right and left hemi-
spheres and paths between higher
(cognitive) and lower (emotional and
survival) brain centres. White matter also connects networks from the
brain to the body and vice versa.
Interrupted connections may slow
down signals, "short-circuit" them,
or cause them to be erratic.

– **Reduced cortical thickness** Studies
found reduced cortical (the outer-
most part of the brain) thickness in
those with screen addiction, reduced
cortical thickness in the frontal
lobe, correlated with impairment of
a cognitive task.

– **Impaired cognitive functioning** Imaging studies have found
less efficient information processing and reduced impulse inhibition,
increased sensitivity to rewards and
insensitivity to loss, and abnormal
spontaneous brain activity associated with poor task performance.

– **Cravings and impaired dopamine function** Research on video games have shown dopamine (implicated in reward processing and addiction) is released, and that craving or urges for screen consumption produces brain changes that are similar to drug cravings. Other findings in internet addiction include reduced numbers of dopamine receptors and transporters.

NOWHERE LEFT TO GO

Looking back, I can remember every aspect of the rest of that day, what with the Liao burning white certainty in my brain. Nothing escaped me, not one single detail. It's seared like photographs on the inside of my skull even now. I can still see a ring of light formed around the sun as a midday cloud strayed through its path. I can still smell the stink of gasoline from a can as a woman, and her teenage son fixed a lawnmower. I can taste the saliva in my mouth and remember how similar its taste was to blood. I remember the sheen of duck wings as they waddled out of a pond, and even the smell of pizza as I rode past a place in the Richmond. But most of all, more than any of it, I can never stop seeing those screens, and the way that woman turned and locked eyes with me.

I'd never seen her before that moment, but she hated me. As sure I was of anything, I knew that woman wanted me dead. It wasn't some passive-aggressive lip purse at the scuzzy messenger. This was different. The gas-blue flame in her eyes said she wanted me torn apart, hacked to bloody bits, dragged behind a car, shot in the back of the head. She was a no one, a tubby grandma from the burbs come into San Francisco for the weekend. She had greying auburn hair, ugly brown pants and a puffy red jacket. She was nobody, and I was nobody to her. Yet the look she gave me was death. Her hatred seared into me. And her eyes. They were a lurid glowing blue, the same blue of the slime I'd seen being fed into people from those things coming out of the screens.

That woman was compelled to turn and look at me. What I saw in her eyes was more than hate. It was recognition. Something in that fat little Midwestern grandma's snarl, the sickening blue in her eyes, those things were looking back at me, and they knew that I could see what was going on. This clarity, this brightness in me, must have made me stand out. As I could now see whatever was there in the screens, so too could they see that I was aware of them. But what was happening to that woman? What was the blue energy doing to her?

I spent the day reliving that moment again and again. It was stuck in a loop in my brain. I rode, and I stopped. I sat, and I watched the world go by. None of it helped take away the Liao's goddamn bright shine, nor stop me seeing that woman snarling at me across the park. I'd done something which I couldn't take back. The Liao had opened a door, and while I was busy looking through it at an atrocity, the atrocity was busy looking back at me.

By seven that night, I'd ridden up and down every back street San Francisco had to offer, stopped at any place that seemed quiet or abandoned. I hadn't eaten or drank anything except some drinking fountain water and a pack of crackers I'd found in my bag. I didn't care. I didn't want a cigarette or even booze. I was avoiding any place where I might see people, but more importantly, might see one of those things, a TV or a screen or a computer. I stayed alone, dodging any place where I might have to witness more of that horrid feeding, or worse, I might again see that woman. I didn't know what she was, but I wasn't going to chance it. She felt around every corner, a demon I could only evade, but never escape.

That day went by at an awful creeping pace. The more I thought of the woman, of the look in her eyes, the more I felt oppressed. I kept looking over my shoulder or starting at the slightest sound. I kept telling myself that it was nothing, that whatever feelings I had, they were just paranoia, stoked by the flames of the Liao in my bloodstream. It didn't help. I couldn't shake this sense of something close by, of a trap closing around me. It was, quite frankly, exhausting. By seven that night, I was worn out. I was done and just wanted to go climb into bed. Tomorrow, I'd figure out what the hell I might do.

Riding back home, I was disconsolately mulling over the world, keeping to the walking and bike paths, weaving my way back towards the Mission. I finally emerged at Kezar and Stanyan, across from the Panhandle, waiting at Stanyan for the light to change.

I heard a noise behind me and turned around to look. He came shuffling out of the tall shrubs, bobbing his head reflexively. He was grimy and in torn clothes, hair matted to his head. A homeless bum, but for some reason, the sight of him had me frozen to that spot. He was stumbling, shambling, weaving towards me, a cackle under his breath.

"That's the thing," he said, eyes locked on mine. "Ya' made a mistake, boy. Biiiiiiig mistake. Shouldn't been fuckin' around with things ya' didn't understand." The old bum wagged a finger at me. "Naughty, naughty boy. Gettin' mixed up in the real shit now. They don't like anyone messin' with their game. They got feeding to do. They feed, and they feed, and we never look away." He shook his head. "Nossir. We don't never look away. And now there's you. You had ta' go get yourself knowin' shit. Now you in it. They don' like no one fuckin' with their feedin'. They can't have that. Nossir. They can't have that, so there can't be no more of you. Hahahahahahahahaha."

I was stiff as a dead branch, my mouth open just the smallest bit. I felt the cold drip of my saliva run down my face, or was it a tear? That old bum kept coming at me. "No need you be fearin' me, boy. I ain't the one comin' for ya. I just told the boy I'd warn ya. The pale boy told me about them, and about you. He whispers to me, tells me secrets, so I told him I'd make good and warn you quick, give you a chance to run. I owed him that much."

He was right in front of me, three steps away. His face was a crooked leer, his scabby knuckles and filth-crusted nails extended towards my face. I could smell shit and piss on him, and the foul stink of body odour and cheap wine.

"The boy, he whispers," he said. "All the time, he whispers to me about them, about what's goin' on, what's comin'. They feed and feed, but we don't look away. We don't never look away." His stare was a vice. "But now there's you, and they know about you, just the same as the boy does. You can see him, can't ya? You see that little pale boy right over there, can't ya?" He pointed back at the bushes behind him.

I glanced, and my heart shot into my throat. The old man was insane, but all the same, I did see the boy. In the shadows, I saw the sallow, emotionless face of a boy staring at me. "He whispers to me," the bum said, and our eyes locked again. "Always whispering." When I looked again, the boy was gone.

The old man's snaggle-toothed grin was twisted like a jack-o-lantern. "Uh oh," he said gleefully. "Looks like time's up for you." He looked one way and the other, up and down the street, and my eyes followed. Coming both ways were the slow-moving silhouettes of people, lank, bone-thin people, with eyes glowing a caustic blue.

"You better run, boy," the old man hissed. "THEY got your number. Hahahahahahahahaha."

The light was still red against me, but I didn't care. I rode like hell through the screaming of brakes and car horns, desperate to get away. The old bum stood there laughing as those things shambled over him, dragged him laughing into the darkness.

"We don't look away!" he screamed as they hauled him off. "The boy won't stop whispering it. He says we don't never look away!!!"

I heard the unmistakable skip of a needle on vinyl. I saw the flash of a smile within a smile within a smile.

. . . The old man's snaggle-toothed grin was twisted like a jack-o-lantern. "Uh oh," he said gleefully. "Looks like time's up for you." He looked one way and the other, up and down the street, and my eyes followed. Coming both ways were the slow-moving silhouettes of people, lank, bone-thin people, with eyes glowing a caustic blue.

"You better run, boy," the old man hissed. "THEY got your number. Hahahahahahahahaha."

The light was still red against me, but I didn't care. I rode like hell through the screaming of brakes and car horns, desperate to get away. The old bum stood there laughing as those things shambled over him, dragged him laughing into the darkness.

"We don't look away!" he screamed as they hauled him off. "The boy won't stop whispering it. He says we don't never look away!!!"

RUN

I rode like mad, tearing along the streets with the horror rising inside of me. The streets were dark, then blinding with the flash of headlights. I was shaken to my core, sweating, gulping for breath as I rode harder down the hills towards the Mission District. I saw cackling faces, sneering stares. Everything blurred into the onrush of cars, the yelling faces of people, the smash of bottles and the tops of buildings holding up a dead and silent sky.

Something was coming for me. That horrible, unbelievable fact raced around in my mind over and over again. I could see them, a grim inspiration made part of terror and part of the Liao. Those glowing eyes, their vicious faces, these weren't people. What I'd seen coming out of the park weren't people, they were slavering, emaciated ghasts. In the cold and the dark, without our knowing, these things had grown in numbers beyond our reckoning, creeping out in the shadows of our ordered world, slouching in the darkness towards some unsuspecting Bethlehem. Who knew how long they had been there, waiting in the low and rotted places? I saw them in my mind again and again, sickeningly clear. Bodies lank and skeletal, fingers elongated, ending in blackened claws. Heads distended and hairless, pointed noses and chins, with their teeth exposed from rictus grins. They were something come staggering out of the Apocalypse seeking terror and flesh.

I'd discovered some awful secret, and now these things in the twisted shape of humans were coming to silence me for good.

I shot into my apartment, slammed the door behind me, tossed my bike down, and ran up the stairs. One of my room-mates was at the top of the landing. "Dude," he said, grabbing me by the shoulders. "Where ya' been? We got some shit goin' on tonight. You should hang!" The Liao coldly explained that I was looking at a dead man, not to stop. I shoved him aside and raced for my room. "Dude, what the fuck?!" he yelled, half-laughing, but I had no time for explanations. If I wanted to stay alive, I had to be gone. I ransacked my room for the few things I needed, then was out. I ran back for the stairs. I would be on my bike and gone before . . .

Looking from the top of the landing, I looked down the stairs to the door to my apartment standing open, and four fig-ures crowded the doorway, silhouetted by the street's darkness.

"Who the hell is that?" my roommate asked, standing next to me. The four looked up with eyes casting a cobalt-coloured pall across their faces. Teeth and noses were too long, blackened lips were curled back, revealing lifeless, inhuman grins. Long nails extended from bony fingers which curled and uncurled like the legs of insects, dragging slashes in the walls and bannister as they climbed the stairs. Fuck.

I ran the other way.

Back along the hall, through the slapdash living room, the kitchen, past my roommates, I was down the rickety back stairs in seconds. I yelled for them to run, to get out, but none of them moved as I shot past. I slipped twice as I stumbled down the back stairs, barrelled across the back yard, and shot over the back fence. My roommates hollered after me, but I just kept yelling to get out, get out now. I couldn't say if they could hear me by the time I dared look back. Yard to yard, tripping and falling in my panic, only to get up and run again, I was over three fences before I stopped and turned. That's when the screaming of my roommates began. Standing in the open back door, a starved shape and the repellent glow of eyes stared after me as screams shredded the night air of the Mission.

I knew for the first time since my childhood what it meant to be hunted.

(the following entry was found posthumously in the private diaries of former CNP police inspector Lutero Bonilla. The entry was dated March 14, 1998, Barcelona, Spain— Translated from the Spanish)

```
They will never find him. Daniel
Vela, I mean.
    I filed my case report today, and
I will do as is expected of me as
an inspector in the CNP. I will go
through the motions of finding and
catching Daniel Vela. He is a wanted
criminal, and it is my duty to pur-
sue him until he is brought to jus-
tice. And to everyone around me, it
will appear I am doing so. I will
follow procedure, and I will chase
every lead. Yet I know we will never
find him. I pray that I never see him
again.
    Him? That can't be right. Daniel
Vela, or whatever I saw. That was
```

no person. Whatever Daniel Vela has become, it is not a thing which should exist in our world.

I would no sooner face Daniel Vela again as I would cross willingly into Hell.

At approx. 2:30 am on March 9th, I was called to the scene of a suspected homicide. Two officers were already on the scene, having been dispatched earlier when neighbours reported a loud and violent altercation in one the apartments.

What the officers found was the mutilated bodies of Camila Ruiz, age 26, and Mateo Herrera, age 29, inside Miss Ruiz's apartment.

I arrived approximately 30 minutes later. It looked like half the police in Barcelona were there. I knew from the look on my partner, Bruno's face that this was a bad one. I knew it like you know death is standing next to you.

I mounted the stairs of what was one of the shabbiest apartment buildings I've seen. People were being asked by officers to go back into their homes, but curious and frightened onlookers persisted. I reached the apartment after a long climb up the stairs. The place was a blood bath. The young woman, Ruiz, she had been torn apart. I do not mean stabbed. I mean torn apart. The wounds were horrific (several of the officers had to leave the scene to vomit). Someone remarked it looked like an animal had done this, and they were not wrong. It was difficult to imagine how a human being could have done this. The savagery of the assault was bad enough. But how could anyone even possess the physical strength required to have done this with bare hands was beyond reckoning. The look on the dead woman's face was a mask frozen in terror.

As for Mateo Herrera, there wasn't a scratch on him. Herrera wasn't beaten, stabbed, or even bruised in any way. For me, that made it all the more gruesome to look upon him. Herrera looked as if he had been aged beyond death. He was shrivelled and desiccated, as if dead for years. We'd never have been able to identify him except for the ID in his wallet. Even his hair had gone white. The body was brittle, cracked and falling apart, like misfired clay. The ME tried to take a blood sample, only to find Herrera had no blood. When she took out the syringe, part of Herrera's arm crumbled away. It took

the paramedics hours to gently move
the body on to a stretcher, for fear
it would disintegrate before they
could move it to the labs.

Both bodies were sprayed or
splashed in some vile-smelling
blueish substance. It had a consis-
tency not unlike saliva or blood,
but it was neither of those things.
Miss Ruiz's chest cavity was pooled
with it. The lab, we hoped, would
give us some idea what it was,
though I'm sure now I don't want to
know.

The apartment appeared to be less
a place for living, and more a place
for running a computer lab. There
was computer equipment everywhere.
Apparently, Miss Ruiz was running
a small tech company out of her
apartment. What precise connection
Herrera had to her we still don't
know.

Our primary suspect was one
Daniel Vela. According to the building superintendent, Vela was rent-
ing one of the rooms in Miss Ruiz's
apartment and had been doing so for
some time. The superintendent said
the kid was maybe twenty or twenty-
one, a film student or some such
thing.

We looked into it. Vela was
enrolled at a small film school in

the city but hadn't been seen in
months.

There was no sign of Vela at the
apartment, but his rented room was
a horror show. There were stains and
splotches of that blue slime everywhere. The room had been installed
with dozens of lights, which were
creating strange angular patterns
on the walls. There was a tattered
mattress with nail or claw marks dug
into it. The entire room stunk of
something worse than death.

Worst of all was the movie. A
videotape was playing through a
small projector on to one of the
rented room's walls. The film was
gibberish. Random images, static,
shifting patterns, the whole thing
had a strobe light effect as the
images in the film changed like stac-
cato. A crack in a wall, a broken
mirror, a close-up of a sallow-faced
boy's uncaring eyes. Frames of riots,
then the flat stillness of a grave-
yard, all of it in black and white.
Numbers, symbols, faces, shapes, it
just kept flashing across the screen
until someone had the good sense to
shut it off. It might have been me.
Gibberish it might have been, but
there was something to it which set
all of us on edge.

We had police out looking for Vela by 3:45 am. If he'd done this, he was on the run, and we wanted him found as fast as possible. A murder this awful, this inexplicable, would make headlines fast, and the Mayor would want answers (and the suspect caught) in a hurry.

We found nothing that night, nor a thing over the next six days.

But the bodies began to show up.

Here, there, across Barcelona. Ten in total in less than a week. Some were torn apart like Ruiz. Others turned to husks like Herrera. All of them were dripping in that blue mucus. Someone in the CNP had spilled to the press about the slime found on the corpses, and that was it. Barcelona was fast gripped in fear as the press ran the story night and day. They called him "El Demonio Azul", the Blue Demon. It seemed no one could talk of anything else. The acting Mayor, Matheu, was apoplectic, to say nothing of our superiors in the CNP and the Mossos d'Esquadra. People were calling in sightings of the maniac night and day. There were even a few priests who were warning the public of devil worship, demonic possession.

The savaged corpses were attributed to our killer in the

press and the public, but so far
no one suspected the shrivelled
and crumbling bodies were victims
of an assault (we kept the details
of Herrera quiet). But we knew.
We knew those weren't just "dese-
crated remains" as the press sur-
mised, claiming Vela was a grave
robber as well as a murderer. We
knew those were murder victims, and
Daniel Vela had killed them the same
as he had Herrera. How he was doing
this, we still were no closer to
understanding.

We tore the city apart, digging
up every lead, chasing every possible place the killer might go. This
was no easy task in the crowded,
labyrinthine back streets and alleys
of Barcelona. Every lead we chased
came up dry. No one who had known
or had any connection with Vela had
seen or heard from him in months.

Who can say how long it might
have gone on? We were having no
effect. We were chasing this spate
of murders cold. We didn't even
have an accurate description of the
killer, beyond one blurry photo from
a classmate at the film school.

It was dumb luck that we found
Daniel Vela. Stupid, dumb luck.

Bruno and I had staked out on
the waterfront, patrolling in around

where the most recent bodies were found. Bruno noted that the homicides seemed to be leading outward in a reasonably straight line from Ruiz's apartment, towards the Gothic district. He figured there was a good chance if Vela was moving across the city killing, we could get ahead of him, perhaps find him or catch him before he struck again.

We were parked out on Carrer de la Mare de Déu de Port, out by the waterfront, when Bruno shook me out of my dozing reveries. It was after midnight and cold. I had my coat pulled close around me, trying to keep from freezing in the car, when Bruno prodded me. "Lutero," he said, pointing. I must have said something, though what it was, I cannot say. I only knew fear at that moment.

It came out of an alley across from us. The hour was late, but there was enough moonlight to show us this abomination. It was naked, lank and bald, with flesh the colour of a putrefying corpse. It moved low to the ground, sometimes lumbering as a drunk, then dropping to all fours like a beast. Its skull and facial features were distorted, twisted and elongated. The nose and chin jutted out in front, with long teeth bared from behind blackened

lips. The hands were curling and
uncurling, ended in long, filthy
claws. It was skeletal, emaciated; a
cadaver made animate.

And its eyes. May Jesus Christ be
my eternal witness, its eyes burned
with a vile blue-black radiance. This
was a thing come out of nightmare,
crossed over somehow into the waking
world. The blue demon, indeed.

I cannot recall what happened
next, for I was paralysed in terror.
Bruno leapt from the car and called
for Daniel Vela to stop, but at the
sight of us, the creature hissed and
snapped, then raced off at an astonishing speed.

Bruno started the car, and we
raced after it. I sat stunned, frozen
in the passenger seat. This thing
may have appeared dead, but it moved
with an unnatural power. Bruno had
the accelerator down, and we were
barely keeping up with it. We chased
it for five, maybe ten minutes, racing north. Bruno was driving like a
madman, screaming our location, and
for backup as I sat in the passenger
seat, still in terrified shock. As we
raced on, I could hear sirens, see
the approaching blue flash of police
lights.

A roadblock had been set up at
on the port end of Carrer de la

Mestrança, with blockades at intersections along side streets. We had
it cornered down a short stretch.
It had nowhere to go. Bruno kept
driving after it, screaming into
the squawk box for blockades to
move from our path, close up behind
us. We raced after the thing until
we had it trapped in the last two
blocks before the waterfront, then
Bruno slammed on the brakes and
jumped out.

Bruno dragged me out of the car
and ran after it, and for whatever
reason, I followed. Bruno had his
pistol drawn, but I only stumbled
in his wake. I have never been so
scared in my life. I looked behind
me. A block and a half behind us,
police were running to catch up, but
Bruno wasn't waiting. He wanted this
capture for himself.

"Daniel Vela!" I remember Bruno
yelling. "Stop where you are, or we
will fire!"

But Bruno was too eager. He
strayed too close. It was just too
close.

This monster, this demon, it
turned and came at Bruno so quickly
there was no time for either of us
to react properly. I was fumbling
then, reaching for my pistol, telling
Bruno to get back, to get away from

it. Bruno managed to fire three times
at the thing, missing once, but two
more hitting it point black. The bullets didn't even slow it down.

Then it opened its mouth, and I
could see by the streetlight that
blue slime was dripping from its
impossibly stretched jaws. It opened
its glowing eyes wide, and Bruno was
bathed in that blue-black radiance.
Bruno screeched, then collapsed,
shrivelling into desiccation and
death in seconds. His remains collapsed to the ground, breaking into
cinders and dust before my eyes.

The demon looked up at me. It
hissed and glared, while I weakly
attempted to raise my pistol. My
arms felt weak, unable to raise the
pistol above my waist. It took two
staggering steps towards me. This
was, I thought, to be my death.

But Daniel Vela or whatever it was
hissed and snapped, then leapt three
meters on to the wall of a building.
As I stared in horrified fascination,
it scaled the side of that seven-
story building in six long leaps,
then was gone over the rooftop even
as I took aim and fired until my pistol was emptied.

Bruno's funeral was today. His family had only ashes to put into the ground. The Chief Inspector ordered me to take some time off with pay, to spend it with my family, to recover.

And so, I did. Yet I will never recover from Daniel Vela. I will do my job, and I will hunt this killer with all the rest of the police, but I pray every night to my dying day that I never again see what I saw that night.

Daniel Vela comes to me in the night as I sleep. It hunts me in my dreams, dripping blue from its rotten mouth, and eyes set ablaze in hellfire.

There is no solace in drink for me anymore, only the promise of dreamless unconsciousness. I will finish this bottle of brandy and slouch towards my bed, praying the dreams will be drunkenly held at bay for another night.

I feel death standing next to me at all hours now. I cannot escape its certainty, no matter how I try . . .

THE HUNT

I ran through the night. I had no idea where I was going, or at least not entirely. I could feel there was someplace I needed to be, but it was vague, just a whisper of the Liao against the roar of my terror. I just kept running, hiding, cutting here and there to be away. Fence upon fence, through the tangle and back alleys, I was ten blocks before I emerged on the streets again. I forced myself to a measured walk. Running city streets in panic was a sure way to get noticed. I couldn't attract attention to myself. I walked, but fast, and with purpose.

I lit a cigarette and kept moving. Don't stop, that was the only thing that mattered. Don't stop, don't look up. Keep boots hitting the pavement. Wherever I was going, it was secondary to being away from whatever those things were. That desperate need to keep one step ahead, that was all I knew. They were out there, those things, and they were hunting me. I had to get to where I needed to be before they found me, wherever that might be.

My feet rose and fell, rose and fell. I smoked and squinted and winced at every scraping sound, every shadow that moved in my periphery. They were after me. I could feel them, hear them somewhere back in the darkness, their asperous breathing and dragging gait, their gas flame eyes hounding my scent. My only hope was to keep moving, that maybe I could keep one step ahead. I hiked past Dolores Park, then up through the Castro and beyond, up into the quiet steep hills overlooking the city. I'd stumbled blindly through the crowded spaces, hurrying head-down as I dodged intersections and following gazes. Every pair of eyes seemed to follow me. I had half-expected some sense of safety in the bustle of people, but no. I felt more alone, more hunted, more exposed.

So, I kept on. I weaved my way up and over Twin Peaks, then stood looking back at San Francisco splayed out for me. It took me nearly an hour to shamble up to the peaks of the city. I wasn't running anymore. I was exhausted, soaked in sweat and out of breath. The Liao was fading fast, replaced with an animal's fear. My mind was a muddle of breathless, dumb panic. I was weak and more than anything else, I needed a belt of vodka to steady my nerves. All around me was darkness and misty, quiet cold. It felt peaceful in that lonely spot, but I knew I couldn't stop. That destination was out there, waiting for me, hiding in the creeping fog of the Pacific Coast.

I had wound down through the back streets of Forest Hill when out of the dark and the cold, I heard a distant screech, then a terrified scream, cut short by gurgling silence. I felt my heart seize painfully in terror. They were out there, behind me somewhere. I had drawn them out of their hidden places, and now they killed with impunity as they hunted me. I hunched my shoulders, pulled my jacket close around me, and rushed on.

I made my way down into West Portal, along Taraval, to where the lights and buzz of traffic rose up again. I was a couple blocks shy of 19th Avenue when I spotted a liquor store. I ducked inside. I knew it was a foolish move, but I was in need of some liquid fortification, something to keep me going.

After the dark and cold of the open streets, the inside of the store was stingingly bright, stuffily warm, and cramped with high shelves. The old guy behind the counter didn't bother to make eye contact but kept at what he was doing back by the register. I went up and down the aisles, not to get anything, but just to warm myself up, and maybe to feel even for a moment that I was safe, part of a sane world. I caught my reflection in the refrigerated section's glass. I was pallid and grey, lines running down my cheeks. My hair was wet and greasy-looking, and my clothes had the rumpled wear of too many unwashed days. I was a long shot off from Mr. Bright Eyes this morning.

I walked up to the register and told the guy I wanted a pint of vodka. He didn't respond. I asked again, this time slapping my money on the counter. I could feel it was time to be gone. I was warmed up a bit but now could feel the panic coming back. I felt trapped, cornered. I needed to get out of there.

When he didn't respond again, I was about to cuss the guy out, when I saw what he was doing. Behind the register, the little old man was watching a portable TV. The tendrils of twisting, shattered glass were pouring into his face, feeding. He turned to look at me, and I could see the glow of sickening blue sinking into his face and watery eyes. He seemed oblivious, a little dazed, as he set my pint of vodka on the counter, but in that glow submerging down into him, some noxious force hissed back at me. From somewhere in the dark of the city, I heard the cry of inhuman screeches. They'd found me. Through this old man, my own stupidity to stop for that vodka, those things knew where I was. They were coming for me.

I grabbed the vodka and ran. The old man yelled after me to take my change. As if.

I ran across 19th Avenue, dodging the confluence and surge of traffic. I was sprinting now, down through the Sunset, past the brief stint of shops and restaurants, down avenue after avenue into the silent expanse of houses. I was alone, a thing hunted, alone on the empty, foggy streets, while the houses all around me were full of dim, unperturbed people. I could see them through their curtains, in silhouette, staring blindly at TVs. Windows flickered in the shadowy theatre of broadcasts, pay-per-view, sitcoms and nightly news. Sports and weather and MTV. Cable, satellite, broadcast. Channel after channel filling screens. Websites and video games. All of it was holding people prisoners for the incandescence of vampires, the draining of their lives, the polluting of their souls. I could hear a sound all around me, an undercurrent of static, a harsh wheezing as of some unclean thing which never could be made to die.

Deeper and deeper into the Sunset I went. The Avenues counted up block by block. The brief interludes of lights and traffic of the inner Sunset were soon gone for good, replaced by the long, unbroken wash of mute, ashen houses. I ran on.

It was twenty blocks later when I could smell the stink of the beach and the muffled groan of the ocean. I was close now; I could feel it. My objective was at hand. It was fast approaching midnight, cold and windswept and lonely, and I was at the end. But I was shaking to the point of collapse. My feet were swollen in my boots, blistered and bleeding. My muscles were cramped and aching. I was still moving fast, but I was too tired to run now.

There wasn't a soul around when my boots finally crunched off the sidewalk and on to the stretches of sandy ice plant at the lip of Ocean Beach. I stood there a minute, then turned and looked back. Across the street, lurking in its decline, was the batshit accountant's house. It was watching me through its boarded windows, grinning at me like a death's head. We shared a silent moment. You were right, I whispered at that death's head. I didn't want to know. Then I turned and scuttled on.

It was the lonely bashing of the waves on the kelp-strewn beach that finally stopped me in my tracks. I looked back, and though I can't be sure, I thought I could see the distant blue pinpricks of their eyes through the fog. I turned away and instead stared out at the water. The Pacific was the colour of lead. Through the mist and dark, I could just make out the white of the sea froth, the dim line separating the ocean from the shore.

I was the last sane man standing upon the earth, and taking a moment, I breathed in the cold air. It made no sense that this would be my final destination. I was trapped. There was nowhere for me to escape. It wouldn't be long before they came down upon me. I was at the precipice, and worst of all, I had no idea where that precipice was going to lead. But I knew this was it. This was my destination, the one my mind had recoiled from just hours before.

Fuck you, I whispered back at those fiends coming for me.

I reached into my jacket and took out the baggie with the Liao in it. I stood stock-still, more scared than I've ever been. The only escape.

I took out seven of the shit-coloured pellets. There was no turning back now. Before I could stop myself, I popped and swallowed them in fast succession, washing them down with desperate gulps of vodka.

I knew it wouldn't be long.

Fuck you.

A LAST WARNING

This is it, Chumley. This is your last chance. Turn back. Pack the pages up and throw this manuscript away. Let it be someone else's problem.

You don't want to know any more. So far, it's been easy. What I've told you so far has been a meek glimmer, a blunder down an ex-junkie's / alcoholic's memory lane.

But now . . .

No one wants to go where angels fear to tread, do they? Avert your eyes.

You don't want to know any more. This is your last chance. You can go back to your subreddits and leaderboards, your binge-watching and your smug self-satisfaction that you have a real bead on things.

You sure you don't want to turn back?

No?

Don't say I didn't warn you.

(Found in the pocket of a dead woman, Košice, Slovakia)

THE NATURE OF THEIR DELETERIOUS EFFECT
INFORMATION LAST UPDATED: 12.26.2019
* *

During the early days of the Network, there was a general lack of understanding of how precisely THEIR feeding and infection occurred. Foolishly, many believed their only ingress was through our eyes, that by avoiding screens, we were freed of potential draining and infection.

This led to several attempts to use other digital mediums of communication. Audio as well as tactile were both attempted, but both met with horrific failure. Not only were such attempts detected and eliminated, but they led to a near complete collapse of the Network in its infancy.

While we are no closer to fully understanding how THEY feed and infect, what we do know is that it is our prolonged consumption of digital information through eyesight which provides THEM the most direct access to the visual cortex and thus the prefrontal cortex.

However, all digital signals provide THEM ingress to feed and infect. Human audio and tactile stimulation are clearly less utilised by modern civilisations in comparison to our visual addiction, but both are powerful senses, and thus offer near equal ingress of THEIR infection and draining.

Attempts to generate audio or tactile information on the internet, or even on a disconnected system, related to the Manuscript or the Network has always led to disastrous results.

We are aware it is the angular nature of our civilisation which gives THEM access to us, but many Network scientists believe it is our use of electromagnetic energies which bridges the chasm between our disparate timespaces. This makes feeding upon our species possible without THEIR need to cross into our curved dimensions.

This is most clearly effective through screens. The light modulation of our modern digital displays appears to be the most efficient means THEY have of bridging a safe

parasitic bond with us, but it is not
the only means.

Whatever you do, do not attempt
to use any form of digital communications. Sound, speech synthesisers,
even braille displays, give THEM
purchase into our reality. How we do
not know, but it is unimportant. At
all costs, avoid any interactivity
with digital systems if you value
your life and sanity.

THE ONLY ESCAPE

I walked down Ocean beach.

I kept walking, slogging, my face wet with sea spray and cloud vapour, my arms and neck shivering against the chill. I was calm then, calmer than I've ever felt. Calm as a corpse. As I went, I stood more and more outside of myself. I could see my own mind from a distance, watch it giving way to something far bigger than all my bullshit put together. Each step I took, I could feel the Liao pushing that brain further and further into clarity. My mind was coming into a pounding focus, split thusly into experience and observation.

A string of screeches came from up the Avenues, and I knew those things weren't far now. I kept walking. Faster than those things, something else was coming. It was the dark corners where Halpin Chalmers had gone to unleash himself, to tear down his own prison, and yes, which became his undoing. Destiny, I thought. That single word hung in my mind. Destiny was coming, with me dangling from its strings.

I was intensely aware then of the sand under my feet, the noisy crackling of the grains grinding into one another. I could feel every aspect of my boots sinking into the sand, and my weight pressing new shapes in the grainy silica beneath me. Wet grit, flung by the cold sea wind, spattered my cheeks. Each particle slowed down to a long, concussive slap. I felt the sand grains one by one, some sticking to the minute grooves and pores of my skin, while others scraped infinitesimal scars in my unfeeling flesh.

The Liao rushed forward, thrusting me ahead of it.

I was being swept aside, and in my place was rising a titan. Rising, lifting, pressing against the fibrous confines of my skin. I felt an intense, awful pressure, a shudder of destruction, and this rising monstrosity split me apart, rose up out of the screaming, desiccated remains. It grew enormous in seconds, a shaft of lumbering death risen from the confines of a wriggling maggot. The titan shattered the skyline with its rising. Ten thousand miles high, a thunderous totem of sand and gore, it had become more than life. The universe turned as it turned, breathed as it breathed. Where there had been a man, now there was a damned, incandescent god.

Larger and larger it grew, until its body stretched up into the heavens. Its heart thrummed the pulse of stars. Its blood coursed in vaulted, tenebrous corridors, great tunnels of gushing magma. Its innards were an atomic bellows breathing fusion, igniting everything in its white-hot gaze. The earth sagged under its weight.

Nothing existed which was not cauterised by its lambent stare. The microscopic world around it recoiled, horrified and screaming by the unfeeling colossus laying waste to their existence. No other being now existed in that primordial fundament, save the dying, terrified mites and this gruesome Polyphemus which I had become.

The Liao advanced. It was exploding inside and all around me, assailing what remained of my brain. Death, that unrelenting spectre of life, now cowered in fear, stood aside to let unforgiving immortality overrun me. I screamed like a star gone nova.

This unimaginable monstrosity which I had become turned its drooling leviathan skull to look out over the alien panorama. From out of the whipping mist and the storming dark, I caught the faintest glimpse of the moon looming over the boiling, algid sea. I halted, eyes burning bright, an angel fallen from its daemonic grace. Roiling away from me was the unfathomable expanse of a bitter and lifeless universe. Beyond that white-hot lunar gyre, I could feel the crushing weight of unending and silent space, the void so absolute and infinite that I stumbled back and crashed upon the sand in my horror. I held up my hands, trying to shield myself from that abomination which moaned back upon me, knowing its uncaring infinitude would remain when nothing of me, of this glimmer of a world, remained.

And the Liao advanced. The breach it had torn inside of me had just begun to split and bleed.

My mind was being ripped apart. All of its paltry tricks and capers were no match for the vision of reality charging headlong into me. The skein of my conscious mind was burned away by it, and I was laid bare to what was before me, before all of us, since before the beginning of time.

I forced myself up and traipsed on. My throat was swollen with gagging screams, with half-spoken madness. Too much, my shredded mind screeched. Too much! It could not bear such a flood of inhumanity, a tirade of unfiltered perception. But there was no wishing this away. I was the Liao's unwilling horror, a bibulous and insane god staggering in the cold, screaming sands. The Liao had me, and it had no intention of letting me go.

My head wrenched and looked back the way it had come. They were coming, those withered revenants, cantering along the sand on bowed legs or on all fours. They loped in pairs or in threes or fours. They were ashen flesh and snapping jaws, eyes burning grisly blue in the night mist.

But I saw past this, saw them for what they truly were. They were carrion made animate, but stretching away from those withered bodies was the same fractured, unnatural bands of light and shattered glass from the screens. The bands wound away into infinity, ending in a rift in the cosmos from whence these things had come. These ghouls racing towards me were nothing more than avatars for those malignant things which had hissed back at me from their angled abyss. Rushing towards me were undead puppets, and those horrors the spectral puppet masters.

The titan roared defiance and hatred at them. I could feel the indignance of the condemned, the wrath of the damned. This was no weak and trembling mortal facing them, no hunted coward. I was burning bright with clarity's hellfire. I'd not die so easily now.

The Liao was dissolving the bonds of my molecules, re-sequencing my nucleotides into unforeseen stanzas. I had only to survive to see what was in store.

The dead came at me like the charge of starving beasts.

CAUSALITY UNDONE

The things leapt; diseased nails extended. I saw distended jaws and the black-gummed snap of teeth.

And the Liao advanced.

My mind exploded. I was no titan now, but collapsed back in on myself like a neutron star, a pounding, unimpeded white fire in the mortal scale of a man. I became a forge, lit from within, torrid with rage and unspeakable power.

Those things slashed, but I struck them away, one after the other. I was burning hot. My muscles were radiant with a grim fury. I slapped and kicked these soulless things, and each blow sent them hurling away into the rocks, out into the sea. But the ferocity and power of my attacks, which would have killed a living thing, merely slowed these things down. Crushed and mangled as they were, they leapt up and came again. And again, I hurled and smashed them without fear or mercy.

There were so many. The more I struck down, all the more replaced them. They were coming down the beach in packs. I smashed them, tore at them, threw them into one another, snapped their spines. But it wasn't enough. The roping energies spinning off into the abyss which infused them with their unlife only dragged the shattered bodies back up, sent them screaming against me again and again.

Something struck me then, a stab of light. A beam of white light splintered my eyes from above.

"Hey," a voice said. "What's going on down there?"

I could see someone up above, aiming two lights down at the beach. The crisp, clean lines of the voice, the forced casualness of the tone indicating authority. The line of flashlight beams terminated in midnight blue uniforms, efficient haircuts. Police, two of them, looking down from a parking lot along Great Highway, training their flashlights on the carnage taking place.

They were caught up quickly.

"Jesus fucking Christ!" one of them yelled. "What the fuck is happening?"

"Call it in," the other one yelled, drawing his gun. "Call it in!"

The things went leaping up the rocks, up at the police the same as they had come at me. Gunshots filled the night air. I watched each bullet explode from the cop's gun, watched it spray through dead flesh. Talons slashed into the cop's neck, while the second cop was pulled down by a pack. For the rest, they swarmed over me.

And right then, the Liao advanced.

Everything dropped to distracted fascination. Everything moved in slow motion. The screams and flailing limbs, the creatures and the cops, even myself, it all reverberated like gongs beneath the waves. Everything went gooey, turned to deteriorating bits in the churn of a cosmic sea.

"Help me!" one of the cops screamed as grey nails rent his flesh. "For the love of Christ, somebody help me!"

It was then that I heard a screeching, metallic voice in my skull. "Ccccconcentrate," the awful voice commanded. "Lloook around you. Ccccconcentrate, and it will begin."

And without questioning, I did what I was told. I concentrated, and indeed, it all began.

Blossoming out of the inferno my mind had ignited, the sweeping curve and flow of timespace came into focus. It was all around us, an inescapable field, warping in every direction like cyclopean tendrils. It was the underpinning of all that existed, all that had ever been and all that would ever be. I felt myself connected to it, moving through it even as I was its part and parcel.

I would not be torn apart by these fiends. There was more at my disposal now than strength. I stretched out my mind and took hold of timespace, and with a thought slowed everything to a standstill. The final syllable of that cop's prayer was a continuous orchestral note. I took a breath, exhaled slowly, and brought the white-hot of my unbounded consciousness to bear on the task.

His screams began to flow in reverse.

"!em pleh ydobemos ,tsirhC fo evol eht roF" he squealed, as I rewound timespace. I stopped, panicked by the realisation of what I'd done. Timespace froze all around me. Bullets froze in the mist, slashing claws stood still in the bloodied air. My panic disappeared. I couldn't stop myself now. I reached out again.

I gently pulled at the winding strand of timespace which enveloped us. I could see the edges of it bend inward, drawn closer to me by the cynosure of the inferno within. Time began to roll backwards even further. I watched the police, the things clambering over them, the gunshots and the zigzagging of their flashlight beams, all of it unwound. Everything was rolling backwards. Causality was undone.

"!ni ti llaC" the cop gibbered. ,knarF ,ni ti llaC"

"?gnineppah si kcuf eht tahW" His partner ranted in response."!tsirhC gnikcuf suseJ"

As I focused, the reversal of time accelerated. I watched the police unwind, turn off their flashlights, step backwards into their squad car and reverse down Great Highway with the rest of the inverted traffic. I watched the dead things lope back up the beach, slaves to time as was everything and everyone around me. The clouds turned back upon themselves; the stars and moon rescinded with the recoiling of the fog. The waves rolled out and in, and the tide drifted away. I looked up and saw a seagull soar back over my head, tail first. Night became dusk, dusk saw the stars fade away and the rise of the sun in the west. I watched the day peel back, then days, then weeks.

And still the Liao advanced.

THE CONTINUUM
OF TIMESPACE

Months, years, decades, they sped away from me faster and faster. But I was not just watching time turn back. With growing confidence, I found that I could bend the edges of space as well, fold the curves so that my location changed as easily as the unrolling of time. Landmasses, lakes, rivers, they swirled together like the mixing of acrylics on a palette. Timespace blurred around me into an unrecognisable fog of colour and motion. I stepped forward, moving through this churning miasma, dazzled and confused by it all. I wasn't afraid, but I could feel the anxious rush of searing adrenaline in my chest. Where was this? I was alone beyond the unknown, drifting in the currents of time, along a path which seemed to span every location which had ever existed.

I could still see one thing, though. There was a gruesome constant in the effluvium of this undone cosmos. Those twisting bands of sickening energy were still there, like parasites latched to a carcass, gorging on its life force, pouring back into their alien timespace from which they came.

I turned away in disgust. I began to see something beyond the whirl and confusion rushing around me. This blur through which I passed was a small part of something far more unexpected and unending. I was travelling along what appeared to be an artery, a vein made up of the time and space I was bending. The artery's boundary was hazy to non-existence nearest to me, but the further ahead and behind I looked, I could see it as a twisting thread weaving off into the beyond. This band upon which I was exerting my will, for I could feel it taut all around me, was the artery of history, and I was running further into its past.

I could see this one artery was only a single thread, part of something infinitely larger. Beyond the boundaries of the thread, there were endless more of these things, strands of timespace very much as the one through which I was travelling. I was moving along a small vein of a boundless, thrumming, vascular network, all of it stretching away into infinity.

I could see interlacing strands like the one I was on, some woven into one another, others spiralling around a greater band that pulsed and squirmed slowly. There were millions upon millions of them, fibres and tendrils interlaced, or split off, or joined to form a greater vein. All of them were swaying slowly like a kelp forest rising and falling with the motion of the tide.

There was an unmistakable vibration all around me, like the beating of some unseen, cosmic heart, pounding in a sough of whispering voices which muttered incomprehensibly. Winding through this, there was the sound of some meandering, high-pitched piping, a monotonous, reedy song playing across eternity. It was a song which had no source, no beginning or end, but I knew instinctively that whatever horror gave voice to that lunatic song was too terrible to be seen by mortal eyes.

I was moving faster and faster through the blur. Around me, I could just make out smatterings of half-formed shapes, flashes of places and animals and people and things. As I rushed through them, I could feel fragments of thoughts and emotions, none of which were my own. It was as if passing through others gave me a glimpse into their lives. But it was all happening so fast, I could only perceive it in a confused jumble. As soon as I was touched by any of it, the river's current rushed on, and whatever I'd felt was gone. Lives and deaths, creation and entropy, it went through me, transformed me, made me a segment through which everything was sieved.

But it was going too fast now. I was losing my control. I had no clue what I was doing, or where or when I was going. I had been forcing my will to bend and control time and space. Now some other force was dragging me along with it. I was caught in some inescapable eddy, a rushing tide that would bash me on some unforeseen disaster. And it was speeding up. The blur of people and places faded to white. The sounds around me dropped to a hush. I was approaching something awful; I could feel it. Something which was not, and yet was always, meant to be.

Out of the hushed whispers and blurred white, came that shockingly loud and grating voice again. "Thiiiiiiis," the screeching, monotonous voice said in my skull. "Thiiiiiis was always meant to be. Do not iiiiiiimagine otherwise."

Something was about to happen, something from which I desperately wanted to turn away, but a something which would not let me go. I struggled to break the bonds, to let the band of timespace go slack, but it was impossible. I was going too fast, too fast. My voice was a deadened, gooey cry.

And then, everything went slack. I passed out of it in an instant, back into normal time and space.

The lights came up on an empty apartment, where a half-naked madman squatted in terror.

HALPIN CHALMERS

The room came into focus, and I was standing on its bare hardwood floors.

The place was empty but for this half-naked lunatic in front of me, a few sheaves of paper and pen in front of him, and nothing else but bare, curved walls. Curved and smoothed like the inside of an egg.

That's when I noticed that the place had begun shaking violently. The madman turned on me, eyes wide with horror.

"Who are you?!" he shrieked. "What are you doing?!"

One look at that white, drawn face and I knew who he was. As ruined as he looked, I knew that face from the photographs in his biography. Halpin Chalmers. This was in 1928, and I was in his apartment in Partridgeville.

I was as scared as he looked, and definitely more confused. He'd asked what I was doing. I didn't know what he meant. But then I looked down at myself and realised. The quake, the shaking of everything, *it was pouring off of me*! I could see the floor, the walls, even the air around me shuddering like violent ripples on a pond. I was the stone thrown into the past's stillness.

"You fool!" Chalmers screamed at me. "They will destroy us both!" The building shuddered all around us. Then came the cracking of plaster. We both turned and saw the splintering of his and Carstairs' handiwork, saw the curves of plaster falling away from the corners of the room. My coming had caused the earthquake, had shattered the plaster, leaving right angles all around him. Yet it was no earthquake. It wasn't the earth which was shaking, but *all things*, and I was the epicentre. I was the unwelcome thing, and the past turned violent to expel me.

"No!!!!" Chalmers screamed. He gaped at me, then turned back to the sheets of paper before him.

"Why?!" he yelled. I had no answer. My mouth gawped stupidly.

"I have to warn everyone!" Chalmers screamed, grabbing the pen and writing frantically. "They're coming! THEY'RE COMING!"

I stepped forward, my hand reaching out to grab him. I don't know what I hoped I could do. Maybe I could pull him into the safety of timespace with me. But as I moved, I could feel myself falling out of this moment. The universe bent inward, drawn towards me. The room grew misty and malleable, and I slipped away, a ghost again, my hand stretching impossibly as the room fell away, and I was pulled back into the whorl of colour and form.

I only had that moment before I was pulled back into the writhing formlessness. In that moment, I saw something which will haunt me the rest of my days. I could see Chalmers frantically scribbling on those sheets of paper, see the shattered room, the fallen chunks of plaster. And out of one of the corners, where right angles had been exposed, I saw a darkness emerge, spreading over the room in billows. Chalmers wrote madly but kept looking up at what was before him. His mouth was twisted downward, terror clear on his face. He began to scream. Coming out of that exposed corner was dissonance. It was a tear of unnatural angles and convex rends in the fabric of all things. This dissonance spread, splintering and slicing reality as it came, a cancer of slashing edges which ripped further into the room.

This squirming void crowded around Chalmers until it surrounded him. It coiled and tensed, an angular field of energy forcing what little remained in the room towards the man until the bits of detritus formed a perfect triangle around him. Chalmers was trapped on all sides by shards and angles creeping towards him. He must have known his doom had arrived, because he dropped the pen and waited, shaking. A single shriek escaped his lips. The aberrant void shuddered and split apart, through which thrust a den of caustic blue tongues. They lashed out and seized Chalmers by the skull. He screamed horribly, and I watched as they drained his life force in an instant. His body shrivelled. His face became a ghastly facade. His eyes went white and unseeing, and his terrified scream became a grimace of death. A diseased blue ichor spurt over his thrashing body as those tongues tore his head from his bloodless neck.

THE HOUNDS

I could do nothing. I was pulled away, dragged back into the whirling contours of reversing succession. The room had dissolved into ephemera. But even as it did, I could see the source of those hideous proboscises which had torn through into Chalmers' room and murdered him. Pouring forth from that fractious rift, awful spectral things were clawing violently into our timespace, swarming over the time and place where I had left Halpin Chalmers to die. These creatures were tethered to that awful nether region, winding out of it. They were the stuff of fractured, unnatural angles, just as I had seen streaming out of those screens. They were slashing, howling edges, serrated blades of light and dark. They were shadows made animate and desperate to feed upon the living.

Chalmers was right: it is impossible to fully describe them. They were far away from me, further with each moment as I slid deeper into the past. Yet I could sense their awful wills coming to bear. There was intelligence there, ancient and evil. Their bodies, such as they were, twisted back on themselves, violently bending into intersections of time and space, so that it was impossible to fully comprehend what I was seeing. They were a coagulation of some primal force, alien and desperately starved. Chalmers had called them *the Hounds of Tindalos*, and I could see why. There was a ravenous quality to them, a gruesomeness in what I saw which was not unlike the ruthless stare and the serrated fangs of wolves hungry for the kill.

And to my greatest horror, with Chalmers now dead, they turned their attentions to me.

And all around me, I could hear it. Above the hushed whisper and the thrum, even above that incessant piping, I could hear their awful breathing. It was the heaving of Perdition, the breath of the damned come crawling from the grave.

Chalmers, in his stupidity and arrogance, had shown them the way to our universe, unleashed them on our curving time-space. Now, I would be their second victim as they began their feeding frenzy.

They recognised me. I could hear it in their sickening breath, feel it like a hot wind searing the dead earth. They knew me, and meant to make good their threat to destroy me.

They turned and began to give chase.

As pointless as I knew it was, I ran again.

THE HUNT REDUX

Whatever had been driving me across timespace to my doomed meeting with Chalmers, it was gone now. I was no longer being thrown along by some unstoppable external force. If I wanted to move forward, it was up to me. I had to concentrate, bring my will to bear, and lurch forward as best I could.

But I was moving too slowly. Every time I turned and looked back, they were closer, loping after me with gaining strides. They would be on me in no time. I couldn't outrun them, but maybe I could outmanoeuvre them. I relaxed my concentration, let the band of timespace around me go slack, and dropped back into some moment of the past.

I wrenched to a halt. I found myself standing on a brick-lined street. Horse-drawn carts trotted along in the early morning light. I could see a trolley car clanging along, and people meandering on the sidewalks to both sides. A pair of drunks, wearing grubby coats and bowler hats, stopped to stare at me, a thing come out of nowhere. And then, as in Chalmers' fateful room, the vibrations shot away from my body as I disrupted this time and place with my unwelcome arrival. I could see everything down the long street begin to tremble and shake, and then riotously sway as the earth and air shook apart. I watched in fascinated horror as buildings shuddered, crumbled, then began their slow descent into collapse. Glass shattered; brick burst apart. People were flung to the ground. The air was already starting to scream with splintering masonry and terrified voices.

Then, pouring up out of the bricks beneath me, that smoky void was writhing up to snatch me, for those horrors to get hold of me.

I pulled the band taut again and rushed further into the past. Their awful breathing was not far behind. I tried to ignore it, to put out of my mind the dreadful feeling that they were just about to overtake me. I was driving myself further from them, accelerating. But even as I sped away, I could feel them matching me. In short order, I could feel they were closing the gap. Moment on moment, they would be on me. I waited until their breathing was upon my neck, and then brought myself to a stop again.

I was standing under grim, overcast skies, surrounded by filthy masses of people and animals. The brutal iron and stone of towers ringed the wet hillside. Armoured, heartless men moved about me, on foot or horseback. Filthy, defeated shapes of peasants bore the weight of sacks and the slough of pointless toil. Some dark age when brutality and oppression ruled from God's flint throne. And again, as before, the earth and sky began to quake with my arrival, sending these foul people screaming from where I appeared. The soldiery unsheathed weapons to strike, only to be torn apart by the shattering force which boomed away from me. The towers exploded and plunged in boneless collapse. And slithering through the crashed masonry was the vile smoke, the twisting of blue tongues. I pulled the band taut and ran again.

Over and over, I kept away from them like this. I rushed further back through time, watching the decades roll into centuries. I would wait until the last moment and then drop into ordinary time and space, hurling myself into some past which could not accept me. Then would come the shaking of heaven and earth. Destruction bursting away from me as I appeared. And if I appeared where there were people, where there were stone and brick and right angles of civilisation, soon I would see that black pollution pouring from buildings, windows, any right angle where they might find purchase into our curving timespace. I would see the dreadful snap of their distorted shapes emerging from the smoke, the lash of their blue tongues. I would feel that foul breath pressing closer.

And when I had exhausted the time of man, when I found myself so far back in the past that only the natural world awaited my arrival, even still I became the cataclysm. The world would tear itself apart with me at the epicentre. In the end, I always had to return to the curves of timespace, and again the Hounds of Tindalos would be after me.

I was a thing unbound in the fabric of the universe, hunted by horrors that would never let me escape.

A SAVIOUR OF SORTS

My strength was fading. The concentration required was exhausting. I was rushing so far into the past that I would soon leave even the birth of my world behind. There was no doubt that no matter how far back I went, they would never stop chasing, never quit until they had overtaken me.

And then that piercing voice spoke again in my head.

"Ahhhhh," the voice reverberated inside my skull. Frightened as I was already, that shock made my heart nearly stop. "Yoooouuuuuuuu aaaaaare still in existence?"

"In your hhhheeeaaad," the awful voice explained. "Am in yyyyyour head." The voice was jittering static, metallic and reedy. "Lllost," it said. "Yyyyyou are lllllost. Ffffollow, please." I had, almost reflexively, turned and looked back, and I could feel something was forming there, a dilation between the fast-approaching swarm and me.

"Ttthere," the voice in my head commanded. "Ggggo there." The dilation pulled me towards it, towards them.

I screamed in protest. "Nnnno angst," the voice assured. "Gödel was correct. Tttttimespace is homeomorphic. Ccccan be uuuused against THEM."

But I wasn't listening to the insane voice. I was screaming, trying to let the band go slack, to get away. It was no use. Whatever was pulling me towards them, it was beyond my control. The dilation drew me towards it like a singularity. I was incapable of pulling away! The horrors bore down upon me. I felt their sickening breath chilling every cell in my body. "No angst," the voice kept saying. "Uuuuused against THEM."

And they swarmed over me.

I passed into the dilation with their tongues and claws all around me.

And then everything was gone.

WILLINGSTON

I was somewhere completely different, and I was screaming loud and clear. I let my scream echo a good minute or more, then collapsed on the ground, shaking and sweating and one heartbeat shy of a heart attack. It took a minute or more, but I finally stopped. I took a couple gulping breaths, stood up, and looked around me.

I was standing inside a perfectly-rounded, opalescent room. It was flawlessly smooth, dully lustrous like the surface of a pearl inverted. Everything was lit by some faint light, yet I couldn't see any source of the illumination. There was nothing else in the room, no objects, no windows or doors. Nothing.

60s Brazilian jazz was playing from nowhere. 'The Girl from Ipanema'.

"I hope you are comfortable," a voice said. A clear, human voice, not that reedy horror that had been in my skull. The voice, like the light and the soft jazz, came from nowhere, and everywhere.

An enormous disembodied smile appeared across from me, lingering just at the edge of the light.

"Forgive us for having frightened you," the voice said, and the smile raced lamely to keep up. "Soothing, yes?"

Um, was what soothing?

"The music. It is intended to relax you. Are you relaxed?"

It was actually making things worse.

The smile puckered thoughtfully. "Ah. We will continue to let it play. Perhaps the restorative effects are cumulative."

Um.

"Can we bring you anything? As this is merely a construct, anything provided will be virtual, but as they say, it is the thought which counts."

I realised then with a start that the white-hot focus I had felt was gone. The burning of Liao still coursed inside of me, but it was . . . contained, as if just out of my reach.

I wanted to know what the fuck was going on. How had I gotten here? What was restraining the Liao inside of me?

"This is difficult to quantify, but let it suffice that in this place, in this construct I have created for you, you do not, existentially-speaking, exist. We are in a form of nil space, and I have trapped you here in order to keep you safe."

And how in the fuck was it doing that?!

"I don't imagine the mathematics would make much sense to you," the smile explained patiently. "But let me assure you that once you are released from this construct, you will again be in full possession of the psycho-chemical power of the Liao and your brain chemistry."

With or without the power of the Liao, and with or without understanding the math involved, I was starting to get a little pissed off and said so.

"Yes, to the point, excellent. First of all, please forgive me. I did put you in harm's way to collect data on THEM, but the risk was minimal. There was a very low probability of your being in danger (variable sample space, inverted at dissecting coordinates and intervals assure the probability ratio accelerates towards 1. Outcome precision 94.4765 percent). It was necessary for my work to see how THEY would respond to your presence in this cycle. It was, to a variance of +-3 percent, as previously measured. Yet, each piece of data we collect on THEM is part of the key to humanity's salvation, or at the very least, to the avoidance of total annihilation." The smile grinned stupidly, while the voice mumbled calculations and statistics to itself in an unending inner dialogue, none of it meant for me.

I didn't understand. Had it done all of this to me? Thrown me through time? Pushed me into that room with Halpin Chalmers?

"Ah, no. We were(/are/will be) incapable of reaching you as such until you were (/are/will be) within the manifolds. Travelling in timespace is (/was/will be) the result of your choice to ingest the Liao, coupled with, shall we say, your unique mindset. You travelled (/will travel/will have travelled) into the curves of timespace, and through a causal loop, you are led (/will be lead/have been led) to Halpin Chalmers' apartment. Your arrival in Halpin Chalmers' rooms, and its deleterious effect on the past was (/is/shall be) predestined to occur, with or without interference from myself. I have watched the paradox unfold thousands of times."

Wait, what? He'd witnessed what thousands of times?

The smile grinned not a little patronisingly. "Your involvement in this paradox, as I said."

I've done this before?

"Before, after, those terms do not apply. Mundane reality has a past and a future, but in the curves of timespace, such concepts are more . . . fluid. Yes, I have observed (/will observe/ will have observed) Halpin Chalmers and yourself thousands of times and have even attempted to change that outcome in countless experiments."

What happened with these experiments?

"Regrettably, the outcome is (/was/shall be), for all intents and purposes, predestined. That term is rudimentary, but it will suffice. More precisely, there is no derivative coaxial timespace stream which does not end in the same result. You were (/are/will be) destined to go to Halpin Chalmers' room. It is your interference which leads to Halpin Chalmers' death, which leads Fred Carstairs to document what he saw. You will be led to read that biography, which will lead you to the Liao, and then back through time to cause Halpin Chalmers' death. My observation and experimentation have led me to conclude that you and Halpin Chalmers are a retrocausal paradox, and as such cannot be altered or undone."

The smile gave me a moment to absorb that bit of nightmare before going on.

"As for myself, I am connected to the paradox, undeniably, but am at best an observer. I am incapable of altering it. The paradox is encoded in the fabric of timespace. It cannot be unmade."

So why the hell bother with me if we've done this thousands of times already.

"Ah, my apologies. I was unclear. While I have (/will have/ had) observed the paradox, my attempts to interfere have never been so direct, nor of this nature. I have guided both Chalmers and yourself, your parents, your grandparents, endless generations in altering directions, but the path always returns to the source. The retrocausal paradox cannot be undone. However, what happens after that, I now realise that this can be changed. Thus, I brought you to this construct, so we may proceed."

A croony sax filled in the silence. I nodded, looking around. All in all, I felt I was taking the loss of my sanity pretty well.

"We haven't long," the voice went on. "THEY will return. By bringing you here, I have only delayed the inevitable. Your scent is known to THEM, and this puts you, not to mention our work, at considerable risk. As long as you remain outside of relative timespace (Lorentzian manifolds as a series of geodesics comprising an infinite conglomeration of Minkowski world tubes), THEY will find you. I was able to trick THEM, lose them in the undulations of our curving timespace. This artificial construct is a temporary sanctuary, but they are already beginning to sense your position.

"Understand that our curving timespace is alien to THEM, but THEY are learning quickly. THEY cannot be outwitted indefinitely. And now (/then/soon to be) that Halpin Chalmers has (/will have) shown THEM how to reach us, they cannot be stopped, only avoided. Correction: they cannot be stopped by direct force. Even still, I will continue my research, hoping to find the requisite mathematics (physics/philosophy/spirituality/music) to, if not defeat THEM, at least return THEM to that place from whence they came."

Was going insane supposed to be so full of scientific jibber-jabber?

"Forgive me. I do get carried away. I have not made formal introductions. My name is Prof. Willingston Willingston, and I am at your service. And you, my unique friend, are Mr. James {NHEEEEEEEEEEEE}." My last name was bleeped out, even as he said it. "It is our great pleasure to meet you. We have (/will have/will) observed you some while, but never before have we met. It is indeed a great pleasure to finally make your acquaintance. You are, after all, incredible, if you'll forgive me saying so."

What was so incredible?

"You, Mr. {NHEEEEEEEEEEEE}. You are incredible. You have, through sheer will and psycho-chemical enhancement, been able to achieve that which I can only approximate with my machine. You must understand, I have had many lifetimes worth of experience in circumnavigating our timespace. You are (/were/will be) a novice, and yet you already can do so much."

The smile and I fell silent, staring at each other. I looked around.

"This place, do you like it?" The voice asked at last. I shrugged, not sure what it wanted me to say. "I hope you do. I made this specifically for you. For us." The smile scrunched. "Perhaps not the most elegant of craftsmanship, I grant you, but if you could understand the requisite mathematics and physics required to create this construct, you would, I think, be duly impressed."

I made a noise which I hoped sounded sufficiently impressed. The smile looked pleased.

"Yes," the voice went on, the proud homeowner taking a guest on a tour. "This place, it exists outside the manifolds of timespace, an artificially constructed dissociative reality. As such, THEY cannot enter here, nor can THEY sense it or us . . . yet."

So where exactly were we?

"Language is insufficient to describe where/when we are at this moment. As I said, it is a construct, maintained at the heart of my machine."

His machine? What the hell was he talking about? We were in a machine?!

"Difficult to quantify, I'm afraid."

What difficult? Were we in a machine or not?

"To be precise, this construct is at the heart of my machine."

Yeah, so he said . . .

"And to be even more precise, it is you who is inside the construct. I am observing you, interacting with you from the controls of my machine."

So, if I was in the construct, and the construct was in the machine, and he was outside the machine . . . ?

The smile wavered. "Again . . ."

Difficult to explain?

"Yes. But we haven't the time to try. THEY are unable to find you at present, but that will not last. THEY already begin to sense you, and thus will soon find this construct, and when THEY do, it is assured that it cannot withstand THEM. We must be quick. I must introduce you to the others."

The . . . others?

To my left and right, two someones had appeared. To my left, a sallow-faced boy of ten with a dead-eyed, thousand-mile stare. The kid from the bushes. To my right, there was a grisly, stuttering, naked shape, convulsing in raging, homicidal agony on all fours. Vicious teeth snarled at me, a single eye hatefully glinting. The thing I'd seen in the batshit accountant's garage.

The smile beamed. "Mr. {NHEEEEEEEEEEEEE}, may I introduce you to our cohorts? The boy is Cole." The kid to my left stared relentlessly. The little fucker had a creepy, otherworldly thing going on, vacant and detached. I stared back, daring the prepubescent little punk to keep it up, but hell's bells if he would not look away. It wasn't aggression I saw in those eyes. He wasn't challenging me. That kid stared with a sociopath's unemotional genius.

"And this . . ." the smile said, then paused. Willingston was at a loss for words. I looked at the shuddering bulk convulsing on the floor to my right and could see why. Talk about non-sequiturs. "Our friend there does not have a name as such but is without a doubt involved."

What the fuck had any of this to do with me?

"Each of us has some part to play in what is unfolding, Mr. {NHEEEEEEEEEEEEE}. We are all tied to the doomed fate of humanity, to the coming of THEM. For myself, my machine has revealed THEM to me as I experimented with unfolding timespace. For Cole, the boy's genetically-engineered intelligence pushes him to another level of awareness, so that he can traverse timespace with his mind. And for—" the smile wavered. "For our friend there, we are unsure how the connection exists, but exists it does." The smile curled almost maliciously. "THEY fear it, and that is enough to make it our ally."

And me?

"Of each of us *inhumans*, we are agreed that you are the most curious. We are intrigued by your involvement, Mr. {NHEEEEEEEEEEEEE}, but more than that, we are captivated with your powers of disassociation."

Disassociation?

"Yes, Mr. {NHEEEEEEEEEEEEE}. Come now. Surely you must have realised your accomplishment. You have done something wholly remarkable, unheard-of in the history of our former species."

He kept saying that. Former species? Inhumans? What the hell did that mean?

"Inhuman. We are inhuman, of course. Cut off from homo sapiens. How could we be otherwise? The four of us. You and I, Cole and our friend there. We have broken through a barrier that was never meant to be bridged by humanity. Truly, we are something else now, no longer human. How can a thing outside of time still be considered human, trapped as our former species are? It is quite reasonable, you see. We have severed a cord, made ourselves undone from the fundamental bonds of mortality. We are inhuman now, something other. Would you not agree?"

I did agree. I hadn't considered it that way, but spelled out like that. Yeah. Something other.

"And of the four of us, you, in particular, are beyond that pale."

Why me in particular? What set me apart?

"Even you must recognise the enormity of your accomplishment, Mr. {NHEEEEEEEEEEEEE}. Cole and our friend there, they have pushed their consciousness, their perceptions beyond the limits of perceivable timespace. That, in itself, is miraculous. I have managed to push both body and mind across that boundary but through artificial means. My machine, it is an artifice, a device which allows me to move through timespace in this way. In all humility, I can agree that my creation is remarkable. Yet you, Mr. {NHEEEEEEEEEEEEE}, have accomplished something far more astounding than all of us combined. With the assistance of that simple drug, you have done what no mortal ever imagined possible. Through some power available only to you, you have driven your physical form beyond the confines of causality. By your inherent madness alone, you have disassociated yourself from mundane reality. Others have dabbled at the edges of that bottomless shore. Halpin Chalmers sent his consciousness out, strayed too far from mundane reality. But only you have forced your corporeal self into the flow of timespace. And how has this been accomplished? By you, an alcoholic, a drug addict, a man who squandered his potential for his pride and the pittance of manual labour."

Okay. Ouch.

"What is it about you which allowed you to do what no one else before or after you will ever do? You are intelligent, but not beyond a point. You are certainly no match intellectually for myself or Cole here. Physically, you are no more or less impressive than most of our former species. Our twisted friend there could surely rend you limb from limb. Your biology, your brain functions, your upbringing, none of it accounts for what you have done. The three of us have slid through timespace, through your life, observing everything you have done or ever been, and nothing can account for this. You are an enigma, Mr. {NHEEEEEEEEEEEEE}, a mystery. You have left not only humanity behind, but us as well, your fellow inhumans." The smile laughed gruesomely. "That must be clear to you by now. By your own conscious effort, you are transformed into a thing without peer, a lunatic god born of its own insanity."

The smile became wan. "And as such, you are THEIR first and foremost prey. You cannot be allowed to exist. You pose too great a threat to THEM. That is why THEY hunt you, and in fact, why you are here. Your ability, your physicality, imbues you with a unique opportunity for our cause."

And what cause might that be?

"What else, but to ensure THEIR ultimate banishment back to their realm. To purge the living Tao of their cancerous presence, and to imprison them once more in the strange angles from whence they came."

And what did that have to do with me? How was I supposed to do anything?

"You have only begun to know THEM. You have inklings of what happened, of what has transpired, and what is to come. You must be shown. We must show you what has happened (/ will happen/is happening) after the death of Halpin Chalmers."

The smile was a crooked line in reality. "This will not harm you, but it will be . . . unpleasant."

I could feel myself being pushed out of focus.

THE HOLLYWOOD
REVUE OF 1929

I found myself seated in a crowded movie theatre. There were people all around me, excited, smiling, eager for the movie to start. I was one of them. I could feel the happy anticipation, the giddy thrill of seeing this picture. It was the premier, and I had managed a ticket! I was a twenty-year-old woman, an aspiring actress working as a receptionist at Wilshire Production Scaffolding. It was June 20, 1929, and my father's attorney had managed to procure two tickets, provided I would accompany him.

The film was The Hollywood Revue of 1929; the place was Grauman's Chinese Theatre.

A cavalcade of stars and famous people were everywhere. Flashing cameras, interviews, so much glitz and glamour. It was like a dream! I smiled and felt the giddy thrill of mixing with so many famous people. There! Was that Stan Laurel? And I could see Jack Benny laughing with Buster Keaton! It was all so incredible. Flashes and sequins, tuxedos and cigarette smoke, the perfume of uncorked champagne and the bright, star-filled eyes all around me.

My father's attorney, a man in his latter forties, with a lot of shaggy hair, a barrel torso (my mother always called such people "heavy set") and black eyes, was nodding around and smiling. His smile came from a twitch in his upper lip which never seemed to stop. He nodded like he was satisfied, then turned to me. He had his arm around my chair. His twitching lip went up as he looked at me, and he nodded some more.

I tried to smile back, but I was nervous and not sure how to act around him. He was my father's attorney, so much older than me, and there was something about the way he looked at me that made me want to look away. But I was here, and he had brought me, so I smiled back. It was incredible! I was at the biggest Hollywood premiere of the year, possibly the decade!

My father's attorney ("Please, call me Terrence") gave me a long look, then turned and stood up to shake hands with a man who had recognised him. They conversed as men do, flippant and harsh, laughing and slapping one another on the arm. When they'd exchanged their back and forth, he introduced me.

"Miss Sylvia Templeton, may I introduce the big man himself, Mr. Harry Rapf." Harry Rapf laughed in a self-deprecating sort of way and put out his hand.

I was stunned. I stood there, mouth open a little bit, eyes goggling. This was Harry Rapf. *The* Harry Rapf! This was his movie! He was one of the biggest producers in pictures, and here I was, meeting him! It took me a moment to have the wits to give him my hand.

"A pleasure to meet you, Miss Templeton," Mr. Rapf said. I nodded and thanked him.

"What'd I tell ya," my father's attorney said, putting his arm around my waist and giving it a firm squeeze. "Is she not the spitting image? Is she not perfect?"

Mr. Rapf looked me up and down and nodded. "If you're confused, Miss Templeton, it's just that Terry here told me about you. He said you were the spitting image—"

"The spitting image, I said!" my father's attorney exclaimed, laughing and squeezing me again.

"—Yes, the spitting image of Dorothy Burgess." Mr. Rapf smiled. "I must say, he was not wrong. Are you an actress, Miss Templeton?"

I told him I was, or I was trying to be. I worked as a receptionist at—

My father's attorney cut me off. "She's ready and willing and able," and he laughed in a way that I didn't like, but I smiled and nodded politely.

"Well, we'd love to do a screen test, if you'd be interested, Miss Templeton," Mr. Rapf said. I thought I was going to faint.

"You just send me the details, Harry," my father's attorney said, pulling me closer. "We'll get the sparks flying!" Another laugh which made me squirm inside. I could feel his hand inch a bit lower down my waist. I felt ashamed and a little sick, but I stood properly and smiled, as my mother had taught me to do. This was my moment. I was going to get a screen test at MGM!

Mr. Rapf said it was a pleasure to meet me. He and Terrence quipped a moment more, and then we took our seats.

The film was about to begin.

And so, I watched the movie, smiled and laughed and tapped my toe to the music. It was delightful. I was so spellbound by the film, but even more, that I was going to be a star! I mean, it wasn't sure, not entirely, but how many girls were asked to MGM for a screen test, and by Harry Rapf, no less! I felt alive, thrilled, and so engrossed in the movie that I thought I might burst!

The movie was a talkie, and so many big names were performing! Singing, dancing, so much glamour! Jack Benny and Conrad Nagel were the masters of ceremonies, introducing every act. Joan Crawford sang a lovely song at the piano. The chorus and dancers made us smile and laugh and sigh. Cliff Edwards sang "Nobody but you" in that dreamy voice of his. We were all laughing as Laurel and Hardy tried to perform a magic act, but only ended punching and pinching one another, and when Oliver Hardy slipped and fell on that giant cake, the whole theatre roared with laughter.

But then, as I watched, I frowned. There was something else. The movie played on, so full of happiness and cheer, and still there grew in my mind something unsettling. It was a feeling of impending ruin, of something creeping closer that could not be named. It was a colourless, shapeless fear, one come out of nowhere, but somehow it felt as if it had always been with me. It felt ancient, like instinct, a fear that went to one's bones. I tried to watch the screen. I hoped it would quiet my mind, that this awful, rising anxiety would subside, but it didn't. It only grew. This feeling, this terrible feeling of some unknown dread was washing against me in rising grey waves.

Everyone around me laughed and applauded at what was happening on the screen. But my laughter was gone. The singing and dancing receded for me. I saw the screen illuminated with shifting blacks and whites, but the shapes no longer made sense. It was nothing but chaotic light splayed on a massive rectangle. I squinted at what I was seeing, but some part of me wanted to turn away, to excuse myself and leave the theatre. But I didn't. I sat and squinted, the fear building in me. The tide was rising fast. And then I saw it.

That movie screen was not just a canvas stretched across a wall. It wasn't just a screen against which light was being projected. That was all anyone around me could see, but I saw that it was something awful. It was an opening in our world to another place, a dreadful place, and the source of my rising dismay. I watched with sickening fascination. This place beyond the screen was lifeless and twisting, like broken panes of clouded glass folding one into the other. The more I looked, the more clear it became. I was looking into another world, but nothing like ours. It was terrible, and as repellent as anything come lurching out of nightmare. It folded and clashed into itself, a stretch of glowing desolation. I could feel it, sense an enmity coming from it. And worst of all was its unfathomable silence. The deathly silence of that place, it shrieked. No living thing has ever given voice to anything like it. An awful, maddening screeching silence, convulsing into itself in unearthly angles.

I was shaking now, face white and eyes streaming with horrified tears. Even my father's attorney had turned to me. I could only catch his concern out of the corners of my eyes. I could see his lip twitching in confusion and genuine fear. He was saying something to me, but I couldn't hear him. I could only hear that silent shrieking of an impossible place, feel the hard clench in my throat as I gagged on the dreadful knowledge of what I saw.

"Ssseee THEM," a voice stuttered in my mind. "Ssseee THEM, Mister {NHEEEEEEEEEEEEE}. This is where THEY found us."

They came sliding out of the endless convulsions of that place. The putrid smell of them filled my nostrils. There were hundreds, thousands of them, and they came slithering to the edge of that open gate of a screen, that hole torn in the fabric of everything by the flickering of pictures and light. I could not make sense of what they were. Their shapes were ghastly and unclean, consumptive demons more awful than anything I could have imagined. They appeared then vanished in the shifting angles and edges beyond the screen. They were evil, the greatest evil that should never be known. These were creatures of malevolence, emaciated and starving.

I shuddered, and my hands tore at the seat rest, at Terrence's jacket, but I was paralysed from looking away. From out of that blood-curdling silence, I heard the sound which pushed my mind beyond the point of sane return. A breathing, a desperate, insatiable death rattle wheezed from those things as they pressed against the screen. They were trapped, imprisoned just on the other side of the movie projection, clawing to get at us, to feed upon us, but we were fish beyond the aquarium glass. Thousands of them slashed and snarled against the limits of the silver screen, pressing as close as they could to get through. To get at us.

And then their attentions turned inevitably to me. I saw them, and they could see me. They could sense my awareness. I felt the squirming of alien minds boring into mine. I stared into the blue, lifeless void of their eyes, and knew them.

The silent shrieking was broken. It burst from my throat as the stab of a gutting knife. I screamed madness and hopelessness at the unsuspecting world. I screamed and screamed, and nothing could stop me. I could find no way to escape it, no path which did not lead me to the madhouse. They were there, waiting for us, swarming to feed upon us. The lights had come up, and the film had been stopped. People were looking at me, rushing to my side, but I could not unsee it. It only made it worse. The rising of the light only hid them from us. In the darkness, on that oblong patch of silver screen, they waited, desperate and starved for our essence. It was only a matter of time. They would find a way through. They would come for us. My scream became the high-pitched silent shriek of that terrible place. I shrieked without hope of any sort of salvation, for we were, all of us, guaranteed a coming doom.

CRACKS IN THE VENEER

I was back in the grey pearl, standing where I'd been before. The smile, the weird kid, and whatever that tortured, hateful thing to my right was were where I'd left them. Herb Alpert and the Tijuana Brass were playing "Spanish Harlem".

The smile smiled. "Soothing."

I looked around. The pearl didn't look so hot. It was crumpled in places, cracked and looked ready to fly apart. Just beyond the unflappable muzak, I could hear that horrible breathing and see the unmistakable slashing of claws upon the surface. They were trying to get in.

The smile seemed to read my thoughts.

"They are being restrained. I will increase output to the construct. There." The eggshell uncrumpled and sealed smooth again. "More to show you," the voice said. "Quickly. I cannot hold them at bay indefinitely."

I could feel myself fading again.

RCA LABORATORIES 1932

I found myself in the back seat of a car. This was Camden, New Jersey. It was September 14, 1932, and the car pulled into the parking lot of RCA Laboratories. My company. It was late at night. There were very few cars in the lot. "We're here, sir," my driver said. I nodded and got out. "You wait here," I told him, waving off his protest. Whatever this was, it was for my eyes only.

What was that Zworykin up to at this hour? The man didn't sleep at all? And why the devil was he rousing me out of bed at this hour? I wondered all of this gruffly, trudging my way to the entrance. The man had called my house in the dead of night, telling me to get down here. If he weren't such a genius, I'd have told him a thing or two, and most likely fired him. Genius or no, I'd considered reading the man the riot act. That phone call had scared my wife half to death. Who calls a person's home at two-thirty in the morning? I wasn't much of a sleeper; too much to do in life to be lying about. Even still, I needed some sleep. Can't run a company on no sleep. Zworykin was brilliant, no doubt, but that was neither here nor there. What was so blasted important that it couldn't wait until morning?

Inside, the place was dark and quiet. I passed a few security guards doing their rounds. They tipped their hats to me. I didn't return the kindness. I was far too angry for civilities. I had a brilliant pain in my neck to question.

I knew where I'd find him. He'd be in his lab, where he always was. I grumbled down the hall, across the cafeteria, into the applied sciences division. Down the hall, fifth door on the left. "Vladimir," I growled, walking into his lab. The man was not there. "Where the devil are you? Vladimir, why is it so blasted dark in here?" His lab was dark as all the rest. It looked like nobody was home. Was he not even here? Was this some sort of practical joke? "Zworykin, you buffoon! You'd better not be playing at something!"

I could see a light under one of the doors. I grumbled under my breath and tromped over to it. Before I could open it, though, the door swung open, and there was the man himself. All my bluster and gruffness vanished the instant I saw him. He looked positively terrible. He was pale as a ghost and frightened half out of his wits. He was visibly shaking.

"Ah, David," he said. "Please, please. You must come with me." His thick Russian accent made me think of my father. At that moment, looking as frail and aged as a man twice his age, he even reminded me of my father. I felt a sympathy for him then and tried to put my hand upon his shoulder. He flinched away. "David, er—Mr. Sarnoff. Please. Come with me. Quickly, please." He scuttled off, and I followed.

Zworykin was mumbling to himself as he led me down another dark hallway, into a smaller laboratory at the far side of the building. "You must forgive me for disturbing you," he said. "I would not have thought to call was it not an emergency. It is so—" He stopped, and by God if the man didn't begin to sob. Now I truly felt pity for the man. I'd never seen him, this brilliant and talented scientist, anything but cheerful. He'd come to work for me and my company two years ago from

Westinghouse, and in all that time, he was nothing but polite smiles and quiet chuckles. Standing before me was a man reduced to tears.

"Come along, Vladimir," I tried, but in all honesty, his breakdown had me nervous. "There, there. It can't be as bad as all that."

Zworykin turned on me, his eyes wide and frightened behind his little glasses. "Oh, but it is, David," he whispered. "It is much worse. For your safety and mine, touch nothing."

We entered the lab.

The room was lit, but it was dim, not much brighter than candlelight. In the middle of the open room were four large devices, each alike. They were heavy metallic boxes with wide camera lenses jutting from one end. Each one was mounted on a tall, spindling tripod for support and balance. They were not dissimilar to the *iconoscope* projectors, the television cameras we were developing at the laboratories. We had countless teams working on our first iconoscope camera prototypes, and Zworykin was our lead researcher in charge of the project. But there was something different about these four. They were larger and more crudely-constructed, as if these were only partially-completed works in progress. Tubes and cables jutted from them and were snaked all over the floors in dark nests. The cameras, if that's what they were, had lenses from one end, but from where I stood, there was no eyepiece on the other, as if the devices only projected from the lens, not used for filming. The four devices were all aimed inward at a square patch between them, with each one occupying one side of this square.

"By God, what is that smell?" I asked, covering my nose and mouth with my handkerchief. It was repulsive, a smell unlike anything I'd ever encountered before. The air was rank with it. Zworykin waved me closer, too upset and distracted to notice. "What the devil is all of this, Vladimir? What are these machines? Is this your doing?"

But I was stopped in my tracks. The cameras or whatever they were, all were projecting some sort of blueish light, shining down on that square of floor in front of them. Lying crumpled in that illuminated square was a sight I'd not forget to my very last. "Oh my God, Vladimir. What is that? Is that a man? Is—is that a body?"

"Eric," Zworykin said, staring at the shrunken, twisted mass in the blue square of light. "That is Eric Gunterman, my assistant."

"But he's—" I tried. I felt sick.

"Or should I say, it was Eric," Zworykin whispered sadly. "He is dead."

"Well clearly he's dead, Vladimir, but what in heavens happened to him? How did he end up like that? Vladimir, Eric wasn't twenty-four years old. I saw him just the other day. He was healthy as an ox. And you're telling me that's him? How is that possible? He's so withered. He looks like he's been dead for decades."

"Yes," the little man with the spectacles murmured. "I know."

I didn't know what was going on, but this was too awful to be real. I moved to examine the body.

"No!" Zworykin cried, pulling me back. "Do not cross into the field created by the projectors! The light is all that contains it."

"It?" I snapped, trying to shake him off. "You're talking about Eric, for God's sake." But then I screamed, as something appeared at the edge of that cube of light. I fell back, held from hitting the floor only by Zworkykin's steadying arm. It seemed the shrivelled remains of Eric Gunterman was not alone in there. Undulating in the air before us was an apparition, a gruesome fanged spectre with hollow gloom for eyes.

It was difficult to make sense of what I was seeing. In one moment, it appeared as a cataclysm of twitching, mottled flesh. The next moment it was nothing but refracted light, splinters of funhouse mirrors distorting everything which touched them. From its dripping, jagged, unformed mouth, a leeching blue tongue lashed out, then recoiled at the edge of the light. The horror snarled and snapped, clawed at the prison holding it.

"Is this some sort of a projection," I asked, never taking my eyes off of it. "Is this some trick?" But I knew the answer to my question even as I spoke the words.

"This is no trick, David," Zworykin said. "That is what killed Eric."

I wheeled on Zworykin. "What are you talking about? That—whatever it is—killed him? How?!"

Zworykin trembled, staring with sickened fascination at the horror imprisoned before us. "I cannot say. It . . . fed upon him. One moment he was Eric, and the next, he was that."

My mind scrambled for any glimmer of meaning to this. "What is all of this, Vladimir? How did this happen? What are these devices?"

Zworykin heaved, finally turning from the awful sight to look at me. "While the work on the iconoscope cameras is my first priority to the company, I have been experimenting with other technologies. Dabbling. These were something I hoped would be a great breakthrough for us."

"A great breakthrough? You mean these cameras?" I asked, pointing at them. "What in the hell are they?"

"They are not dissimilar to the iconoscope cameras, but these are fitted with a new projection tube which I have created. These tubes are much more powerful than the iconoscope prototypes. They are not limited to projecting two-dimensional images. These would allow us to project three-dimensional images! Imagine it. Three-dimensional images, as if the things they projected were actually real!" His scientific excitement of that moment faded with one look in the direction of Eric's corpse. "Four cameras, each projecting one side of the three-dimensional object, all focused on a central space where the object would appear. And it worked! It actually worked. It was to be my greatest invention. Eric and I had been working on this a few nights each week for the last year, and it was working. It was not fully-realised, but it was promising, David. We were making real progress. I call it the *alithiscope*, the true light projector."

The monstrosity weaved from side to side, watching us from its illuminated cage. "Is that some sort of illusion, then?"

"I do not know what that is, David," Zworykin replied, taking off and cleaning his glasses. "But it is no illusion. It is most certainly real."

"But it's like a—a ghost," I protested.

"Whatever it is," Zworykin insisted. "It is clearly not bound by the same rules of physics as we are, but that does not make it any less real."

I could not bear to look at the horror. Beyond its gruesome appearance, the thing was clearly studying us. I shuddered at its eyeless gaze. This was not some mindless brute. I could sense intelligence in that gaze.

Instead, I demanded Zworykin tell me precisely what had happened.

"Eric and I came to the laboratory at seven this evening. Our attempts had been promising if a little crude. We were both sure we were close to a breakthrough. We had made refinements on the alithiscope tubes, and tonight we were to test them. I installed the tubes in the projectors, while Eric calibrated for our tests. We began our testing just after midnight, and the improvements had worked. We were projecting a three-dimensional image of an apple upon the floor. The image was weak, so we increased the output to the projectors. And that's when IT appeared. Eric thought it was some false image, a glitch. He walked into the light, and . . ." Zworykin trailed off. He looked at the floor and was silent for a time. He finally looked at me, and my heart felt broken for the poor little man. "I have witnessed many things in my life, David," he said to me. "But the scream, Eric's scream, it was awful, the most terrified and agonising sound one could ever imagine. Whatever IT did when it lashed its tongue to him, it devoured him from the inside out."

"What do you mean?" I whispered.

"It was as if it drank his life away," Zworykin murmured. "It fed not on his flesh, but on his soul."

I had heard enough. This had gone on for far too long. What we would tell the police, Eric's family, I didn't know, but at that moment, I didn't care. This had to end. "What will happen if we turn these machines of yours off, Vladimir?"

"Only a guess, but I would think it would simply disappear. This creature, it must exist outside of our reality. My projectors have, somehow, brought it into our world. If we turn them off, I believe it will return to wherever it comes from."

"You believe?" I asked. "And what if you're wrong? What if that thing doesn't disappear, but is set loose?"

Zworykin nodded. "In that case, David, we will end up as Eric did."

So, there it was. The decision rested with me. "Turn it off," I said. Zworykin looked at me a long time, then nodded and started for the control board.

I took him by the arm. "But do it slowly," I said. "If it looks like it might escape, turn the projectors back to full and keep it trapped."

I turned, and despite my revulsion, I watched the thing. I was terrified and sickened, but I'd be damned if I would face my death any other way. "Go back to whatever hell created you," I whispered, and the beast hissed viciously back at me.

Zworykin began reducing the power. I could hear the whine of the projectors diminishing. The blue light grew fainter. The creature sensed what we were doing, for it began to thrash and whirl about like a cornered animal. It was crashing about in its cage, sending harsh bursts of light and shadow in its frantic wake to be away.

Then it did what neither of us ever imagined. It turned on Eric's desiccated corpse and rushed inside of it! Both Zworykin and I gasped and then screamed as the body began to twitch and convulse. It was moving almost involuntarily, like a man seizing under electrocution.

"Keep going!" I yelled at Zworykin. "Don't stop, man!"

Zworykin was dialling down the power, and the light was faint now. That's when Eric Gunterman's lifeless head lifted from the floor. It turned and stared at us. Its shrunken lips were pulled back from its teeth, baring blackened gums and a blue slime which ran from its mouth in a nauseating drool. A rasping came out of the dead man's mouth. And then I looked into the corpse's eyes . . .

The machines fell silent. The light was gone. The corpse crumpled back to the floor, lifeless and still.

The next thing I knew, Zworykin was at my side. I started at his touch. "David," he asked. "Are you alright?"

I said nothing but instead gave him a weak nod. The thing was gone, that was all that mattered.

I knew then that I would never tell Vladimir what I saw in that final moment, for it was too awful for anyone to bear. I only looked into those eyes for a fraction of an instant, but that was more than enough. What I saw, it was very nearly my undoing. Everything which is foul in this world, every evil I had read of in scripture, it was staring back at me from that dead man's eyes. An unending cruelty and hunger cast its gaze upon me, a malevolent intelligence far surpassing that of men.

Ancient beyond any scale of time which our fragile minds can reckon, it and its kind knew of men, and were ravenous to feed.

THEY ARE ALMOST THROUGH

I was back in the pearl.

Gillian Hills was crooning "Zou Bisou Bisou".

The pearl was cracked and crumpled again, looking worse than before.

The smile was an austere upside-down scowl then, and Willingston's voice was hushed and low.

"There are incidents which have occurred since the paradox, isolated encounters with THEM, but which have gone unnoticed by most of humanity," he said. "And why would the human race take notice? Humanity cannot imagine the wondrous and the horrific beyond their own egotistic limits. Our former species is unprepared for what is coming," Willingston said. "But you will be, Mr. {NHEEEEEEEEEEEEE}. You must be prepared if you are to save some fragment of humans from total annihilation."

Why couldn't we just go into the future, warn ourselves, others, of what's coming?

"Come now, you must already realise that such a thing is impossible."

Why? Weren't we travelling through time? What was stopping us?

"I would have thought that self-evident by now. Why did you see so many curving bands of timespace? Why so many pasts? The future, as you call it, is no straight line. Time is the amalgam of infinite variations. Yes or no. This or that. The shift of a quantum from there to here. All of these variations, they are nothing but potential. If you choose to do this or that, if you stumbled and fell or managed not to slip in the first place, each one is a variation in timespace, and both are true. Each of these variations is a divergence from the present into two distinct futures, and these futures split again and again and again with every variation, every potential. The multiverse, it is the eternally branching of futures splitting into futures splitting and splitting and splitting. We call it *the Potentiality*, and for all intents and purposes, it is nothing but chaos. The Potentiality cannot be traversed, Mr. {NHEEEEEEEEEEEE}, for it is the static wave of constantly branching outcomes, all of them true, and none of them converging again. Time spreads like a radiation of diverging potential, infinite numbers of sibling universes spawning an infinite number more. I have attempted to go there, as has Cole, and I assume our gruesome friend as well. It is unbounded possibilities, and as such, a timespace without an anchor of substance to it. It is, to paraphrase Heraclitus, as if attempting to step on the same water twice. THEY spread across this virulently, across the infinite variations of splintering universes. There will soon be no future we can know where THEY have not infected. There is, in effect, no escape from THEM on any of the variant timelines, infinite though they might be."

And the past?

"In a way, the past can be affected, for what is the past but simply a form of the present, distinctive to the observer? You have seen this. You have changed many times and places with your violent arrival in those pasts, but this has not affected some present or future you might ever know, for you are only a variant in a swarm of variance. You, like all other input, only create more divergence, more futures, more potential, more chaos. What has been changed in one strand of the multiverse has no bearing upon the other strands. It only serves to create more and more strands."

And why couldn't I exist in the past? Why did I always start it shaking, tear it apart?

"There is no place for you in the past, just as there is no escapable future for you in the Potentiality. You have a destiny, Mr. {NHEEEEEEEEEEEEE}. This is encoded in the fabric of existence as we know it."

That wasn't really an answer.

"I can tell you that the math checks out. You are a universal constant. A small one, a transient one, but a constant, nonetheless. Removing you, or Chalmers, or THEM from this span of our timespace unravels everything else."

The smile bounced up quizzically. "Shall we press on?"

I was pushed out of focus again.

VIRTUALIS HQ, 1998

It was March 8, 1998, and I was in Barcelona, and not the best part of it by the looks of it. I was walking fast, making my way to Camila's apartment. Camila lived on a shitty side street of El Raval, close to the port. Every building for blocks around had bars on doors and windows, including hers. Graffiti and garbage were everywhere. It was hardly the kind of place you wanted to be wandering at night. The taxi wouldn't bring me to her building but dropped me a couple of blocks north. I couldn't blame him. Why the fuck did she live here? I was none too pleased to be here at this time of night, but Camila had contacted me, told me to come here tonight, so here I was.

When I made it to her door, one of the plexiglass doors into the apartment building stood wedged open. "Real fucking safe," I grumbled. I read the little name plates by the front door. I could see she'd listed the name of her company on the apartment listings. "Virtualis" it read in her finicky handwriting. She was running her new business out of her apartment. I buzzed four times; no answer. Tired of waiting, I just went in, pulling the door shut behind me.

I hadn't seen Camila in over a year. We'd worked together for a stint over at this shit tech outsourcing company called QualiSol. QualiSol management liked to think they were a player in the tech game in Spain, even across the EU. They were not. QualiSol was just another shit outsourcing company in a sea of shit outsourcing companies across Europe. The only reason I stayed at QualiSol was that I was a lazy bastard who had suckered my way into a sweet deal when I got hired. Camila was hired two months after me, and we worked together for two years. We both knew what the place was, and we joked ruthlessly and often about how little the place mattered. Then, one day, Camila up and quit. She bailed because she said the place was a paper-pushing career killer for anyone in the IT game, and she'd decided to go work on her pet project she claimed was going to make her stinking rich. As lazy a bastard as I was, it was Camila bailing that led me to bail a couple of months later. Camila and I stayed in contact via email, but not much. We exchanged maybe four in total, all in the first two months, then nothing. She went her way; I went mine.

Then just last week, I got an email from her. She said she was ready to show someone her project, and I was the first person she thought of. I have to admit I was flattered. As smart as I liked to think I was (and trust me, I was pretty damn smart and happy to run it up everyone's flagpole), I knew Camila was so far out in front of me it was scary. Camila had brains, both in tech and business. She knew her shit. Whatever she'd been doing for the past year, I was damn sure it was going to be good.

I took the stairs up to her apartment. Syringes and beer cans, old newspapers and crumpled Ducados packets. Someone had spray-painted a horse fucking Bart Simpson on the second-floor walk-up wall. This place was one-meter shy of a slum. I grimaced and kept going. Third floor, fourth floor. The lift was broken open on the fifth floor, smelling like cat piss. I made it to the sixth floor, then down the hall to Camila's place. She had a sign on the door with a logo and the company name on it. I banged on the door. "Camila, it's Mateo." A long wait. "Camila?"

Finally, I heard movement inside. "Mateo, shit," I heard her say. "Sorry, I'm coming."

She finally opened the door. "Jesus," I said. "You okay?" She looked like hell.

Camila waved me in. "Yeah, I'm fine. Come on in. Sorry, I fell asleep."

I walked into a dark apartment with computers set up all over, not to mention takeaway cartons and about a million empty red bull cans. It looked little better than the stairwells. You could've been forgiven for thinking she was squatting there. The place had the basic shape of an apartment, but anything beyond that was incidental. Camila had turned the place into a modern-day mad scientist's lair. Beyond the couch and one armchair, there was nothing left to mark it as a place where humans lived. Standing in the living room, I could see the kitchenette near the window. Not a pot or pan in sight. She'd taken out the refrigerator and everything else that wasn't bolted down and stacked it up with servers and monitors. She'd set up an air conditioner on a folding table near the windows to keep all the servers and PCs cooled. Tech crap was everywhere. It was all so illegally wired up; the place was using so much electricity from all the equipment, I couldn't imagine how the cops hadn't marked it for a drug lab. Camila brushed a bunch of junk off the lounge chair and waved me to sit down. "So, you don't entertain much," I said.

Camila fell back on her couch. "Sorry, I was expecting to be ready for you. I just—look, I'm going to have to have you back another time." Pasty and monitor-tanned as Camila always was, she looked particularly wan. Whatever she was doing, she was clearly not sleeping much.

Now, on the one hand, I had nothing but pity for her. She looked like she'd been burning candles at both ends, and most of it taking toxic chemicals. On the other hand, I wasn't taking no for an answer that easily. "Come on, Camila. I've been champing at the bit to see what you're working on for like a year. Don't leave me hanging."

Camila gave me an exhausted half-scowl. "Mateo, don't start with me. It's been a fucked-up week. I really don't have the time or energy. Can we just pretend like I didn't send that email, make some bullshit chitchat and go our separate ways?"

Nope. "Just a peek. I just want to see whatever you're doing. I came all the way across town, and this neighbourhood is a shit hole. I thought I was going to get murdered or tagged with Bart Simpson porn on the way here."

She huffed and got up. "Fine." She started for the bedroom.

"Well, let's go." I jumped up.

In the bedroom (which had no bed, no dressers, not even shit in the closet, aside from what looked like a SAN backup. How the hell was she living here?!), there was a whole bunch more equipment, cables and a speaker setup that would make an audiophile hard. In the middle of the room was a flat square of linoleum (I wondered if she had dumpster-dived it or had just cut it up off the kitchenette floor) with an office chair sitting on it. Next to the linoleum and chair was a black stand with a helmet and goggles on it. The helmet and goggles were wired to a console.

"Whoa," I said, catching on immediately. "Have you been building VR?"

Camila nodded. "VR."

"Dear God," I said. "Is this what you've been building all this time?"

"Yeah. I had a couple of guys who helped me with the software and the sound integration, but the helmet, the goggles, all the custom hardware, yeah. That was me."

"Amazing," I said, nodding. "Absolutely incredible!" Camila smiled wanly and nodded.

VR. Virtual Reality. A helmet and goggle setup to feed the wearer simulated reality via sound and graphics. There had been a fair number of attempts by some big-name players in the IT industry (most of them weak), but corporations had millions to drop on R&D. The fact that Camila had put this together on a shoestring was only further proof of her genius.

I gave her a high-five. She weakly reciprocated. "Wow," I said. "I figured you were up to something incredible, but not this incredible." She shrugged. "Can I try it? It's ready, right? You wouldn't have pinged me if it wasn't ready."

I sat down in the office chair and reached for the helmet.

"Don't!" Camila said, pushing my hand away. "Seriously. You do not want to do that."

"Why not? Is it gonna give me a seizure or something?" She said nothing. "Wait, is it?"

"Look, Mateo, I have to get back to work." Camila was giving me the wave to go. "Sorry you had to drag yourself across town. My mistake, completely. Anyway, thanks for coming by."

"Camila, what the hell is going on? You call me over here, all excited to show off your wares, and now you're chasing me out after five minutes. What is up?"

"It's nothing, alright?" she said. "I'm just not ready to show it off yet. It's got too many bugs."

"That's bullshit, Camila. What are you hiding?"

Then I heard it. We both did. There was a sound from somewhere in the apartment, a sound of someone or something, and it wasn't us.

Camila and I looked at each other for a good long stretch before she sighed and slumped her shoulders.

"Fine," she said at last. "Look, Mateo, you gotta swear you're gonna keep this between us. Just us. Nobody else. Things got fucked up, and nobody can catch wind of any of this. You gotta promise me. Promise."

"Okay, I promise, fine." More banging sounds. "What the hell is that?"

"Come on," she said, leading me out of the bedroom. We crossed through the living room to another door on the other side.

"Stay back," she said, reaching for the door. "And whatever you do, don't scream."

"Don't scream?" I asked. Then she opened the door. It was a good thing she told me not to scream. I just might have.

The room on the other side of the door was brighter than bright. The place was filled with lamps of every size and shape, all of them aimed every which way to illuminate every corner. The lights crisscrossed, creating slanted, dihedral patterns on the walls and ceiling. Projected against one wall was a compilation video of a jumble of images and video clips, all of them strung together and running in silence. There was a mangy mattress on the floor, with a single occupant.

Naked but for some tattered jeans, emaciated, and the colour of a long-dead corpse, the occupant was riveted to the projected images on the wall. Its head was all but bald, with only the last wisps of human hair on its head. What I could see of its face was bony and angular. Its nose and chin were freakishly exaggerated, and its lips were pulled back in a violent death grimace. Its teeth were sickeningly long, making it look like it was grinning horribly. Whatever the thing was, it was hissing and snapping quietly at the movie, as if it was a lunatic in an asylum engaged in a madman's conversation with no one. It was enthralled with what it saw, clawing the mattress with its skeletal fingers as it watched.

"What the fuck?" I gasped uncontrollably. The thing turned towards us at the sound of my voice. I only saw the briefest glimpse, but the eyes, sunken deep in its skull, were glowing a gruesome blue-black.

Camila slammed the door. "No!" she yelled, and then we heard the whatever it was slam into the door, slashing and hissing like mad.

"Jesus fucking Christ, Camila!" I snapped. "What the fuck is that?!"

The thing on the other side of the door was going crazy. Whatever it was, it wanted out, and attacked the door for a good five minutes before lapsing back into silence.

Camila and I went back to the couch and chair and collapsed.

"That's Daniel," Camila said at last.

"Daniel? Daniel?! Jesus fucking Christ! Who the fuck is Daniel?" I asked. "And why in the hell did you let him into your house? Are you insane? He looks like a goddamn demon!"

"Mateo, he didn't look like that when I met him. Do you think I'm an idiot?"

"Well, I don't know! Who the hell is he?!"

"He was my tester. I couldn't afford much, and he needed a place to crash, so I paid him with room and board and a bit of cash. He was my guinea pig on the VR helmet. He gave me feedback, and I kept him from living on the streets."

"So, I'm assuming he wasn't anything like that goddamn junkie ghoul in there when he moved in."

"Again," Camila said. "I'm not an idiot."

"Well it must have been clear to you at some point he had to go. You must have seen it coming."

Camila got up and went into the kitchenette. "I need a drink. You want one?"

"Yes. Clearly, I want a drink. Camila, what the hell is wrong with him? He looks—" I couldn't bring myself to say it.

"Dead?" she said, handing me a glass of rum. I drank half of it in a single gulp.

"Yeah, dead. I mean, dear god. He actually looks like a corpse. Some evil zombie corpse. And what the hell was that with his eyes?"

"Mateo, I don't know. I don't know how he ended up like that. Six months ago, he was normal as anybody. A little scrawny, a little down on his luck, but he was just a student. He was a film student working on a project and needed some-place to crash. I needed a tester. I had the spare room, and so it seemed a good match. It was fine at first. It wasn't until, I don't know, maybe two, three months ago that I started to notice it."

"It?"

"The smell. Don't you smell it?"

Camila was right. There was this pervasive stench just under the surface, something sickening but undefinable. "What is that?"

"I don't know, and I don't know when I first noticed it. I thought maybe it was something in the building, the pipes or something. But I did start to notice Daniel was losing weight. I didn't think much of it. I figured he was just working really hard, and a poor student. He wasn't really eating, not really sleeping. The only thing he wanted to do was to test the helmet and to work on his movie."

"Is that what he's watching?" I asked. "His movie?"

"That's it. When he moved in, he was working on a differ-ent movie. Some art-house piece. But once he started testing the helmet, he told me he wanted to make a multimedia piece, something which would go great with my VR helmet. I figured, shit, if he wants to do that, I'm not going say no. Start-ups need all the help they can get. So, he worked on it, and I worked on my VR.

"He finally showed me the first cut of his new movie. It's what you saw projected on his wall. A bunch of random clips, all strung together. When he showed it to me, I couldn't make sense of why he chose the clips he did, but I pretended to like it. Even if I didn't end up using what he'd made for a demo reel, I figured if it kept him in the project, let him go nuts. But the thing was, he knew I didn't like it, or didn't get it, so he started changing it, making the tiniest of changes. Like single frame changes, something no one would ever notice. He edited and re-edited that film, but as long as he kept testing the helmet, I didn't care. That was his thing, whatever. As long as he was doing the work, I didn't care what he did with his own time. I don't know when it was that I finally noticed he'd stopped eating, but by then, he was too far gone.

"A couple of weeks ago, my cousin invited me to get out of town, and I figured why not. Daniel was really scaring me. He never came out of his room, except when I was asleep or out. The smell had gotten so bad, I had to leave the windows open all the time. I knew it wasn't the pipes. It was him that was giving off that horrible smell. I didn't know what that stink was, or why he smelled that way, but I knew he had to go. The VR was good enough to take to investors. I didn't need him anymore, and besides, he was watching that movie on an endless loop in his room. Just watching and re-watching that fucking video. It got to the point where I didn't even ask him to come out of his room. He looked terrible when I did see him. He'd lost so much weight, I thought he might have cancer or some sickness. Or maybe he was a junkie. I didn't know. But he was still just Daniel, the sullen art student I'd met. More angry, more secretive, but it was still him. I guess I should have done something then, but I thought it would sort itself. I don't know." She finished off the rum in her glass and went to get some more. When she came back, she sat looking at me a long time.

"I figured it was fine. I've dealt with assholes and freaks before. My cousin had contacted me and asked me to go away with her for a few days. It was a good excuse for me to get out of the city, away from my work, away from Daniel and all of it. I was exhausted. I needed a break, even a small one."

"When was this?"

"That was two weeks ago, when I sent you that email. Exhausted as I was, I was excited. I knew it was getting close, that the helmet was ready to go to market. I wanted to show you what I'd been up to before I got all tangled up in investor bullshit. I thought you might want to come work with me. I'm going to need a good team, and I trust you. I figured when I got back, I'd give Daniel his final pay, thank him, and tell him to pack it up. Fine, right? Then I got home. I found him in there with the helmet on. I knew straight away. I knew he hadn't left that chair the whole time I'd been gone. He was watching his video on an endless loop through the helmet."

"Whatever happened to Daniel, it happened fast, in less than a week. He looked like he does now, a horrible goddamn skeleton. I swear, when I saw him, I thought he was dead. I was crying, terrified. So, I took the helmet off—"

"Wait a minute," I said, catching on. "You took the helmet off first? Why didn't you call the cops, an ambulance?"

Camila flustered. "What would that do? I knew if the cops turned up and found Daniel dead with my VR helmet on, they'd start asking a lot of questions, wondering if he had a seizure, something like that. Mateo, I couldn't risk that. My project would be ruined."

"Your project?" I asked. "Camila, your project? You thought a man was dead, and you were worried about your work?! What were you planning on doing? Were you just going to dump him in his room and say you found him dead when you got home?"

Camila stuck out her chin. "Yes. What else? Come on! The guy clearly lost his mind or died of drugs or cancer. What difference did it make if he was found in his room or the chair?"

"It makes a whole lot of difference, Camila. A huge amount of difference!"

"Would you shut up and listen to me? Yes, okay, I was going to drop him in his room. I'm a monster. You can berate me later. The moment I took off the helmet, he leapt at me. He came flying after me, shrieking and clawing."

"Oh my god," I said. "What happened?"

"I nearly didn't get away. He was fast and strong. He grabbed me, threw me on the floor, and that's when he looked in my eyes. Jesus, those eyes. I only looked in them for a second, but I felt like everything was doomed. I could feel myself dying, shrivelling up, turning to disease. I felt totally hopeless. But some part of me fought back. I knew he was going to kill me. I grabbed something, I don't even remember what, and I bashed him across the head as hard as I could. I must have hit him hard enough to knock him out, because when I finally got up, he was out cold on the floor. I dragged him into his room and dumped him."

"How did you know to turn on his movie?"

"I didn't. It was already on. He had it playing on a loop with all those lights on. I just threw him in there, locked the door and came out. At first, I wasn't sure if I'd killed him, but then I heard him in there. I could hear his creepy breathing and him hissing to himself. I looked in on him a couple of times, really quiet, but he didn't seem to notice me. Just kept watching that movie. It's the only thing that calms him down. It's like his heroin or something. He never looks away from it. It's the only thing that keeps him from attacking the door."

Camila went into the bathroom and came back out with a towel. She handed it to me, and the smell of it nearly made me vomit.

"What the fuck is that?!" I asked, dropping it. The towel was covered in some blue slime which smelled horrible.

"That," she announced. "Is his blood. Or whatever is inside of him. I mopped that off his head and off the floor after I clobbered him."

I kicked the towel away, sickened.

"Camila, what if he is sick? What if he does have cancer? He needs help."

Camila sat and considered. "Mateo, you saw what was on the other side of that door. Do you think he is just sick? Does that thing look like a sick man to you?"

I shook my head. "And what of your equipment? I know this sounds crazy, but could your VR helmet have done this to him?"

Camila shook her head. "I've been going over that thought a long time, but I can't see how. It's a couple of tiny screens inside a pair of goggles, hooked to a computer program. How could any of those do that to him? It's not done that to me."

I saw her point, but even still. "Then why didn't you want me to put on the helmet, Camila?"

She wouldn't look at me. "More testing. We just need to do more testing. Make sure it's safe. I'm sure it is, but just to make sure."

We sat in silence and polished off two more glasses. If I listened very carefully, I could hear that thing dragging its claws on the mattress in there. Camila and I stared out the window. The rum was gone.

"I need your help, Mateo," Camila said at last. "I know this will sound insane, but whatever that thing is, that's not Daniel anymore. It's not human. It's not right. Whatever that thing is, I have to get myself and everything about my project as far away from it as possible."

"What are you saying, Camila?"

"We have to kill it," she said. "We have to kill it and get rid of that corpse." Camila waited a long time, staring at me, then finished her thought. "I'll split the company with you, sixty-forty."

I sat with the empty glass shaking in my hand, sickened not only at the monster that I'd seen but in the knowledge of what we were both about to do, the monsters we were about to become ourselves.

"How do we want to do it?" I asked, wishing there was more rum.

THE SHATTERING
OF THE SPHERE

"You understand now, yes?"

The sphere was collapsing in on itself. Still, the smile, the kid and that twitching thing were to each side of me.

I *didn't* understand. I didn't know what any of it meant, or what the hell they expected me to do in all of this.

"Is it not apparent what is happening? These were isolated incidents since the paradox, but they are becoming less isolated. The addicts grow in number, and THEY are the cause. THEY are using humanity's primitive synaptic response mechanisms to reach all of us."

How were they doing this?

"Through screens, Mr. {NHEEEEEEEEEEEEE}. Through our screens. Our televisions, our films, our phones, our tablets, our displays. THEY can use the disruptions in the electromagnetic fields, coupled with the geometry of angular timespace, to pass into our world, and thereupon feed on humanity. You have seen this, though you had no way to prove this empirically. I have observed THEM for many lifetimes. I can assure you, what you saw—the exchange between the viewer and the viewed screen, that phenomenon is real."

So, they feed on people?

"Feed, yes. The creatures (THEM), THEY consume the bioplasmic energies which power our cells, our molecules. These are, chemically-speaking, what gives us life. I am no chemist, but I have observed THEM as THEY feed (breakdown of nucleic acids, macromolecular dissolution and recombination), and worse still, what THEY inject into us each time THEY do so."

The blue ichor.

"Indeed. The blue ichor. The substance documented (/to be documented/will have been documented) by Doctor James Morton when he examined the 'blue slime' they found (/will find/will have found) on Halpin Chalmer's corpse. I can only speculate as to what this substance is, but it is not placed in humanity without purpose, that much is clear. Whatever this substance might be, it infects us, alters us, in ways which are deleterious to our psycho-chemical and physiological well-being. You have seen the results. Humans being fed upon through their addiction to screens, I call the *screen dead*. The more exposure to the substance, the more base the intelligence of the subject, the more rapidly a victim is drained by THEM, and thus the more damaging the effects. Diminished memory and focus, a lingering sense of gloom and malaise, painful surges in fight or flight instinct, triggered by fluctuating dopamine response. The grey matter recedes; biochemical dissolution, weakening emotional and structural centres of the entire organism. The screen dead are any persons currently, or recently connected to THEIR network as a food source. These humans are the most easily controlled through subliminal programming, and act as the unwitting eyes and ears for their masters(/predators/parasites).

"Those corpses which pursued you across San Francisco. They are the ultimate outcome of this exchange. In time, the organism will succumb to the toxins of the blue ichor. THEY then take control of the residual physical form, and use the corpse as their tool, their weapon, against any of our former species which is deemed a threat. The bodies have been twisted and remade to suit THEIR purposes. These animate cadavers I call the *departed*. These hide in the darkness, creeping in the places where humanity fears to tread, waiting to fulfil their masters' will. In the time you came from, the screen dead are already growing in number, but that is only the genesis of their ranks. In the years to come, the infection will spread with the advent of mobile technology, and in time the screen dead will outnumber the living. The departed's numbers will swell, growing to hundreds of millions. THEY will control you, dominate your civilisation, and become your true masters."

At the heart of all of this, was the most obvious of questions. What are these things? Where did they come from? Why were they doing this to us?

"THEY? There is no word which can accurately describe THEM. THEY are creatures from a reality which is utterly alien to our own. THEY are ancient beyond understanding, the desiccated remains of creation. Halpin Chalmers called THEM *the Hounds of Tindalos*. His name for THEM was based on his occult understanding, severely biased by his cursory observations, his highly agitated state, and the stimulant effects of the Liao.

"I have refined his name for THEM, as a species. Whatever else THEY might be, THEY are assuredly a species, though as alien and unlike any species we have ever encountered. For me, these creatures (THEY) are *the Tindalosi*. THEY are apex predators, utilising their concealment from humanity's senses to gorge upon and corrupt us. Yet we are more than mere provender to them. My observations have led me to conclude that THEY are poisoning humanity for some other, fouler purpose."

What purpose?

"Inconclusive data, but it is assuredly terminal in nature."

Not even a clue as to what they might be doing, aside from enslaving and poisoning and devouring the human race?

"Again, inconclusive data, but I can hazard a guess. The word 'cataclysmic' seems an apropos postulation of what is to come."

What the hell was he, was anyone going to do about all this?!

"Do not imagine that I have not tried to alter this outcome. It is impossible. As with you and Chalmers, the Tindalosi (THEY) are part of the retrocausal paradox. They cannot be stopped at the source, which is that self-same paradox. Believe me. I have tried. For each attempt I have made to undo the damage done by Chalmers, or by you, there have been reactions, a correction if you will, which sets things once more on the course which cannot be altered. I can no more change the outcome of the paradox than I can undo my own existence. Only you can save our former species."

Me?

"Yes, you. You see, unlike us, you have already become untethered from reality. You are not mere consciousness projecting itself through timespace like Cole here. Nor the product of hateful madness, as our writhing friend. You are not constrained by a physical machine, as am I. You are untethered, Mr. {NHEEEEEEEEEEEEE}, physically, mentally, in all ways. You are disassociated from the ties which bind. You are a part of the paradox, and you are outside the bounds of all things, all time and space." The smile widened. "You must concentrate, focus your mind and go to the place where you will find the next clue."

What clue?! I didn't know what he was talking about.

"With the collapse of this construct, the Liao's overwhelming clarity will rush over you again. There are answers which you have not considered, Mr. {NHEEEEEEEEEEEE}. Go back to the place where this all began. Return to where you entered the paradox."

I didn't understand! I didn't know where that was, and even if I did, wouldn't I just destroy that place/moment the same as all the other places in the past I'd been?!

"In your present state of consciousness, that would be true. Yet we are not without our talents, are we? We will do THEM one better. You will go to a new plane of disassociation, to a timespace which even the three of us cannot perceive. You will go up to the next level."

I was not liking the sound of this.

"I must be blunt. I do not expect you will succeed. Most likely, you will be lost forever, or just as likely destroyed by THEM. But if you wish to survive, you must concentrate. Do whatever it takes. Return to the place where this all began. Find Wǔyè Yuándīng."

I knew that name! The batshit accountant had told me the same thing.

"Yes, it is that which holds the answer."

Where the fuck was I supposed to find it, whatever it was?

"I have traversed curved timespace for what you would consider to be many lifetimes. In doing so, I have concluded that there is more to the cosmic order than the curves and angles of timespace. Where the four of us have moved beyond humanity, there is more beyond even what we have grasped, other planes which supersede this reality. Places where even the Tindalosi have not reached, nor can they, for they are not you. Layers upon layers of infinity, each one comprising the one beyond it, each step outward leading to a more advanced stratum. You must rise again, Mr. {NHEEEEEEEEEEEE}, keep pushing further until you find what you seek. Leave THEM behind."

How was I supposed to do that?

"Oh, I think you know. You must push your consciousness even further over the precipice, as it were. The Liao, Mr. {NHEEEEEEEEEEEE}. You will take the rest of the Liao."

I could see the egg was falling away. I could see the swarm of the Tindalosi beyond its tattering edges. Unnatural angles and the lash of blue tongues, the metallic serration of fangs glared back at me. Claws like shattering glass tore to get in, to get at me.

But more terrifying than those awful shapes desperate to get at me was the thought of taking more of that dreadful drug. What would become of me?

The smile seemed to read my thoughts. "I cannot conjecture what will happen to you if you take more of the substance. Truly, you have already consumed as much as Halpin Chalmers did on that fateful night, and even that amount was the man's undoing. I can only imagine what wonders; what damnation awaits you. But after all, what choice do you have? You must escape, and it is once again your only means of evading THEM."

I took the bag from my pocket, hands shaking. I still had a little bit of the vodka left. Just enough, as it turned out. I consumed every last one of the pellets of Liao and let the empty baggy fall to the tattering floor.

"I wish you well, Mr. {NHEEEEEEEEEEEE}. If you somehow survive, I hope that we might meet again."

I could already feel the Liao overloading my senses. What was going to happen to me?

"What else does one expect to happen when one goes beyond the boundaries of reality? Madness, of course."

I didn't want to go mad.

"I thought you would have realised by now, Mr. {NHEEEEEEEEEEEEE}. Your madness has always been a fore-gone conclusion."

Before I could say anything more, I was already gone.

A THING OF
UNIMPORTANCE

The thrum of a heart, the squirming of vesicles, the rush of fluid in arteries and capillaries. Electro-chemical dynamism, the firing of synapses across the chaotic lattice of a nervous system, culminating in the viscous addendum of a brain. Organs processing, glands secreting, marrow replenishing, and bones holding sinew to fibrous muscle. The sweating sheen of follicles, stinking flesh. Ragged breath, lungs expanding and contracting in sickened, unconstrained panic.

No thoughts, no reason. No cerebration, no intellect. Even the voice of a voice of a voice is lost now, the ever-retreating coagulation of parts which form the lie of a self. There is none of that, no more paradox comprised of memory, fear, desire, and discernment. The organism is void of purpose. It cannot reason or rationalise. It exists, nothing more. Its lifespan is meagre and brief. It is pathetic, a dying clot of gore which twitches and starves, thirsts and suffers. It desperately clutches and thrashes after its own survival. It had long laboured under the delusions it was an apex of creation. This is washed away.

Lying there was an evanescent droplet in the transient spray of evolution, a spurted seed of biological impermanence. It would fade from reality so quickly that it could hardly be thought to have existed at all.

And yet it lived. It breathed. It was a fluidic, an organic machine, the construction of trillions upon trillions of hive-minded cells, all of them guided by a blueprint in double helix. It seemed as unlikely as anything that such a thing could ever exist, and yet it did. It floated in amniosity, naked, staring, cast beyond the shores of time and space. It had somehow escaped these things, risen above them. The wriggling maggot had elevated itself into this unimaginable stratosphere which supersedes such notions.

There was no curving past, no splintering future. There was no mad fluting here, nor the horrific breathing, nor the fracturing horror of angular timespace. Nothing, not even the Tindalosi, could find a way here (wherever here was), no more than a shadow can chase its way back to the object which casts it. The thing floats alone in this place without time or space. It waits without purpose or reason.

There was a flash, a gasp of breath, and once more, I was.

I found myself outside of it all, a formless mind manifested in the dark. I was consciousness, nothing more, and I could perceive all things which were in this place. At that moment, this tiny blob of life was all there was. Me and this mycoplasma, we were the strange co-habitants of an undiscovered country. What a pair.

It hovered there before me, sad and alone and isolated. It squirmed and trembled, and I observed it with a cold but intrigued dispassion. I was the scientist and it the amoebae on the wrong end of the microscope. How could I think of it otherwise? It was unimportant, a pointless gob of ooze. It barely twitched with the most laughable rudiments of life. How could such a thing even be aware of itself, of the universe around it?

No. This was electrical impulses, cytoplasm and tissue, all of it encased in a blanched, vulnerable film.

But watch it I did. I knew that such a short-lived thing would soon be gone. It would dissolve away, and I would be left alone. Because I so feared unending loneliness, I gave this slime my attention, my perfect clarity. I basked in its rudimentary company.

I observed this grub for so long that I soon began to know every part of it, know when it would move, when I would see the wet rush of fluid beneath its skin. What I was looking at was a first step, something primordial, a primitive living thing alone in lifelessness. It had no other purpose other than the clinging will to live, and yet was that not enough? Was that not the basis of all life, the pointless scrabble to hang on even as destruction inevitably approaches? Pathetic though it might be, there was something . . . precious to that. The fact that this thing was the only life in this desolation. I wondered idly if it knew where, or even what it was, how it was unique in this stratosphere.

Another flash, the deep intake of breath, and the one burst outward into the many.

Radiating away from this tiny grub were the countless moments of its senseless life. Reflections of reflections spun away in every direction, filling that place with nothing else. I was no longer looking just at the wriggling source, but at every instance of its existence radiating away from it. From before its conception to the fading echoes of existence after it had gone. Catalogued before me was every moment it had lived, as well as every moment it might have lived. A Potentiality in singular, this one thing's existence fracturing into incalculable variations on the same writhing theme. I was seeing every possible outcome of this organism's lifetime, and my eyes were scintillated with their reflections.

And there was something else as well. Another inhabitant to our own private Idaho. Lying next to my feet was that twitching, agonised shape from the batshit accountant's garage, from Willingston's egg. It lay there in its sickening pain, thrashing and baring its teeth. I could not think of a more unwelcome guest. I watched it trembling and snarling. It lay beside the source of this place, the maggot from which all of this began.

Another flash. Another gasp. And that hateful thing cawed like an animal, then forced itself to its feet. Hunched in agonising, hateful pain, it rose to a stand and began to drag itself across the lifetime of this grub, this wriggling source. I had no choice but to follow. It was to be my guide, reprehensible as that idea was to me.

My guide stopped at the various moments of the clot's existence. It was there huddled in a corner at the moment of the clot's conception, watching viciously at the grunting of the father into the mother.

It was there at the thing's squalling birth, a blind, wet dab of life which shrieked without end.

I followed the gnashing, naked creature deeper.

We were there as the clot grew and thrived in its colourless existence. The clot had weak eyes, so that by the age of nine, it was forced to wear glass lenses strapped to its face. It was strong compared to other young of its species but was uninterested in their senseless games. Instead, it spent much of its time with books clenched in its claws. It was unwelcome and abused amongst the other young of its kind. It suffered beatings, abuse, isolation. It was alone, so often alone, and it retreated further into its books, further into its brooding silence and sullen looks. Soon, it was unwilling to communicate willingly, to most any of its kind.

We were there at every moment, every stage of its development in a world which was hostile to it, and hostile to its books, its quiet melancholy. We were witness to its confusion, its unhappiness, saw it live as an outcast in the small hick town where it grew up. It hated the place, hated its life, but knew it was a prisoner there. It was trapped until it was grown.

We went on. The clot lived its childhood in a soliloquy of lonely days, watching from an isolated bench on the playground. It persisted, and it fought when it could, and it read. I admit that I couldn't help some modicum of pity for the little smear. There was a cheerlessness to its experience, something too cruel even for something which mattered so little. My guide went on, and I followed.

Soon we reached its pupal stage, its transformation to maturity. It suffered still, but it had found others like it. Grimy and excluded, angry and loud and damaged. They came and went in a pack. They held only their own council and knew the secret dark places to go and hide, to celebrate their distastefulness. The stink of intoxicants, the crash of harsh music, of screaming into late nights. Running from authority, mangling property, lying whenever it suited. At long last, this throng of untouchables made the little clot feel like it belonged, gave it the safety of numbers, the raucousness of laughter.

But even still it continued to read. It donned its glasses and read whenever it could. It excelled at education, even as it was dismissed and disgraced by those which educated it. Unfit, unclean, never to amount to anything. It didn't care. Intoxicants and music and the written word, the dizzying light of the edge, that was all it needed.

We were there when it plumbed into the unmade with hallucinogenics, crashed a car with its blood sloshing with alcohol. We saw it fight. We saw it run. We saw it find a voice full of thought, full of cynicism and complexity. We watched it reach out for an edge that was never as far out as it hoped. It kept reaching. It reached and reached, until it reached right through to leaving its dilapidated home behind. A canvas bag, a sling of well-worn albums, blue plastic crates overfilled with books. It intended never, ever to look back.

My guide went on, but I was less willing now. I wanted to go back, to return to my shadowy place of distant equanimity. I wanted to be the scientist again, impartial and removed. But my guide only stared with its baleful eye, gnashed its teeth, and I had no choice but to follow.

It led me through the clot's meaningless race into adulthood. The drugs, the philosophy, the unrepentant blaze of freedom. The advanced courses, the chopped and snorted lines, the rags of ether. The harsh rancour of discordant guitar. The increasing complexity of language, of mathematics, of philosophy and thought.

And somewhere along the way, it managed to accidentally find something more than itself. It found something more than its toxins and its words and its music and its freedoms. It found another. It found the confusing jumble of love.

So, the it had become a they, two clots of life which had suffered so much in their individual lives, felt so much the pain of isolation, humiliation and loneliness. Now they had found one another. They spoke and touched and fought, helped and hurt, found new meaning in their connection.

It was no longer alone. With this other one, it had found the missing part, and I felt the tears well up in my eyes. I watched that little thing, and for the first time, I saw it approach something close to happiness.

The flash, the gasp, and my guide shrieked until I could hear nothing else. I tried to turn back, to run away, but the way behind me was closed now. The moments come before drove me forward.

A flash of the lighter under the spoon, the gasp of breath as the junk hit its vein, and then the glossy eyes stared at nothing as it fell back, too high to undo the belt from its arm. The moments went bad for a long time after that, slurred and pointless and sinking and worthless. It was one long haze of the flash, the gasp and the needle, through which I barely looked up to see her leaving.

No, I murmured. Not this. Not again.

THE BASEMENT

My mother's basement.

My body twitching and naked, I was half wrapped in the greasy cling of soaking wet sheets. My teeth were bared in a vicious, animal snarl. Heroin sick was crawling all over me. I was cussing in a diseased whisper, telling the universe to go fuck itself. I hated everyone, especially my mother, who had locked me down here with bottled water, boxes of crackers and a puke bucket.

I'd already tried kicking the door down but hadn't come close to denting it. In the early 70s, my old man had upgraded our basement into a bomb shelter. Nothing short of levelling the whole house was going to take out that door.

The fiends of heroin withdrawals were having their way with me. My body was starved for endorphins, for their opioid replacements I'd been injecting for years. I'd cut rug on San Francisco and gone home to that shit show I called my hometown, back to my mom's house, to give it all up. That's what I'd told myself, what I told her when I moved my shit into her basement. I'd come to clean up, to leave the junk behind. I moved in, uninvited, and settled myself in the dark anonymity of rural town nowhere. I was going to get myself clean the old-fashioned way: cold goddamn turkey.

Addiction always has other plans.

The first couple of weeks, I'd made a passable show of going clean. I went through the motions for myself at first, tried to believe my own bullshit that this was the catalyst to my quitting. Yeah, right. A dump like my hometown, there's heroin around if you know where to snoop, and I definitely knew that, even after all these years.

It took about a month before I accepted the game I was running, and once I did that, I basked in it. This made things easier overall. It reduced the amount of lying I had to do by half. I went from lying to two people, to just lying to one: the one being my mom. I'd lied to her most of my life, and this was no different. I kept up appearances, and we both went along with the little game she and I played. I lied, and she believed me, and as long as no one said anything else, the lie was the truth.

I'd sneak to the next town over, to this shithole bar by the river where an old Mexican lady poured drinks and sold junk on the side. I'd tell my mom I was going out for a couple hours, to get some drinks, to get some fresh air. Meanwhile, the old broad at the bar would keep me fixed, so I was free to lay low in my mom's basement, keep the fix going indefinitely, no one the wiser. Yeah, such a goddamn genius is the junkie, right? The perfect crime. Who would ever suspect a junkie of having a supply nearby and lying their ass off to keep fixed?

I thought I was so fucking smart; thought I'd set myself up with a comfy new life. I had ten thousand bucks up my sleeve, cash I'd conned, been owed, or cajoled from suckers before leaving San Francisco. The bar lady's heroin was good and cheap and plentiful. The old lady was ready to sell night or day. My mom was old and trusting and witless, so I could snow her as long as I liked. Her basement was the perfect spot to carry on. No rent, no bills, so I could stretch out my money on smokes and heroin for maybe nine months, maybe even a year, before I had to make a move.

But I wasn't as smart as I liked to tell myself. Old and trusting as my mom was, she wasn't an idiot. She might have been a retired high school librarian who grew up in the 1950s, but she knew me, and she'd lived with my lies since I was a kid. I wasn't fooling her, and she played me right into her hands. The perfect setup. I was going to get clean whether I wanted to or not. She was holding me to my resolution, one way or another.

One morning I got up to go on my daily junk run and found she'd trapped me down there. At first, I thought it was a mistake, or the door was jammed, but then I saw the crackers, the water, and the puke bucket. I knew. My mom had set me up, and nothing shy of a demolitions expert would free me from that basement prison. I was a mix of insane rage and terror of what was about to come. I don't know if my mother was on the other side of that door while I screamed and kicked and begged and called her a worthless old whore. She never said a word. I was on my own.

I held out for three days on the remaining stash I had. I stretched it thin, just enough to keep myself from the sick, but even still, I knew it was only a matter of time. The heroin wouldn't last. It never lasts. As thin as I stretched my supply, there is an end to all things, and soon enough, I would be at that dreaded finish line.

Time ticked on, a couple more days at most. The last of the H ran dry. Two days later, and I was the tank running on empty. The sick crawled over me.

Blue tongues darted from the dark corners of the basement. Pain and diarrhoea became my keepers. I screamed and twitched, raged and cried. Blue ichor gathered in the back of my brain. I pulled the soaked sheets around me, pulled them over my greasy, sweating head and stringy hair and cawed like a dying animal. I craved gasoline and ash, the singed taste of human flesh. I wanted to shred my lips, tear off my red-hot eyelids. I frothed and raved from a podium at a crowd of lunatics.

Fever overran me, and with it, delirium. I coughed until I puked, but there was nothing in my stomach but bile heaved up in a navy-coloured plastic bucket. The stinking wet sheets wrapped themselves around me, constricted like snakes around a bloated rat. From the light of the static-filled TV playing across the room, I could see silhouettes moving along the walls, but nothing was casting them.

Please, please, I hissed through clenched teeth. Make it stop. Just one more fix, then make it stop.

And then I heard it. From our family piano upstairs, my mother had sat down to play. Quiet and even, the song sank down through the shitty shag carpet, down through the floor, to me shuddering in that basement below. She was playing Erik Satie's Gnossienne No. 3.

That measured, tempered, horror movie music was a funeral march, a plodding nightmarish tranquillity that I had to escape. I wanted to drown it out, to crank up any sound to make those songs go away. But the record player was across the room, and I was too weak and sick to go over to it. The needle was still thipping at the end of the album as it had all night long, but now its sound was as loud and grating as that piano music raining down from above. The TV was hissing static, and too far away to crank up its volume, already eating into my brain like caustic fumes. I couldn't move. The static, the thipping of the needle, the rattle of my laboured breath, these were the chorus of that unsettling ambience of Satie's reveries. They were eating me alive.

Shut up, I whispered. Just shut the fuck up.

But no one was listening. Not the TV, not the record player, not my mother, not even those silhouettes cast upon the wall by nothing. They just crept closer to me, soundless except for their slashing blue tongues, and my gruesome breathing.

WǓYÈ YUÁNDĪNG

And like that, I was somewhere else.

I had lurched forward in time somehow. I don't know how, but I was now lying on the couch of that old mutual friend's apartment. It was that night we'd reunited at the bar, when he'd helped me back to his place. My eyes were bright and sickeningly aware, blazing with the calefaction of the Liao. I could sense everything in that room, and it filled me with a fear I couldn't name. The rabbit in me froze, watching but not wanting to see. Where was my mother's basement? Where was the sick? How had I gotten here?

The room was exactly as I remembered it. The pictures on the wall, the Turkish rug on the hardwood floor. Everything but the music, and his chair.

The music he'd been playing that night, Gnossienne No. 3 had just completed its last dismal stanza and the record spun down to an end. The last notes played, and like a coffin lowered into a grave, fell silent. That silence lasted only a moment, replaced by that same distasteful sound of the needle thipping at the end of a vinyl as in my mother's basement. Huh, thip

. . . huh, thip . . . huh, thip. An unending leak of static that repeated over and over again.

I could still hear my mother's piano playing from some-where above, or was that only in my mind?

I looked around his living room. Yes, it *was* the same, but somehow something was wrong. I stared at each thing in turn, and there was no denying it was exactly as I'd remembered it. So why was it terrifying me to look at it? I couldn't quite put my finger on what it was. I kept looking from spot to spot in the room, but nothing *I looked at* seemed out of place.

The chair where he'd sat: that was different, awfully so. In this new, strange place, whatever this place was, the chair was turned with its back to me. I couldn't see who was sitting in it, but I knew someone, or better put, *something* was sitting there. Whatever lurked in that chair was dead silent, and that silence terrified me. I didn't want to see whatever sat there. I knew if I did, my mind would be lost forever.

Whatever was sitting with its back to me in that chair, that's what had the rabbit in me frozen. That chair was wrapped in a silence like an event horizon. Every sound disappeared into its cold, inescapable silence. That's when I noticed it. It wasn't just silence which poured away from that chair. *Everything in that room* was somehow emanating from the chair. The room, its contents, the couch where I lay, even me, all of us were pouring out of that chair like water from a wellspring. The chair was the focal point, the silent heart, and from which everything ended and began.

Wherever I looked, there was a crisp normality to what I saw, clear as it was on that night. The table, the rug, the stereo, the pictures on the walls, they all looked real. It was where my eyes were not looking, this I couldn't quite catch. Whenever I turned my head to look, everything was solid and real. But my peripheral vision showed a very different reality. There was a smeared liquidity to everything, like turgidly swirling oil paints being mixed in a jar. Outside my direct line of sight, this place, this reality, was nothing but a viscous illusion. I was a part of this solvent existence. Everything in the periphery was a melted, languid dance. As for what was in front of me, this silent chair, it held the answers I didn't want to know.

I whispered to it, asked what it wanted. Nothing. No sound came out of my mouth. I asked again, more forcefully. Silence. I screamed at it. *Where was I? What was this place? What the fuck did it want with me?! Why didn't it just leave me alone?!* No sounds came out of me. No noise came from anywhere. Everything was liquid silence, and I was raging futilely against it.

And then I knew why. I wasn't actually speaking. My voice was just trapped, screaming in my head. Everything beyond my skull was a gooey quiet, and I was an awful spectator floating in it. I was a caricature, a figure in acrylics and oils painted on a canvas, lying on a painting of a couch in a painting of a living room. None of it was real, just an illusion created by the silence of the chair.

Soon even my screams gave up to that silence. I let myself fade into it, get lost in the undercurrent. I became just another prop on that gelatinous stage. Nothing was left but that torpid, devouring silence pouring from that chair.

And then the silence was destroyed utterly.

"Close," a voice of voices thundered from the chair. It was as if the silence had never been. A shock wave of voices in chorus shook everything all around me until the edges of reality blurred.

"THEY are always close now," the voice of voices said from the chair. "Close to finding you, to catching you. Your evasions have been successful, but transient," it said. "You, a flashing speck of timespace, THEY sense you. THEY close in."

As soon as the last word completed, the voices were utterly gone. The silence rushed in, restoring the void.

I was paralysed on that couch, every ounce of me wanting to flee. The fear was growing. I did all I could to focus on just one question.

Where was I? I asked in my mind. What was this place? I could feel my thoughts fly away from me like ripples towards the chair.

"This place," it said. "It is your mind."

All of this was just a hallucination?

"When have you ever known otherwise?"

I could almost hear the slushing rise and fall of a tide all around me. Ocean Beach, Willingston's smile, Cole's blank eyes, the snarl of the shuddering thing glaring up at me, they formed and dissolved in the edges of my sight.

"The *Objar*," it said. "Those who give this liquid *placelessness* a name, they call this the Objar." The silence whorled in. "Is it not glorious?" it asked.

Yes, I had to admit, looking past my terror and confusion. It was exactly that. Whatever this was, it was glorious.

"You have found me," it said. "Found me in this place which is no place at all. You cannot last here. Alpha to omega cannot exist within nothingness. I will show you why you came."

And like that, the liquid world on the fringe coagulated sickeningly. Something was taking shape.

"THEY slither at the edge of your mind," it boomed. I could almost see the Tindalosi, or some semblance of them, clawing at the boundaries of my sight. "Lurking in the uninhabited voids of your timespace. THEY feed upon you, poisoning your minds, altering your genetic code with THEIR essence. But you know this already. But what is unknown to you, that is why you have come here. THEY are plotting the ruination of your world."

Everything fell back to gooey silence. Only the *huh, thip* . . . *huh, thip* . . . *huh, thip* played on.

"THEY drain and infect your species with purpose. Not only to feed but to control, to rule over you. THEY reshape you in THEIR image, turn you into something other."

I knew all of this or at least suspected. I needed something more, some way to stop them.

"THEY cannot be stopped," the voices said. "Your planet is doomed. Your civilisations are dependent on the technologies, enslaved to them. Dopamine addiction driven by light pulses feeds directly into the cerebral cortex. Shrinking grey matter, malfunctioning white matter, diminishing capacity for restorative sleep. Social and personal anxiety rise, as does the drought of empathy. The dependence feeds upon itself, driving more consumption, furthering the failing brain functions and the collapse of proper structure in consciousness. Your species enslaves itself to its own demise, feeds its own cancer. The brain, weakened and starved, is made easier to feed upon, and to infect with the blue ichor."

There had to be a way to stop them.

"Your empires are too weak to resist THEM. You know this to be true. You have seen it, watched as your puny societies waste the earth, squabble over position and arrogance, murder endlessly in the name of commerce and sovereignty. The arrogant solipsism, the death cults, the ruthless need to destroy and to revel. Yours are stupid and carnivorous civilisations, flagrantly dismissive of all life save their own. All are guilty, save the weak, the very old, and the very young. Your species' age upon your world is already destroyed. You have only to wait to realise it. Your kind will be wiped from the world because of your civilisations' greed and cancerous nature. Only the very few, the very small, the very old, will manage to be saved. And they *will* be saved. This is why you are here."

Why?

"You will save them."

The voice stopped, and the silence crashed back. All that remained was the huh, thip of the needle playing on, and it made that silence all the more unbearable. Huh, thip . . . huh, thip . . . slow and steady. Mindless repetition in monotone.

"Listen," the voice commanded. "Can you hear THEM? You must know THEM so that you can save your kind from complete damnation. Listen to THEM. Know THEM, and fear."

The needle on dead vinyl, there was something increasingly repellent in the sound of it. Everything was stretched and gaunt. Each repetition of that sound of a needle on the blackened, grooved flesh slowed and deepened. Something waited in that sound, and it drew me in.

The TV was across from me. I lay on that mattress in my mother's basement, too sick to move or to even look away. The box was broadcasting radiation.

The needle thipped, and I jerked in terror. I kept trying to pull myself back from an edge I could not see.

Their breathing. It was the wheezing death rattle of a child molester shanked in a prison toilet stall. It was the sound of a cannibal choking on a chunk of twitching flesh. The gagging of a meth fiend's last hit before her heart explodes. The laboured pant of squalling wildlife dying in a toxic spill. It was the sound of all things coming to unnatural ends.

The smell of them washed over me in rank coils. I fell headlong into their angles.

It smelled like a shit-stained body shaking under basement sheets. I could see them crawling in the shadows in the corners of my eyes, feel the breathing in my own burning, aching, heroin-deprived lungs. They were beyond the static, past the irradiance and the electromagnetic chaos.

They are an unquenched thirst. They are starvation, famine, a shuddering want. It wastes them, leaves them shaking and desperate with need. But this ravening is the innermost of what they are. They are a horrible inversion of creation, an unfulfilled hollow of it. Not death, but the eternal hunger to feed. All life, all sanity must be drawn into them, until there is nothing living or sane left. They have waited starving in their grey desolation since the shattering of the Tao in its two pieces: yin, the creation, and yang, that which devours it.

My arms clenched, and my fingers turned to desperate claws. The junk in my veins was long gone. I ground my teeth and spat at my traitor mother for locking me down here. The twisted tinkle of Gnossiennes on her treasonous piano spat down on me from above.

Their abode is a dreary, barren waste, a fractious cosmos of angled timespace which runs askance to our own. They were trapped there since time was time, trapped for endless aeons in that gaunt abyss. In all those unbroken cycles of cosmic existence, they only distantly sensed curved timespace, but nothing more. The thought of curves, of life and its fluidity, these were utterly alien to them. They loped aimlessly through those unimaginable angles, trapped there. Perhaps they had been imprisoned, or maybe just the whim of existence had left them bound there. Whatever the reason, however such ancient horrors came to be, and why they were the denizens of that dimension, Chalmers was right about one thing. The Tindalosi were something unclean, an afterbirth at the creation of time-space. They are an anathema to all that lives.

They existed there on the pale shores of their unwholesome perdition, the embodiment of deprivation. And in listening to their breathing, I had fallen in with them. I was amongst them, a part of their pack.

I listened to that awful breathing. And sickening as it was, I was able to make some sense of them. The breathing, it was what they were. It was their language, their telepathy, the thing which projected them into existence.

I saw the long line of starved nothingness which was their lot. Across the span of eternity, they were alone. Moving, searching, starving for they knew not what. An addiction without a drug.

And yet I caught flashes, quantum-level rarities of intruders to their angled timespace. Squirming abominations appeared, utterly destroying anything which strayed too close. Chittering insectoid brain stems had once come, moving telepathically across that limbo before vanishing. The unimaginable corpse of a formless titan erupted out of a rift, then fell screaming back to wherever it had come from. And more than once, there was a blazing comet of green light which streaked across the gloomy heavens, its shape that of a coffin clock, and inside the unmistakable form of a man. Each of these encounters with alien things was spectacular but ultimately lost in the scope of their desolation. These were little more than images, ghostly shapes tattered in the angles. The Tindalosi dwelt in so much endless privation and hateful agony that such events, momentous as they were, were faded beyond memory sesvigintillion years before another occurred. These moments were separated by the black distances between the stars, confused and incomprehensible flickers in their collective consciousness.

And then, there was the coming of a faceless avatar with flesh the texture of cold space. It had appeared to them, whispered to them, while it held them captive in its eyeless gaze. This thing, this crawling chaos, it whispered of creation, of the curves of timespace. It told them of life, of the eventual coming of Halpin Chalmers . . . and of me! It spoke to them of madness, and of corruption, of the mad piping at the heart of chaos, and of life upon which they might feed until nothing was left. It hissed of a cabal to both their benefits, leading to the ruination of the pitiful species and their world, and then to all life and sanity which lay beyond. And then the crawling chaos was gone, and the Tindalosi starved and waited.

Hundreds of millions of years came and went before Chalmers' fateful crossing into their realm. Their hunger had at last found its source, and they gave chase. Long they had waited, and at last, their chance to feast had come to pass. They had been caged forever in their domain, but no more. Chalmers had shown them the way out!

Yet once in our curved timespace, they found it alien, so unexpected and vibrant from what they had imagined. They were trapped outside of this living universe, suspended in the spaces between it. It was impossible for them to cross into curving timespace without some medium for doing so. Only sharp angles gave them purchase into our existence, and then only for a brief time. Our atmosphere is toxic to them, as is the searing radiation of the sun and our stars. The Tindalosi may have found themselves into our universe, but they were unable to reach into it for anything more than an instant, and then in agonising pain.

Yet Chalmers and I, we were the ones which led them to our century, to our technology. This was their salvation. With our advances in the 20th and 21st century, our movies, our televisions, our monitors, our phones and screens and displays, they had found the perfect inroad to feeding on us, and to put into effect their plot with the crawling chaos.

The hiss of the static withdrew. The TV and the huh, thip were gone, and I was alone on the couch again. The chair with its back to me once again devoured everything into its silence.

What are you? I wanted to know.

"I am Wⵙyè Yuándīng," the thing in the chair said. "*The Midnight Gardener.*"

The silence wrapped around the chair, drawing me in.

The voice of voices went on. "I am what your mind cannot accept. I am the anathema. To your regressive species, to THEM, to the crawling chaos, and to those which it serves. I am that which cannot be reached. All things fear me, for there can be nothing but fear for what one can never comprehend. I am what you and THEY cannot accept."

I didn't understand.

"You are not meant to understand. You have only to fulfil your purpose."

Which was what?

"Only you can go where they cannot reach. Your existence is *sui generis*. In your timespace, none have done what you have done, and so it must be you who does what is needed. You will escape THEM again. Escape one last time and write what you have seen. Only then will you die. For in the end, THEY will find you. There is nothing you can do to stop that. You will have only the briefest of your years to write what you have learned."

What then?

"Then THEY will come for you. Nothing can make this otherwise."

Why couldn't it stop them? Why couldn't it help me?

"You cannot be saved. The Willingston has proven this. You are what was needed, an apotheosis. You are the needle on the completed record of your former species. Events long before your birth, before the creation of your world, have set you in motion. These cannot be unset.

"Do not hesitate. Write, and then you will die. Your words, your warning will spread as rumour, as a whispered fear of what is to come. In that, you will be the saviour of some fragment of your species from annihilation."

I lay twitching on that sweat-soaked mattress, wrapped in those nasty sheets, begging for this not to be how it ended.

I remembered the gruesome death of Halpin Chalmers, how the Tindalosi had poured through the cracks in his apartment walls, and torn him apart, body and soul.

I still didn't understand how or where or when I could escape to write.

"You will."

And from the silence surrounding the chair, something reached out and touched me between the eyes.

Please, please, I hissed through clenched teeth. Make it stop. Just one more fix, then make it stop.

"Time for you to go," the voice of voices intoned. "No place for alpha and omega here. You must return to complete your task."

I could feel myself being pushed out of focus. The liquid periphery began to close in.

There was one last thing I had to know.

"Wait," I said. I had to know before this was all taken away. "Are you god?" I asked.

"No, *Umnya*" it replied emptily. "Are you?"

THE BASEMENT REDUX

In an instant, I was out of that horrific time in my mother's basement. That moment had turned me back, sent me wandering forward through the scenes of the squirming clot's existence. I stepped over so much of it, letting it slide past me as I pushed past it. Moments drifted around and through me. Things felt more and more familiar. I was drawn by a magnetism which had no name. It drew me along, through those speeding moments, until I passed into the dilation which was my destination.

I was alone, standing in shadow.

I stepped forward through the darkness, groping with my hands for anything to guide me. For a long while, there was nothing, and I moved in absolute black. I groped forward a long time, and then there was the smell of burning kerosene. The smell caught me off-guard. Inching along in the dark, following the smell, I found I was approaching the source of that stink. Ahead were pools of light. There were five of them, equally positioned from one another.

I emerged at the edge of the pools of light but couldn't go forward into them. I was restrained for some reason from stepping forward out of the shadows. I tried to press forward, but each time that I did, I was wracked by an awful, thrashing pain. I tried again and again but always recoiled in agony. I stood at its edge, looking in. As I watched, the flaring brightness of the light dimmed, and I was looking in on the concrete floor of a basement garage.

There were two men in that basement. One of them, a wild-eyed Chinese man in a filthy, tattered suit, was standing outside the balls of light. The other stood inside the light, his back to me. I couldn't see this man clearly. He kept stuttering in and out of focus.

"You know who I mean!" the man in a tattered suit yelled at the other. "THEM!!!!" The man pointed around the room. "No way in. This is the only safe place in this house, in this whole fucking country!"

The pools of light were coming off five kerosene lanterns.

The man in the tattered suit stood nearby, waving a gun. He turned and looked into the shadows where I stood. Our eyes locked a long while. The man in the suit finally tore his eyes away and turned back to the one in the middle of the garage.

"Tell me why you came," he demanded, then without waiting for the other to respond. "Tell me!"

The one in the middle of the light spoke, but it was muffled and incomprehensible, as if he was speaking underwater.

The one in the suit didn't like it. "You're full of shit," he yelled, nearly whimpering, looking between the one in the middle of the room and the shadows where I was trapped. "I'm not sure which of you is telling the truth. You might not be the same, it might be a different curve. You could be working for THEM!"

I yelled that it wasn't THEM, that I was the right one. But I knew my voice, like me, couldn't get through the barrier of the light.

The one in the centre still spoke in muffled burbles, but then out came a name. "Halpin Chalmers," he said.

The one with the gun nodded, then looked at me trapped beyond the corona of light. A harsh grin crossed his face. "So, you do know," the one in the suit spat. "Yes, Halpin Chalmers. And what he saw, what he found out."

He lowered the gun and laughed. It was a ruthless, corroded sound. "But you don't know. I can see it on you. You don't have any idea what's going on, what you're getting yourself into, do you? You're just some idiot who that kid from next door knows, asking about this stuff." He laughed again, pulling a baggy from his pants pocket. "Yes, I have what you want." The two men's eyes locked, and a grisly smile spread further up the sides of the suited man's filthy cheeks. "But you sure you want it? You sure you want to know?" He shook his head at the other one. "You should listen to me. You don't want to know."

The other one said he did.

I was pressing again, trying to make myself heard, to break through that barrier. I was frantic, slamming myself into the burning, invisible field.

"No," I screamed. "No, no. He doesn't want to know! Don't tell him!"

The one in the suit turned back at me. "He said he wants to know! Don't tell me what to do. He wants it. That means he already has it!"

I already have it, I screamed. I have it. Not him. Don't drag him into this. Let him go.

The batshit accountant started to raise the pistol, but gave it up, looked at the baggy in his other hand, then chucked it to the one in the middle. "Take it. Take it and get the fuck out of here. Don't ever come back here. You come back, you come near my property, I'll shoot you. I swear, I'll shoot you dead if I ever see you again."

I steeled myself against the agonising pain and forced myself forward. I dragged myself into that torrid light until it was all around me, searing my flesh from the inside out. I collapsed to the concrete floor, trapped in that corposant of searing pain. I thrashed and twitched, my face wrenched upwards, one eye glaring about hatefully. The fire in that light burned through me, scorched the clothes off my burning back so that I was left naked, shuddering, gagging on the awful anguish.

I knew I could go no further. The pain was tearing me apart. Through gritted teeth, writhing in that daemonic light, I managed to squeeze out a name. It was a desperate last ditch, a prayer to a dead and uncaring god. There was no way to stop the batshit accountant from giving him the Liao, but at least I could steer him in the only direction he had left. I ground my teeth and repeated the name again and again.

The batshit accountant's eyes flinched in recognition. "I know!" he yelled.

"You," he said to the one in the centre. "You have to find Wǔyè Yuándīng. That's what he said to tell you. It's the only way you'll be safe. Find Wǔyè Yuándīng. It won't save you, but it'll keep you safe long enough . . ."

I tried to say more, to tell the batshit accountant what I knew, a warning, anything to speak to the one in the middle, so he would know it was me, know I was warning him not to take the Liao. I kept saying things through my gritted teeth, fighting with all my might not to rush back out of the fire that engulfed me.

The batshit accountant turned and told me to shut up, shut up, SHUT UP! "You want to lead them here?!" he demanded. "I didn't have to help!"

And then, the one in the middle, he turned and looked at me. I was clenched and shuddering, my eyes red and my mouth a snarl. I saw recognition in his confused eyes. It was only an instant, but I saw repetition, the endless regression of this moment into eternity. I saw him and heard the shrill screams of a madwoman strapped to a gurney. I saw myself in his eyes in a rounded room that wasn't a room. I was looking at him, and he was looking down at me.

We both repeated the words in that mirrored reflection of each other.

Find Wǔyè Yuándīng, we both said, and I realised who he was.

Damn that grinning Willingston: I was looking at me.

THE TWO-DIMENSIONAL FUTURE

I knew now what had to be done. I knew what the silent chair expected me to do.

I followed myself through the moments stretching on ahead. I saw myself in my apartment, saw myself looking at the Liao, stood staring at myself as I languished hidden in the ether outside my own consciousness. I stood waiting beside myself, watching me ponder whether or not to take that foul substance. I was looking at the man but also beyond him. I watched him, watched the infinite variations of myself splintering away from that one moment into the potentiality of this wriggling maggot, and I began to trace their courses until I found the one I was meant to follow.

I followed one of the strands of time, which lead away from the decisions I had made, away from the man I had become. I moved slowly, stepped carefully. I was picking my way through each decision these fissioning versions of myself were making. This one waited another week to take the Liao. This one took it all and was found mutilated a day later. This one took the first dose, then the second, but never went to that cafe or that bar. This one was unable to evade the watchful eyes of the screen dead. Another was torn apart or laid to waste by the departed. Another was hunted for years before being murdered in an alley. I retraced my steps countless times, returning to some crossroads in its existence, then set off down another path to see how my alter-self had fared. Endless variations of my life were played and rewound, abandoned for another, then another, and on and on. I traced my steps through a bleak parade of my own failed existence, each time ending only in ruination and death.

I couldn't say how long this went on, but as I've said, I went slowly. There were so many paths to follow, and so many little moments, which led me to some conclusion or path which didn't suit my needs. I was rewinding and fast-forwarding my own timespace, slipstreaming through the lens of my own potentiality. I had no hunger, no thirst. I had no need of sleep, nor any biological function. So many dead ends or failed paths, and I had no choice to redact, to back up, to try again. I can only imagine how much time it took for me to find what I was after. It would have to be measured in terms of centuries, millennia; nothing less. Infinite paths take time . . .

But in the end, I did find what I was after. I found the point which would lead me away from the Tindalosi, to keep me safe from them as long as possible. I could have kept searching, looking for something even better, but I could feel the Liao beginning to recede in my bloodstream, evaporate from my brain. I had to go now, or potentially be lost in the endless spans between timespace.

I followed the path to my chosen destination.

My steps touched back down on a two-dimensional world. It was a place of bas-reliefs and vedute, a landscape world of which my alter-self was a caricature. I was standing on a still frame of Ocean Beach, loitering at the flat edges of Sutro Baths.

It was late at night. The sky was a dome of clouds and stars. It was the very night I had left my own timespace behind, but this one was flat.

Let me be clear: This life, this timeline I was stepping into, it wasn't me, not the me that had left time and space so many hundreds or thousands of years ago. This was an alter-me, a version of myself on another timeline branching off from that wriggling maggot I had left in that timeless oblivion. This was a life I never lived, and I was inhabiting some hidden corner of this alter-me's consciousness, the quantum field of his mind. This was how I was to hide from the Tindalosi. I would take refuge in a timespace where I had never done the things so many of me had done a million times before. This would be my safe port, this alter-me's existence, and in doing so, would avoid detection for some time.

I could feel little differences, tiny variations in the substratum of this man, this causal sibling of mine. I could hear differing thoughts and memories from my own. This version of me had never taken the Liao, not ever. He had spent the weeks after his encounter with the batshit accountant pondering who he was, what he had become. He was appalled and sickened by himself, a man who couldn't stop chasing after the next fix. That night I ran to Ocean Beach, he had instead ended up riding his bike to the water's edge, then walking up and down that stretch of coastline, thinking things over. That version of me spent the better part of the night huddled behind some rocks at Sutro Baths, chewing over his next move in life.

This version of me wasn't destined to go spinning through timespace for aeons. He had turned away from its draw, turned away from my obsession, and instead took a long walk up and down that beach to ponder what kind of man he was.

He'd spent his time thinking about what a dead-end he'd reached in his life. This latest fiasco of chasing after Halpin Chalmers and the Liao was just one more in a long line of pointless attempts to keep the party going. It was all fun and freaky, but it wasn't going anywhere. It was another dose, another dumb distraction to keep him from facing the facts. He was never going to get any further in life if he didn't do something to change it. He had to knock off this bullshit and actually do something. What the fuck was he doing? Riding a goddamn bike for a living? At his age?! He was too old, and his knees were too fucked to be dicking around with that nonsense anymore. He had outgrown it, and yet was living like a goddamn college kid in a shithole apartment with a bunch of stupid party boys. How long had it been since he'd actually taken any real pleasure from his lifestyle, his life? Where he'd gone to, what he'd become, he was sick of it now. He had to move on, and this was his shivering wake-up call on that desolate stretch of beach.

Tired of waking up hungover, sick of seeing that box of stash under his bed, he was over being up until the crack of dawn every Friday night and lurching into his pointless job every Monday morning. He was done. He was going to take that job his friend Marty had been offering him all these years. He was going to go to work in landscaping. He was going to leave the City, get out of his apartment, get a place to himself. And though he didn't think it exactly, some voice in him was sure it was time for him to quit his lifetime of drugs and booze. Get himself out of the same old goddamn thing, the same stupid rut that was taking his life in one big fat circle leading nowhere. That's how I found him, wandering away from the beach, back up Geary Street as the cold San Francisco sun came up.

None of this was mine to remember. I was there, sure. I was in his head, watching it all, feeling memories of a night that I'd not lived. I was a spectator in the skull of an alternate copy, a two-dimensional avatar in some parallel flatscreen world. I watched as he caught a bus a few blocks up and headed back to the Mission, ready to start again.

Sitting on that bus, staring out the window at the empty grey streets, he and I let the fog-blurred lights and the illegible street signs blend together in a smear. It whizzed past and melted in the cold. He ignored it all. It was background chatter, a submarine ride through an indistinct haze as he thought his thoughts. At that moment, knowing he was about to embark on a new phase he'd put off for too long, he thought now more than ever, he could really use a drink. We laughed together. What a goddamn irony that was.

And then I felt the Liao recede. It's psychoactive grip on me faded. I felt myself drop. The bus, the world, everything in that planar existence lurched forward, then halted far too fast, as if too much momentum was suddenly stopped by too much force.

Six months had passed. The days and nights rolled past like pages in a flipbook. The moments jumbled, and then I was hit with a hurl of memories, those of my flat alter ego's life being taken apart and put back together again. I watched him moving out of his apartment in the Mission, his home for far too long. I watched him packing, throwing out more of his old junk than he actually took with him. In the end, he only took his futon, his clothes, a dresser and a single trinket by which to remember his old life. Everything else was up for grabs or went in the trash. The last things he chucked into the garbage was his old stash box, the book from Caliph Gary, and the book our old mutual friend had given him all that time ago.

I saw him calling Marty, finally accepting the landscaping gig that Marty had offered him a dozen times or more. I saw him quitting his messenger job, and then two weeks later dropping his last package with not just a little bit of wistfulness. He packed the last of his trifles off his empty bedroom floor, stuffed them in his messenger bag, and left his old apartment for good. I watched him catch the Bart train for Oakland. He rode to MacArthur station, rode his bike to his new apartment, and there spent a few days getting settled before he started his new job.

And while staring out the window of his new apartment, gazing out at the streetlights and the quiet drone of traffic, the Liao receded again.

He was on his own for almost a year by the time that next lurch subsided. He'd been off the booze the entire time. It was dumbfounding, seeing him swear off. He slept a lot and read a lot. He worked extra hard at his new job, so much so that his co-workers were shocked at how he never stopped. An easy task for someone trying to quit old habits. His anger, his frustrations, the clawing cravings at the back of his neck, he threw them into every hammer swing, every shovel of dirt, every bag of compost he hauled.

Early on in his sobriety, we watched the days and nights tick by in the slow procession only a recovering addict can know. They dragged, those days, and he paced and smoked cigarettes, and growled and cursed and wanted nothing more than to give in. His throat was dry like jerky. He was depressed, unhappy in everything except work and unconsciousness. Those first weeks, the old lusts refused to die the fuck down. At night, that's when the cravings were always the worst. He could almost smell the alcohol under his nose. He hated that time, and so did I.

I kept screaming at him to stop all this bullshit and just have a goddamn drink already, even just to cut the edge. One fucking drink, what could it hurt? But he wasn't listening to me, or he couldn't hear me, or he didn't want to. He stuck it out, a year-long nightmare where he had to actually deal with his own life. Boredom, pain, the desperate, pathetic need to escape. He weathered it. And much as I hate to admit this, that 2-D version of me, he had more balls than I could ever hope to have. He held tough and refused to lift a glass or light a joint. He smoked pack after pack of cigarettes until he was sure he would fill up with cancer, but he didn't go back to the drink or the drugs. He refused to let himself lose this fight. He wanted a new reality, to push the edge. This was it. He wasn't going to push past the boundaries where most people feared to tread. He was going to push past the ones where he feared to tread. Every day he passed the test of not drinking was another day added to the list of his endurance which he couldn't betray. He had to get to the other side. It was the worst and the best year of his miserable life.

And again, the Liao receded.

When the lurching finally stopped, things were well and truly changed. I was still in a world that felt flat and incomplete, but it was far more real than before. Everything around me had gained a new fullness. People and things no longer had that cut-out quality to them. There was something more lifelike, something which was fast approaching normalcy.

It was then, in this surge forward, that I figured out what was happening. Why, I'd wondered, did the world have a deplorable vapidness, a lack of dimension to it? Why was I just a passenger in this guy's skull, a squirming ghost in his poster board brain? Why was this world of his so empty of any range or depth or detail? It had, since my arrival, felt imprecise, even sparing in any real detail. But with this recession of the Liao, I got it. Everything had begun to feel more complete, closer to life as I knew it. It was still not quite right, but there was more to it now, and more importantly, there was more to this alter-me. The thoughts in his head were more jumbled and varied like you find in a real person.

And as I thought back, I realised each lurch had been like this. Each jump had made things the tiniest bit more real. At first, I'd assumed this was just the nature of this alter-me's reality. He lived in some Flatland parallel to what had been my life.

But no. I could see that what I'd been experiencing wasn't some fundamental difference in our realities, but a perspective I'd not considered. I wasn't racing through his two-dimensional life. I was catching up to him somewhere up ahead. Every time the Liao receded, I was closing in on the real him. I was living out his past, reviewing in fast forward his memories.

I got it now. The last moment I had known in my timespace was on Ocean Beach that night, so that's where I'd picked up. This version had long since left those moments behind. While I'd been off roaming the mad halls of infinity, time had marched on for him. He was somewhere up ahead of me. I was lurching forward because the Liao's effects were wearing off, and I was returning to his present, riding the ghosts of his memory to get there.

When I stopped again, seven years had gone by. It was 2010. Things had changed a lot for him in those seven years, way more than I imagined they ever could. He'd gotten thinner, in his body and in his mind. He still struggled with the cravings, but only once in a great while now. The cravings he'd learned how to handle. What he struggled with more was far worse: the long stints without cravings. All addicts know what you never can, Chumley: there is a kind of glory in addictions, one which reaches far beyond the thirst for the drug. To have this gone from inside of him left him diminished, a lesser man. This he missed most of all.

But he'd never relented. He was living his life clean and sober, wistfully accepting the advent of middle age. He was 43 years old, a man too old to do manual labour except recreationally. Luckily for him, he no longer had to. His job in landscaping had gone well, and with hard work, some help from Marty, and a small loan from a bank, he'd given up the day-to-day labour and started a landscaping business of his own.

Over time, they had gathered a small but growing list of loyal clients. He and Marty started their new business with just a handful, but this was all they needed to get going. Their customers liked them. They liked their personal touch and how much care they put into their work. They trusted him and Marty, knew they would do what it took to get the job done right. Most of their clients were internet or lawyer types, doctors, architects, wealthy homeowners out of North Oakland or Marin. Their clients were the kind of people who have friends and neighbours who didn't want to look like they couldn't keep up with the Joneses. It tallied up to a growing demand for their services.

They started the business in 2005. After a year of going it alone, they'd made enough to hire employees. Marty ran the sales side of the company, and he focused on services and the staff. They contracted a bookkeeper and hired three guys to do the labour. They rented a small office in West Berkeley, where he spent a lot of time managing things, keeping the people who worked for him gainfully employed, and keeping his customers upping his name to their wealthy, well-paying friends. After eighteen months, they were making more money than they could have ever anticipated, with a windfall in a San Francisco sub-contract to refurbish an old playground. He threw himself into the business the same as he had the manual labour he'd done years before. It was his whole world.

He had a car and a reasonably nice house out in Lafayette. He had a nice mountain bike and a barbecue and a smoker. He began reading again, so had amassed an impressive personal library. He collected local art and donated to charities. He landscaped his own back garden so well that it had won state awards.

At work, he was the kind of boss he'd always wanted. He treated the people who worked for him as if they mattered. He made sure that when the company succeeded, the staff did as well. People were loyal to him, and because of this, wanted him to see they cared because they could see that he did.

In his personal life, such that it was, he was best described as friendly but aloof. He had few friends. He had Marty and a few contacts with old eccentrics from his past. Even still, amongst them, he was considered odd. Something had changed in him. He was the same guy, but now he'd lost the edge. The addict in him was gone. He wasn't the same jittery-handed bundle of brilliant self-destruction. That fire seemed to have gone out, and in its place, he had his business, and a quiet, solitary life. But those who had known him back in the day, they didn't seem to mind. It suited him, this new quietness. Those who only knew him more recently, they couldn't imagine him from the stories his older friends would tell. A drug addict? A loud-mouthed alcoholic? A loose screw? None of it made sense to see this quiet, industrious, lonely man.

What social contact he had in life, it was staid at best. He would go out for coffee or dinner sometimes, or he would join friends and would play pool or chess, or even meet sometimes to see a movie. He had dinner with Marty and Marty's wife. He was always friendly, but rarely attended social events of more than two or three people. He kept to himself. He didn't chase after late nights and was usually the first to head home. Many people thought he was very lonely. No girlfriend, no wife. Just a fat dog he'd gotten from the SPCA and his books to keep him company. People had tried setting him up, but it never went anywhere. In the end, they'd stopped trying.

Thing was, he didn't mind how he lived, his quietness and the lonely distance he maintained. He wasn't restless or in any way put off by his self-imposed exile. He preferred it. He ate out alone three or four nights a week and spent his weekends hiking or reading, sleeping late or just sitting alone listening to music. His was the life of a recluse, but not a miserable or pointed one. He kept to himself because there was something in all of what he'd been through which now demanded silence of him. It required he be alone with the dog and his books in a world which fears and distrusts loneliness.

There was a lurch as the Liao once more receded.

Five more years had gone by. He was rolling up on 50. He'd met Nicole in the intervening years, a woman not much younger than him. She was divorced with two kids, one in high school and the other in college. They'd met at the SPCA, where she volunteered a day a week. He'd brought in his dog for a check-up, and he and Nicole started talking. It wasn't long before they were dating, and not long after that before they were a couple. He didn't move in with her, nor did she want him to. They were both too old to entertain romantic fantasies. They liked one another and kept good company in the times they weren't living their own lives. He was kind to her kids, and she was an anchor for him, making sure he didn't drift any further from the human race than he already had. It was nice and easy, and he let it happen because he realised he needed it. He was a little taken aback that in so short a time he developed such strong feelings for this stern, kind-hearted woman, but there it was. He had been alone for so many years. Enough was enough. For the only other time in his life, he let himself find a bit of happiness in his love for her.

He attended her daughter's high school graduation. Nicole took him clothes shopping and made sure he got out amongst his own kind. He bought her little things from thrift and antique shops because they seemed like something she'd like. She helped him build bookshelves, so the piles of books on the floors of his house now had a home. When the dog died of a failed liver, it was Nicole who was there to help him bury her, and it was Nicole's shoulder he cried on in his grief.

I watched all of this and winced. Here was this guy, this alter-me, who had a nice, tidy middle-age. I'd never have pictured my life turning out like that, reclining my way into stoic, quiet decline. He was my Ned Flanders, my version of that old mutual friend. Here was a guy who had done just what I'd swore I'd never do. And yet I wasn't so blind as to ignore that this guy had so many things I'd always needed. He was, in his own way, happy in a life he'd made for himself. And his reasons for doing what he'd done weren't sappy or sentimental. I could follow his reasoning, and that scared me. That could be me. I could have done just the same had that Liao not been in my pocket. I guess in a way, I did do just the same. This was my life now, hijacked though it was. The guy I was in my old life, the one I'd left on Ocean Beach, he was gone, lost to the entropy of the cosmos. He was trapped beyond the folds of creation, fizzled to an end, a failed story spawned from the wriggling source of his own potentiality. I was this guy now, a stowaway on a lifeboat I didn't quite recognise.

And then the last of the Liao faded away forever.

RUINING A MAN'S
PRESENT

I had arrived in my alter-self's present. Another year had
passed. It was the latter part of 2015, and he and Nicole were
at a free concert in Joaquin Miller Park, up in the Oakland
Hills. He sat in the dark, surrounded by strangers, listening to
jazz. Nicole loved jazz, and they'd spent plenty of their time
together hiking in the redwoods of the park. It had been a long,
hot summer and now autumn was finally settling in.

The two of them had eaten dinner at a Korean BBQ place
over on Telegraph, then come up to catch the outdoor concert.
He was feeling sleepy, a little dreamy when he settled down
on the grass. Nicole sat next to him, drinking a beer, and he
sipped iced tea from a giant plastic cup. They ate their dessert picnic-style, putting their legs together and laying napkins
over them, making a crumbly mess as they nibbled a churro.

The show had been going for an hour, with a Dixieland
group doing Cole Porter covers. When they finished and
ambled off the stage, he was listless and only too happy for
a moment of silence. Nicole loved jazz; he tolerated it for her

sake. He looked sleepily around at the crowd, a wry smile on his face. How far the wicked have fallen, he thought to himself. How the fuck did I end up here? Listening to Dixieland?! We both laughed at this.

Not that he could hear me. I was in his present, but I was just as much a mute phantasm as I'd been before. I rode the train of his thoughts, felt the evening breeze over his skin, the drowsy hush of his body as he lounged on the lawn. I might as well not have been there, for all he knew of me. I spent the first part of that concert yelling at him. I could feel something, some shift in our quantum fields, a closing of the gap between us, but nothing. I was still on the other side of some cognitive impasse, buried back in his subconscious, an alien intelligence just beyond the periphery.

So, he sat with Nicole and waited as the next band got set up on stage. It was cooler then, so they wrapped in a blanket together and waited with everyone else. The crowd was quiet and not just a little listless. Everyone was winding down after a long, hot day, and the last act of the night, the headliner, was about to begin.

She came on stage. She was the reason Nicole had wanted to come tonight, a favourite musician of hers. He'd never heard of her (beyond what Nicole had played for him), but that didn't matter so much. He looked over and saw the girlish excitement in his girlfriend's face, and he knew coming here tonight had been the right thing to do.

The jazz musician began her set, taking time to chat amiably with the audience between songs. She played numbers on her guitar while her band backed her competently. Nicole was thrilled. An hour went by this way, with him only half-listening, grinning stupidly and sedately as the meal and dessert napped peacefully in his belly. He was half-asleep, his mind meandering in that nowhere place where dreams and waking life mingle without contradiction.

The musician's set was half over, and she put down her guitar and went to the piano. She said more things, talked about this or that. Everything was quiet and sleepy when she started to play. She opened with a favourite classical piece of hers.

Gnossienne No. 3

And that's where he found me waiting.

I'd been calling out to him, screaming his name, begging him to hear me all that time, but now that he could see me there inside of him, all I could say was hello.

Hello, he whispered back, so quietly that no one could have heard him, nor seen his lips move. The happiness he had constructed for himself over those many years, the carefully manufactured path which had led him to something like a normal life, it all fell out from under him as we looked into one another's mirrored eyes. I had no choice; I showed him what I was. I was sick to have to do it, but I did. I showed him everything. I showed him what had happened, and what I'd been through when our lives diverged. I showed him the Tindalosi, and Willingston, and the Potentiality, and Wǔyè Yuándīng. I was a hijacker, a fucked version of himself who had not only damned myself but had damned the human race. And now I'd damned him as well. This sappy, ageing version of me, one who had found some modicum of peace, he was the sacrificial lamb, and I was the stone upon which he was to be killed. The Tindalosi would be coming. They would find us. They would kill us. We only had the tiniest amount of time before it would be too late. We had to write down what I'd seen, and hopefully do our work before horrid death came calling.

And I have to admit that he took it better than I would have. Yes, silent, miserable tears ran down his face, and his jaw trembled with unrequited horror at what I'd shown him, but he looked around at the world he'd made for himself, looked one last time at the woman he'd come to love. Then he stood up and walked away. She called his name, first in confusion and then with growing concern, but he never looked back. He kept walking away until he had wandered back into Oakland, back to his apartment. Hands shaking, he unlocked our door, and we went inside to gather what few things we would need.

And like that, he disappeared from his life, and no one he knew would ever see him alive again.

THE COMING OF RECTANGULAR GODS

It's been a year since that sad, broken version of me left that Oakland park and disappeared from everything he knew and loved. I have to live with it every day. I'm the pile of shit who made this happen. I took everything away from him that starry night, and in exchange, I gave him horror, the promise of damnation, and imminent death.

Not a day goes by that I don't ask for his forgiveness. I pray he can somehow find it in himself to forgive me for dragging him back into a mess he'd never wanted, or even created. I was the one who did this, and yet he will be the one to suffer for it. I beg him to forgive me, to know how sorry I am, but he never answers me, never accepts my apology. He's silent now. I don't hear anything of him anymore. When I'm awake, he is nowhere to be found. I'm the only voice in this head. I steer his body around. While I sleep, I think that's when he must be awake. I can't say for sure, but somewhere in the recesses of my skull is an image of a red-eyed catatonic, a miserable fuck who has lost everything that mattered to him, staring morosely at nothing.

He is dead silent now, a distant ghost that just gave up and fell back into the blackness. He never came outright and blamed me, but I figure that was self-evident. If he doesn't blame me, then he's a fool. He should lay this all at my feet. This is all my fault. I should be left alone. It was always my burden to bear.

Maybe it's better this way. It's my crime, so why should it be anyone but me to face the noose?

We drove out of the Bay Area that very same night. We drove off, and for the next couple of days, we just rolled. At some point, we were well and truly gone from everyone and everything we'd known. Nobody would know us where we were. We'd become no one, cut all our ties.

I won't tell you where we went. It doesn't matter. We were in a smallish city somewhere. It was that kind of smallish city that couldn't catch a break. Never big enough to matter, too big to have any small-town charm. It was depressed and scavenging to get by. Too many broken windows and dusty 'For Sale' signs. Way too many bars and check-cashing places. Downtown had the charm of a rusting girder. A dying machine parts factory was the only thing keeping the town afloat.

We found a shitty hotel in the worst part of town, the kind of place where you pay by the day or the week. No one ever cares who you are in a place like that, as long as you have the money. Names don't matter; who you are or what you've done doesn't matter. Just keep your mouth shut, keep to yourself, and pay on time. People in squalor know how to keep their mouths shut, how to mind their own business. Everyone has something to hide in a town like that, a neighbourhood like that. As long as you stick to the rules, and don't cross someone else, no one will cross you. Last thing anyone down in the shit wants is to get noticed. It was perfect.

We got a room with its own toilet, shower and phone. In a dump like this, those kinds of luxuries meant more dollars a week, but it also meant absolute privacy. We paid four months in advance, in cash. The hotel manager was happy to see the greenbacks and wasn't bothered by not taking down any identification for the money we shelled out. His look said it all: he didn't know us, he wouldn't remember us, and as long as the rent was paid, he didn't give a shit to know anything about us.

We spent the first couple hours in that room doing absolutely nothing. My alter-self was a babbling shitstorm in our collective head. He was a mess, an emotional basket case, trying to munge together some sense to it all. I didn't blame him for trying, but I knew it wasn't going to happen. I had to let him get there on his own. I couldn't console the guy, and to be honest here, I didn't even try. There was nothing to console. This wasn't going to get better. It wasn't going to go away. He knew what I knew now, that the human race, our world, was going to be wiped from existence, and before that, we would be murdered. The only time we had left had to be dedicated to trying to get all of what I knew down before the knife cut our throat. What the fuck was there to console? I let him have his breakdown in peace.

It took a couple hours, but eventually, he got something of a grip and said he had to make some calls. He had to tell people things, say his goodbyes. I didn't think it was a good idea, but I knew from the edge in his voice that my opinion didn't matter. He wasn't asking; this had to get done. What did it matter, anyway? I'd ruined his life. How could I say no to this one last request? Let the guy have his final moments.

He called his office, which was closed, and left a long rambling message for Marty, for the staff, and told them he had to go. He said the business was Marty's now, but that if it was okay, to keep paying him as his fair share. Just keep putting his paycheck in his account each week. He asked them to deal with the loose ends which anyone leaves when they leave their life so abruptly: He told them to never try to contact him, or find him, or do anything beyond what he'd asked. He had to go, and he couldn't explain why. He called and left a similar rambling message with his accountant, his lawyer. He made it clear that he was out, and all he expected was the paycheck and to be left alone. They were to consider him as dead.

Those were the easy ones. Then he called Nicole. He wanted to just leave a message, to record his last words to her, but we both knew it wasn't going to play out that easily. She answered. I wished more than anything that she would be away, but no. We both knew deep down she was right there waiting for his call.

In all that I've done in my life, all the miserable, fucked-up things I've pulled, I have never felt shame like that. I felt sick as she cried and begged him to explain, to please come back home, and they could make it okay again. He sobbed and told her he couldn't, that he had to do this. She didn't understand, she just wanted him back. She cried and cried, and he sobbed even harder than she did, but he never told her anything, never gave any clue where he was, or why he'd left. She wanted to know if it was her, if she'd done something. Why was he leaving her? Weren't they happy together? And he said through his blubbering that he was happier than he'd been in forever. It wasn't her; she was the last person in the world he ever wanted to hurt. He had to go, he had to go. And though she begged him to stay on the line, to let her convince him that she could help, he whispered one last time that he loved her, that he had to go now, and then he hung up.

I made the only suggestion which ever made any sense to me at a time like that: We needed a drink.

And right there, that was it. That was the worst thing I have ever done in my life. This miserable fuck, his life ruined, horrific death doomed to catch up to him, him in the most pathetic state of his life, and I dangled what I knew he couldn't resist in front of him. He acquiesced. He let me carry him down to a liquor store. I got us a pack of smokes, a disposable lighter, and a litre of okay vodka.

He drank it at first in sips from a plastic cup, sitting back on his rented bed and looking at the room that would most likely be the scene of his murder. He drank and smoked, drank and smoked, and yet I felt nothing. I could feel him growing quieter with every sip, drifting into that dismal silence that only booze can bring, that medicinal numb which vodka adds to the soul. He was slipping down, settling to the bottom like unseen silt on the floor of a lake. I could feel this all happening, but what I couldn't feel was the booze.

I didn't feel a thing. No warmth, no dizzying euphoria, not even the lovely spin of booze on an empty stomach. I made him drink more and more. He drank, and he sank, but I was still standing on the shore. I felt the same sickening clarity that the Liao had thrown on me another lifetime ago. He drank and drank until he was so far gone that I had to lift the cup to our lips for him, and still I felt nothing. I wanted to feel something, anything else, something stupid and angry and blurry. I wanted to slip away like I could feel him doing, sink into the bottom of that cup and drink myself away like I used to. But no. I was a shiny bright penny while my alter-self sloshed deeper in the growing grip of alcohol. I threw the cup aside and tipped the bottle back, pouring it down in searing gulps. I might as well have been upending water for all the effect it had on me.

Come on, I growled through his lips, drinking more frantically. I had to feel something, anything. Any feeling to kill my insides, to make me sigh and forget what I'd done to this poor sonofabitch. Make me dizzy and bleary and lost in my own drunk. I needed it. I had to get away from this shame, this regret. I drank like a fiend, guzzling the vodka in huge mouthfuls. Nothing.

"COME ON!!!!!" I screamed, downing the last of the bottle and letting it fall out of my hands. I couldn't feel anything except cold, undiluted sobriety hanging me up by its noose. It was no use. Only the clarity, that goddamn brightness from the Liao indelibly burned into me. I got up, desperate to get back to the liquor store to buy some more, but he fell sideways into the desk, unable to stand. His body lurched across the room with legless momentum, stumbling and bashing into everything in its path. I tried to grope for the door, but my alter-self's eyes were blurred and crossed. The knob slipped out of his twitching fingers. And finally, this drunken corpse I couldn't drive flung itself into the bathroom, heaving up booze and bile into the toilet. It heaved and vomited up the poison until there was nothing left, and it lay coughing on the floor, finally passing out.

I went into darkness still clear, still sober and bright, and begging to feel anything else.

When I came to, I was alone on the bathroom floor. The alter-me was gone, leaving behind only a long last hushed murmur from where he'd drifted away. The body was mine now, this aged body that had done so many things I'd never have had the guts to do. I'd stolen it from him, taken his life away, so now this body was mine to do with as I pleased. Except get wasted.

Over the coming weeks, I tried everything. Booze, weed, meth, coke, pills, acid, mushrooms, ketamine, you name it. I got my hands on them in a place like that with ease, downed them in near-lethal doses, but none of them made the slightest difference. Sure, this body I'd stolen suffered their ill effects, but I got nothing in return. I felt nothing except their after-effects, the pains. What I knew beyond that was only that perfect clarity, that awful, damning clarity that the Liao had forced on me and now refused to take away. All other substances, their faint flicker stood no chance in the Liao's harsh light.

I was alone. My alter-self was gone, a dead or silent passenger in the nightmare of someone else's damned existence.

Where had he gone? I couldn't say. Maybe he was still there, buried somewhere in the gruesome darkness, lost in the phantasm of his peaceful past. I would wake from dreams filled with sadness and regret, with a loss which wasn't mine. Was it him? It didn't matter, I guess. No matter what, I was alone now. I was the sole survivor, the conductor of this runaway train. What other choice did I have but to start what I'd come to do? I bought this typewriter, and I began to write it all down. I made a routine of it, writing every morning and every night. For my afternoons, I spent them wandering, going anywhere my legs decided to take me. And that's when I learned first-hand how bad it had really become.

You have to understand, when I'd left the world, all this internet shit was brand new, still in its gruesome infancy. Mobile phones were little more than bricks with buttons. PCs were for nerds and hipsters who could bother to afford them. TV, movies, they were widespread, but not like this. My time in this dead man's skull had been mostly me playing catch up on his memories, so the world around us had been little more than a fleeting sideshow. Now I was seeing it first-hand, and I was seeing that it had already become a nightmare.

Everywhere I went, I saw them. Everywhere nothing but screens. Every face gawking into them. Staring, all the time staring, mouths gaped. Games, social networks, videos, pictures, streaming content. One in a hundred wasn't hypnotised by them, one in a thousand. Everyone staring into them, and I can see THEM draining everyone, vomiting THEIR blue ichor into the screen dead.

Every store, every building, every train and bus, there are screens. There is nowhere to turn that they don't now inhabit. The screens look down on us and lure us into looking up and worshipping them. A rectangular pantheon of horrific gods which entrance and mesmerise, transform all in us which is good into something foul and evil. People are hooked, unable to put down the screens for even a moment. Phone on the bus, phone on the street. PC in the office, phone going home. TV for five, six hours, then start again. Junkies stumble everywhere in the name of news, of current events, of entertainment, of productivity and being connected. Endless connections everywhere I looked. They have become THEIR eyes and ears, THEIR experiments, THEIR chattel.

I looked away. I couldn't let THEM find me, couldn't let myself be caught in THEIR sickening web. I looked away, but in a world where there is nothing but the unspeakable angles of screens, where could I look but down at my feet, cowering my sight for fear of being found? The human race gawks blankly, complicit in their own poisoning and destruction. I saw them siphoned day by day, watched as the blue ichor festered down into their hindbrain, mutating their genetics, turning them against all that is natural, all which is good in the human race. I heard whispers on the radio, read flashes in the last scraps of newspapers. There is a rising anger, a desperate fear on the streets. Brutal tyrants are coming up, and ethics have become fake news. Racism, sexism, violence erupting around the world. Everyone keeps glued to their screens, staying tuned for next week, for the cliff-hanger to come to its fateful conclusion. The screens are above everyone. THEY rule humanity now. There is no one else, no one who can or will fight against them.

For ten long months, I wrote, getting all of this down as fast as I could. I could feel time was running out. Willingston and the Midnight Gardener were right: it was only a matter of time. Eventually, I'd be caught. I could only look away so much. The screens surround me. Every bank, every store, every office and train station and theatre and mall, all I saw now was the shattered glass of the Tindalosi bleeding through into our existence. I began to avoid it all, a self-banished pariah, going out of my way to avoid anywhere where these horrible rents in reality exist. I looked away, looked down and cowered, just to keep ahead of THEM a little longer, but it couldn't go on forever. The end was closing in.

I caught looks from people sometimes, those close to final screen-death. There it was, that blue-tinged stain to their eyes which filled me with hopelessness and dread. I could see it, in those flickering moments, that something was in them now, something looking back at me with suspicion and ravenous hunger. Sunken eyes, hollow cheeks, eyes full of rage made from unrequited loathing and paranoia. I saw it more and more each day. Every day, more and more people's eyes grew lossy and craven, drained of themselves, and filled up with THEM. The screen dead grow paranoid and hateful, strung out on fight or flight.

A year to the day of my arrival in this shit town, and some dread instinct told me I was being hunted. Cars and busses would speed up as I crossed the road, aiming to hit me. Groups of screen-dead teenagers would follow me with hateful looks. I bought a gun and kept it on me at all times, even when I slept, which was almost never. In the long, late hours of the night, I could swear I heard that horrible breathing prowling somewhere close by, see the sharp lash of blue tongues in the corners, in the shadows.

One day, I saw two men standing across from my hotel as I came home. They watched me intently as I went inside. I went up to my room and looked out the window. They were watching my room.

My phone rang. I jumped at the sound and only stared at it as it rang and rang and rang.

"ANSWER THAT GODDAMN PHONE!" someone yelled after a long while, so I did.

A reedy, jittering, metallic voice came back at me. "Yyyyou must flee, Mr. {NHEEEEEEEEEEEEEEEE}," the voice said. It was Willingston. "Ttthey have found you. Fffffflllllleeeeeee now, or you will be killed. The manuscript must be completed."

The line went dead, but I knew Willingston was right. If I stayed there even one more night, I'd be a corpse by morning. Without thinking, I packed in darkness, and snuck out down the back stairs. From the obscurity of the alley, I peered from behind a dumpster, and the two were still there, staring up at my window, their mouths moving silently. In the darkness, I could see the awful blue burning coming from their sockets, and almost make out the splintering tendrils leeched to their brains, the writhing strands of their puppet masters out in the angled grey of timespace.

I slipped away and drove off into the night. I knew there was only one place I could go to finish this. I was going home.

HOME

It's been four months since I came back to San Francisco, and I'm writing these last pages by kerosene light.

I'm in a dilapidated house on the loneliest stretch of the Outer Sunset, the last safe place left in all the world. I don't know why I drove here. Maybe it was instinct. Maybe it was a reedy voice just on the outskirts of my perception. I had no sane reason to come back to this house. The batshit accountant warned me never to come back or he'd kill me. But I was desperate, and there are far worse horrors than being gunned down. Maybe I wanted him to kill me. I knew there was no place else for me to hide from THEM. The only safe place is this garage, with its rounded walls, with the pools of kerosene light, the lines on the floor forming the trace of not a pentagram, but of the *elder sign*. It is a protection against THEM, against all intrusion from the angles and the things which serve them.

The batshit accountant is dead, a drained and mangled corpse desiccating in one of the stinking bedrooms upstairs. I found him there when I broke in. I'd half expected him to come charging at me, gun already firing, but no. The moment I was inside, I knew from the stink there would be no word or action from him. I found him, or what remained of him, sprawled on a mangy mattress in one of the empty bedrooms. What I could see of his face was wrenched in a terrified screech.

I've wondered since I returned home what finally drove the batshit accountant to go upstairs? He'd stockpiled this garage with enough supplies to last. He had food, water, a toilet, a shower, a bed. He could have stayed down here indefinitely. This basement is the only safe place in all the world, and yet he'd left it. I guess in the end, no animal can stay penned forever. Even the safest cage is still a cage. Even if it means death, eventually all living things have to breathe freedom. Then again, it's just as likely the screen-dead tracked him to this house, same as they're trying to find me. Maybe the departed came in the night, dragged him screaming from the garage to that bedroom, to tear him apart, or to let their masters have their final remittance. I imagine this is far more likely. I have no delusions. That's my fate as well.

I'm at the end. I can feel it. I hear THEIR breathing all around me, see the blue flick of THEIR tongues at the edges of my perception. The scratching of shattered glass scrapes the walls, but can't cross in. I can feel eyes on the house, smell the foul stench of the blue ichor. No fortress is forever. It won't be long now. The needle at the end of the record has nearly skipped its last.

Willingston has come back to me. He comes out of whatever timespace that mad scientist has created for himself. He's promised to take the manuscript away before THEY can seize it. His smile appears to me out of the darkness, to encourage me, to coax me on, and to tell me my time is almost up. He won't tell me exactly when. He won't tell me exactly how. He just smiles and explains it is all playing out as it should. How goddamn encouraging. I'm so pleased that my death is right on track.

So Chumley, here we are. As I tat out these final lines, I get one last chance to gloat and say I told you so. You didn't want to know, did you? Now you have it in your skull, how will you look again? How will you goggle at your computerised dependence now? How will you ride that train, stand at that intersection, sit in that restaurant, all the while seeing the screen dead rising around you? How will you face it, seeing them draining, sinking, curling into deadened husks as the blue ichor gluts them with disease and raging enmity? How will you look away, lower your gaze, wish it all away? How will you keep your sanity intact in a world you know will soon be dead and gone?

You figured you could sit atop a dying world while you wandered your virtual paradise, and somehow it would all work out okay.

But now? Well, now you know otherwise. You know now that you're nothing more than some dissolving organic goo being lapped up by a billion proboscises. You are THEIR eyes and ears, THEIR source of power, THEIR food. You and all like you are being turned into something else, something *other*. You're an idiotic participant in your own destruction, doped to complacency for THEIR ends.

Do you see the screen dead, Chumley? The ones with their faces turned only to the rectangular gods. They're all around you, aren't they?

Yeah, they are. The blue-tinged eyes, the crazed hate and paranoia. The screen dead gawk and glaze down into their phones, lapping at the pixels while THEY feed. They are the unwitting spies of the new masters, little more than hunks of putrid flesh left for the ghouls at night.

I'm guessing about now your fellow citizens aren't the folks they used to be.

Protests on the nightly news turn to bloodbaths. Gun-toting goons are cawing for insurrection. The left and the right are coming apart at the frays. Desperation and mania haemorrhage from the ruptured sides of nations. Everywhere, the online world is running with disease and set ablaze.

Uncle Donnie has gone full-frontal MAGA while he yells at the TV. THEY slither from the flatscreen to gorge themselves on what's left of his mind.

Mom is dosed on game candies coming off her phone; Dad hasn't turned off the news or his secret porn stash in months.

Grandma is planted in her recliner in front of the idiot box. She's sick of all this namby-pamby crap, these snowflake brats and their filthy immigrants. She's frothing at the mouth, eager for violence, for power, for any kind of revenge. Blue drool bubbles at the corner of her blackened lips.

Your friends and neighbours chase conspiracies, clicking link after link to find the final page or video that will bring the whole cabal to light. They chase after proof, the one last thread that will untangle all these deep fakes. Down they go, spiralling into that web of red strands that link the conspiracies together. They tumble deeper and deeper, following the money, chasing chemtrails, one more click to the grand Conspiracy. They race down into the devouring maws of THEM.

THEY have your family and friends, Chumley. THEY have your neighbours and co-workers. THEY have your nation, your world.

And what the fuck do you know, but THEY have you too.

Deny it all you like, but it's true. Can't look away, can you? Try as you might, knowing what you know, you desperately want to free yourself before it's too late, but you can't put the screen down. A moment or two, an hour or a day at most, but then you're back. Your jittering hands and junk-sick mind can't help themselves. And way deep down inside, in that place inside that you won't admit exists, *you want it to keep going.* You're hooked and have no interest in being otherwise. Junkie, addict, you want THEM to feed on whatever you have left.

The blue ichor stings going down, but the thrum of your heart, the rush of adrenaline and toxic desire is just too much to be denied.

One more game, just another episode, one last like or retweet and you'll quit.

You swear it. You'll break away. But in the end, you'll keep looking. THEY will drain you beyond emptiness; you'll become one of THEIR puppets, one of the feral undead, one of the departed. Even to the last, you'll keep staring, and your only thought will be of one more hit, one more dose. Just one more.

HAHAHAHAHAHAHAHAHAHAHAHAHAHAAAAAA AAAAAAAAAA. Welcome to the edge.

No amount of internet is going to undo this, jackass. You can't get out of this with another hit from your mobile phone or shooting up another video game. You can't go back to that virtual paradise which now you know is nothing but a digital hell. You can't click your way out of this one, pal. **404: Easy Out Not Found**

I told you, Chumley. I told you to put it down. I told you to put the goddamn manuscript down. Why the fuck didn't you listen?

Because you're an idiot, a junkie, and you let yourself get lulled. You and all the rest of your species let your guards down. You fell in with THEIR connected age, THEIR digital revolution, THEIR golden age of wireless, and you didn't have to care or think about anything. You dropped your guard and thought it was all hunky-fucking-dory.

That's all a predator needs, dipshit. Any herbivore knows that. A predator just needs that one chance, that one opportunity when you're not looking to lunge for the jugular, and it's game over. Lookee, lookee: the whole goddamn human race gave THEM their chance, and THEY took it.

And as it goes on? As the violence and the hatred and the madness spread? As the world comes apart, and the truth is made just another commodity, another trick of the light, same as freedom, same as justice, same as humanity, same as life? What then? Can you keep pretending everything will work out? As THEY spread like a blue cancer, and as the screen dead outnumber the living; as the departed skulk in growing numbers in the outer dark, THEIR avatars upon this earth, whatcha gonna do? Just gonna let yourself go numb, fall further into it all, feel THEM crawling in the back of your brain, in your every thought? What's your game plan there, Chumley?

I have a pretty good idea of how you'll be going out.

Not how you figure it, no. You're not some video game or movie star hero, some quippy urbane all devil-may-care like you always figured. No. You'll be barricaded behind some door, crying and begging down on your knees, cowering from THEM, but more important, hiding from the one thing you never could face: Yourself.

Oh well.

Sorry, Chumley. That's not my problem now. That's all you. I type these final lines and will let Willingston carry this manuscript away into the curves of timespace. I send with him a gift as well: the last trinket of alter-me's former life: his baggie of Liao. It was the one thing from his old life my alter-self couldn't part with. It's all yours now. Whoever you are, maybe it will convince you of what these pages can't. I can't stop you now. My time is up. Do whatever you want.

And if you won't take it, if you don't believe me or don't have the guts, then find that old mutual friend of ours. Do that for me, will you, Chumley? Find him. Give him the manuscript. Give him the Liao. He'll believe. He'll take the Liao and follow where I've gone.

I take back what I said. That old mutual friend of ours, he was no Fred Carstairs, just a little bit less desperate to live at the edge than I am. But he'd follow me. He'd throw away his life, his family, and his mind to see what I've seen. He'd find Willingston. He would throw it all away, let his everything turn to nothing, and go seeking Wǔyè Yuándīng dressed in a costume shaped like me. If you won't do it, Chumley, then at least go find him and give him the chance for damnation. I've ruined so many lives, so what's one more, right?

Whatever you do, whatever you choose, remember: Avert your eyes from worthless things, and revive yourself to the living world. You haven't long before it all comes crashing down.

The syringe sits clean and ready beside me. The tie-off, the spoon and lighter are next to it, as is the balloon of heroin. Enough there to kill a junkie, and more than enough to stop this man's heart. THEY will be here soon. I can hear footsteps outside, the awful breathing of things not meant to inhabit a sane and living world.

I should be getting along now, Chumley. I'm sure I've taken up enough of your precious internet time already. Besides, my words and time are all spent.

If you'll excuse me, I have to get to my last and final fix. I won't let THEM find me any way but dead.

(Pages found in a tattered and blood-stained notebook, Ocean Beach, San Francisco, CA)

Folie à Deux ("madness to two") is a syndrome in which two or more individuals share a common set of delusions.

It is an old term, first coined in the 19th century by psychiatrists Charles Lasègue and Jean-Pierre Falret. In modern times, we refer to this syndrome (and those similar to it) by the all-encompassing and less romantic classification of **Shared Delusional Disorder (SDD)**.

Sufferers of the still-misunderstood malady are often close, related by ancestry, emotional attachment, or marriage. The disorder is known to have a high correlation with people who are isolated outsiders, in close proximity to one another, and of similarly dysfunctional backgrounds.

To date, there is no identifiable cause for such shared delusions, beyond speculative theories. Most psychiatrists attribute a majority of such cases to abusive or distressing backgrounds, stressors from without and within, as well as isolation from society.

There are many documented cases which lend some credence to this theory, wherein two or more individuals who have led dysfunctional and isolated lives are felled simultaneously by some shared delirium.

Christine and Lea Papin, sisters from an abusive and isolated background, were maids in the household of René and Léonie Lancelin. Considered quiet and unassuming, the sisters simultaneously fell to a violent rage, and murdered Mme. Lancelin and her daughter.

The Tromp family, who fell under the spell of their father's paranoid fantasies, followed him on a delusional road trip off the grid to escape unseen forces.

Nathan Leopold And Richard Loeb, two young men who, in 1924, murdered 14-year-old Bobby Franks in the backseat of a rented car, then attempted to concoct a bizarre kidnapping scheme to cover their tracks.

The majority of cases prior to the latter part of the 20th century were primarily of the sort described above. Close individuals share delusions, usually driven by a dominant delusional (known as **the primary**) passing their delusion on to the more submissive or receptive delusional (known as **the secondary**).

In more recent times, there are any number of well-documented cases in which much larger groups of otherwise sane individuals were suddenly and without reason struck by a collective psychosis.

* The Marching Band Collapse In 1986, students were gathered on the Hollinwell Showground in England's Kirkby-in-Ashfield for a marching band competition. Witnesses reported that suddenly, hundreds of students fell silent, and nearly 300 of them collapsed. No adults were affected. There is still no known reason for what happened.

* The Sri Lanka "virus" In 2012, over 1,900 school children and teachers in Sri Lanka were afflicted with a malady that had no apparent cause nor treatment.

* The Satanic Daycare Cabal From the latter 1980s through to the present, a persistent and virulent mass delusion continues to spread through highly-conservative English-speaking communities. Known as the 'Daycare Ritual Abuse' hysteria, the delusion centres on morbid fantasies of daycare workers engaging the children in all manners of satanic ritual abuse.

One must consider for a moment the changing nature of our society, particularly as it pertains to the internet and social media in the last three decades. As digital media has become increasingly ubiquitous, many health officials have begun warning of the potential dangers in excessive computer or screen usage. Such usage is not only potentially harmful to abusers, it is also a breeding ground for social isolation and dysfunctional, addictive behaviour. The risk of both increased stress and a growing sense of social isolation cannot be overstated. As with any form of substance abuse, the higher the daily

dosage, the greater the risk of deleterious effects compounding.

Factor with this the idea of meme
theory. Meme theory states that an
idea spreads from person to person,
much in the same way many living
organisms (particularly viruses and
bacteria) move from host to host.
It is believed the meme transmutes
by a form of natural selection, not
unlike biological evolution. Memes
do this through the processes of
variation, mutation, competition,
and inheritance, each of which influ-
ences a meme's reproductive success.
Memes keep spreading through the
behaviours which they engender in
their hosts.
    Meme distribution was once only
possible in localised groups, as
regional boundaries and vast distances were often the barriers to
a meme reproducing further. Without
the ability to leave a local region,
a meme would remain confined, unable
to spread. However, we no longer live
in such a restrained system. Given
our distributed and world-wide digital communications networks, we
have allowed memes to expand virulently. Memes now have the power of
an informational biohazard of sorts,

one which cannot be quarantined nor restrained without some yet-unknown technique.

One need only look a short distance to find lesser or greater degrees of memes moving among us regularly and in growing numbers across the internet. Most memes are generally harmless, such as popular content or imagery spiking usage and interest. However, memes can also take on a far more destructive element: That of the distribution of a mass delusion.

Never before has it been possible for so many secondary delusional minds to be so readily available to primaries. Ideas are no longer confined to local regions or even to groups. Ideas can now spread and metastasise in the minds of millions. Never in the history of our species has so much madness had access to so many willing and delusional participants. Conservative estimates show that followers of false beliefs or conspiracy theories number in the hundreds of millions, all in a surprisingly short time frame. Such delusion is spreading via the internet, leading to more sharing, and the production of more like-minded content.

It is difficult to imagine how such highly-distributed insanity can be stopped, even contained. The distributed nature of our interconnectedness means that ideas have become the breeding ground for an unrestrained psychological pathogen.

An example of such a distributed, wide-spread mass delusion currently sweeping the globe is known as the **Network Delusion** or the **Network Conspiracy.** Since the latter part of 2016, a persistent and recurring *Folie à Deux* has spread to growing numbers of people. This mass delusion appears to be based upon the idea that some portion of the human race are *outsiders*, belonging to a secret society known only as **the Network.** This secret society has information about a coming doomsday, and because of their knowledge and actions, are being hunted and destroyed at every turn. The Network is believed to be a collection of people who have, for one reason or another, disconnected themselves from digital communication and content, and live among us in an effort to disseminate the knowledge of this fast-approaching apocalypse, albeit without the internet to assist their efforts.

This delusive meme has no known basis in fact. There are no records of such an organisation, nor any verifiable evidence anywhere to corroborate this delusion, and yet it persists. This *Folie à Deux* has had such a growing impact in the last four years, that it has led to other, loosely-related paranoid and hallucinatory group fantasies. Among the more intriguing and persistent are

* Growing unease and feelings of despair Large number of people have been documented in the last 18 months complaining of a growing dis-ease involving the internet and digital media. Individuals from all diversities across the world report finding themselves gripped by a growing fear and dismay, particularly when using the internet or consuming digital content. Those who were interviewed described a feeling of weakness, of being drained somehow, with just as many horrified to admit to sudden and irrational feelings of uncharacteristic hatred and intolerance. Others complained of being watched, manipulated, even infected while using any form of digital media.

* The 'Grey Men' or 'Grey Ghouls'
delusion Sufferers claim to have
seen grey-fleshed people moving in
the dark, dead things with distorted
features and with glowing eyes. Some
describe these 'grey ghouls' as moving in packs, while others have seen
a lone such creature moving at night.
In all cases, the affected claim
the creatures are both gruesome and
savage.

* The Disembodied Smile This shared
hallucination has spread increasingly
since 2017, apparently by motifs
or images found on the internet.
Curiously, many of those questioned
about what they saw were unable to
recall ever having seen any such
imagery prior to their hallucinatory
experience. Hundreds of thousands of
people across the globe have claimed
to have seen a large, disembodied
smile, or better put, a series of
smiles, one inside of the other. This
hallucination of the smile appears
briefly, then vanishes, never to
return.

One is compelled to wonder at this
most virulent of mass psychoses, the
largest and most all-encompassing

Folie à Deux in recorded history. We are witnessing a global delusional pandemic which is spreading across the world, borne on the wings of the digital age.

(page bloodied and unreadable beyond this point)

ACKNOWLEDGMENTS

No writer is an island.

The writing of *Screens* was a massive endeavour for me, and I would be remiss if I didn't take a moment to thank the people in my life who helped to make all this possible. I may have written the book, but it was ya'll who made sure I never gave up. None of this would have been possible without you in my life.

I'd like to thank my kids, Lydia and Hugo, for their encouragement, their enthusiasm, and their patience as I've plodded my way to the finish line. You guys inspire me to create the cool and creepy. Never forget how proud I am of you both.

To my brothers Barry and Eric, who have been there supporting me and always championing my writing, much gratitude. It is so much easier to keep on when you know people believe in what you are trying to do.

I want to thank the folks at Smith Publicity: Sarah Miniaci, and especially to my publicist Andrea Thatcher for keeping me moving forward and always being willing to deal with my quirks and foibles. Much love for all your help and excitement.

To Christina Henry de Tessan and the team over at Girl Friday, a massive thank you. Alexander Rigby and his team were always there to answer my questions and guide me in the publishing and design process. I specifically want to thank my pal and marketing lead at Girl Friday, Georgie Hockett, whose sense of humour, energy, and brilliant insights re-inspired me when my energies were dropping low. Big props, Jersey.

I want to give thanks to my illustrator and friend, David Slebodnick, for his illustrations which made the Manuscript look like the awful and wonderful thing I'd hoped it would be.

I want to thank my therapist and mentor, Christopher Swayne, for helping me to circumnavigate my psyche these last few years as this book has grown into what it is.

I especially want to shout out to two very important people in my life:

To my brother Wes, words cannot convey, man. Through all my writing, he has been there as an editor, as a confidant, as a like mind and wise man. Wes, I can't put into words all you've done for me over the years, and I only hope somehow to repay you for all that you've given me.

And most of all, I want to thank my wife and partner in crime, Mary Rose, for never giving up on me, for believing in me when no one else would, and for putting up with my crazy ass when no other person would have. Without you in my life, this book would surely have died on the vine, and I would never have become the man and writer that I am today.

AUTHOR BIO

Christopher Laine is a writer, software architect, and founder of several business and tech ventures.

He studied literature and writing at San Francisco State University. His interests include world mythology and religions, philosophy, science, cooking, and martial arts.

Originally from San Francisco, he is a world traveller who eventually settled in New Zealand with his partner Mary and two children.

"There's not a lot to know about ourselves which art and literature, mythology and psychology have yet to teach us. I write from this perspective, that we are not at the end of our story as a species, but clearly just at its beginning."

Made in the USA
Middletown, DE
20 February 2021

33514797R00201